MW00395828

In the House of Transcendence by Amanda Ross

Published by Amanda Ross

www.amandarosswrites.com

Copyright © 2022 Amanda Ross

Cover by Tajae Keith

Edited by Erica James of MasterPieces Writing and Editing LLC

Interior formatting by C. M. Lockhart of Written in Melanin LLC

ISBN: 978-1-7349854-4-3

Printed in the United States of America

First Edition

In the House

of

Transcendence

Other Books
By Amanda Ross

The Witchkind Series:

To Astera, With Love
To Ilaris, In Desperation

Anthologies:

Girls of Might and Magic
Kindred Kingdoms

Author's Note

This book contains some scenes and instances that some readers may find disturbing. They are: drug use, violence, anxiety, and murder. If these trigger you, please be mindful when reading.

As you read In the House of Transcendence, here is a playlist to make you feel as though you're dancing at Nightingale's, traipsing through Bonaventure or exploring Savannah right alongside Zora. Prepare to transcend.

For all the queer Black fantasy fans who long to see themselves as the hero, the love interest, the friend, and the villain. You are transcendent.

Chapter 1

"People who say New Orleans is the most haunted city in America have never spent time in Savannah and have obviously never met a necromancer. This city crackles with the energy of the dead and dying, and it's only by virtue of the House of Transcendence that I haven't run away or lost my damn mind."

Spell Book of Marquitta Transcendence, 2018

Zora McNair was anxious. She was in a city she didn't know, sitting at a table outside of a late-night dessert bar alone, her coffee tepid and the frosting on her slice of cake melting in the not-quite-summer but not-quite-fall heat. Cars cruised by the restaurant as waiters took the patrons' orders, yet the echoing of her heartbeat drowned out the sounds around her. Even when a coffee mug connected with the ground, Zora's composure remained intact. Her poker face was immaculate. She'd learned to affect the appearance and vibe of serenity, of ease, no matter the situation at a young age. And so, to the people passing by on the street and walking past her into the restaurant, she looked content. No one would know she was lonely, or that she was afraid of the ghost that loomed over her shoulder.

Of course, they'd never be able to see the ghost unless they were like her—unless they were necromancers or mediums. Hell, even some witches without the Sight could sense the latent energy that ghosts give off. But no, no one could see the ghost at her shoulder, or the trio of spirits across the street at the Maritime Museum, or the ones who lingered at the corner all dressed in their finest early aughts clubwear.

Boots with the fur, Zora thought, a random lyric from a song she hadn't heard in ages. The lyric floated in and out of her memory, along with thoughts of how long ago crop tops and denim jeans ruled everything.

No one would see Zora sitting by herself and think she was in need or want of company—at least, that's what she believed the passersby and restaurant patrons thought. But when she heard the screech of an iron chair sliding across the sidewalk, Zora looked up from her phone, where she'd been scrolling through TikTok with her volume on silent. A woman not much older than Zora stood across from her.

"Can I join you?" the woman asked. She tapped the back of the chair with her long, dark nails. Zora glanced at the other tables and noticed a few openings between the crowds. She wondered why this woman had chosen this seat, but when she saw the woman shift from one foot to the other, Zora nodded.

The woman smiled a smile so beautiful that it made Zora's breath hitch. Once she sat, Zora got a better look at her, at her brown skin and close-cropped blond hair, expertly finger waved. At her high cheekbones and full lips. At the long lashes and ample cleavage. At the black, silk suit and black lace teddy that fit a tall, plus-sized body not too dissimilar from Zora's. She fixed her gaze on the gold chain around the woman's neck that ended in a bird-shaped charm.

The woman seemed to be examining Zora in much the same way and Zora leaned back, figuring if she was going to be assessed she may as well give the woman a good look. She allowed her orange sleeveless cardigan to fall to her sides, revealing a white tank top and dark blue denim jeans that accentuated her own curves. After several seconds, the woman extended her hand.

"Thanks, most of the other tables were taken. I'm Birdie."

Zora smiled and shook the woman's hand. "Oh, like the . . ."

She gestured toward the charm around Birdie's neck and Birdie nodded. A waitress walked over toward them, a peppy blond with a ponytail that seemed to keep moving long after she stopped.

"What can I get you?" she asked, holding a menu out to Birdie.

"I'll take a cappuccino and a piece of tiramisu cheesecake," Birdie said without looking at the menu.

The waitress nodded and smiled. She turned back to Zora. "More coffee?"

Zora looked down at her mug then back up at the waitress. "Yeah. Thanks."

"Absolutely!" the waitress said before prancing back into the restaurant, her ponytail in full swing.

Zora turned her attention back to her phone, shrugging her shoulder slightly as the ghost, a woman who looked straight out of the '40s, leaned in closer to Zora, her hand inches away from Zora's shoulder.

Don't fuckin' touch me, Zora thought. She wasn't in the mood for memories, didn't have the energy to have the very last moments of this random person's life flash before her eyes as it so often happened when a ghost touched her. She wanted a moment of peace, free from those whose souls refused to rest.

"I didn't get your name?" Birdie asked, her tone light, bringing Zora back to the present. Zora looked up at the woman, tilting her head slightly, her long braid falling over her shoulder.

Why did she choose this seat? Zora thought. Part of her wanted to tell the woman, "Thanks, but no thanks. I'm not here for the chatter." But the other part, the lonely part, ached at the thought of someone being interested enough to talk to her. Apart from the waitress, it'd been nearly ten hours since she'd spoken to anyone. Anyone except for her mother, of course, but though Zora wanted to talk to her, she hadn't wanted to talk to Zora. Not for four years . . .

"Zora," she stated. She set her phone down on the table and skewed a piece of cake with her fork. She half expected the conversation to end there, but Birdie smiled and remarked:

"Beautiful name." She leaned forward. "So, Miss Zora, you from 'round here?"

The waitress brought their coffees and Birdie's slice of cheesecake before Zora could answer. They both smiled at the waitress and when she'd gone back into the cafe, Birdie focused her attention on Zora.

Zora felt her shoulders tense, but she took a deep breath and released it slowly before replying, "No. Memphis. You?"

"Atlanta."

"Hmm, ATL," Zora responded. She took a long draw of coffee reveling in the warmth of it, in the way it made her whole body buzz.

Birdie chuckled. "Yep, that's right. So, how are you liking Savannah so far?" she asked as she took a bite of her cheesecake.

"It's beautiful," Zora replied. "I love the architecture, the food the vibe."

"Yes, Savannah certainly leaves a mark on you," Birdie paused.

Zora nodded and grabbed her coffee cup.

"But I imagine the ghosts do that, too."

Zora nearly choked on her coffee. *How did she know about the ghosts?* she thought. She took another deep breath and regained her composure. When she looked up at Birdie, she'd slipped her unaffected mask back on.

"Ghosts aren't real," Zora scoffed.

Birdie side-eyed her and waved her away, her long black nails looking like claws.

"I know the look. My fiancée used to see them, too."

"Used to?" Zora asked.

Birdie's lip twitched. She held her cup between her hands and sighed, looking down at her coffee. "She died. A month ago."

Zora's heartbeat skipped. She'd never lost someone she loved, but she'd been to more funerals than she could count. She'd seen the devastation that death could cause, especially when the deceased was young, and the death was sudden. She didn't wish that type of heartache on her worst enemy.

"I'm sorry." Zora reached out and touched Birdie's hand and Birdie smiled tightly. She squeezed Zora's hand with her other hand then they unraveled themselves.

Birdie smiled, her eyes glassy. "Thank you."

"How long were you together?" Zora asked.

"Two years. I proposed to her the day before she . . ." Birdie cleared her throat. She took a long sip of coffee and dabbed at her bottom lashes with the edge of her nail. "She was murdered."

Zora's brows knitted as she simultaneously felt sorry for this woman's loss and wondered how she felt so comfortable telling a stranger about her fiancée's murder.

Murder. Another version of death Zora knew all too well. As a necromancer, she'd seen her fair share of final moments, the first memory she'd get when a ghost touched her. She never knew why—was it like their life flashing for her but in reverse? Zora had never maintained contact with one long enough to see a full trip down their memory lane; she never wanted to. Though these specters made her uncomfortable, she couldn't say the same for the grief stricken. Unlike most people, she was well versed in comforting the grieving. It had stopped being awkward for her when she was eleven.

Zora finished her last bite of cake and set her plate aside. She settled back in her chair, sipping her coffee.

"I'm sorry. That must've been devastating."

"It was. I still don't know who—" Birdie inhaled then dabbed at her eye. "Well, anyway. She'd get twitchy, too, whenever a ghost was near."

"Twitchy?"

"Yeah. Lots of random shruggin' and shiftin' in her chair. Just like you did a few minutes ago," Birdie replied.

Zora paused, trying her best to keep her poker face on. The waitress strolled over and asked if they were enjoying their meal and if they needed anything else. Zora and Birdie replied "no" at the same time, but all Zora could think about was not how this woman had surmised she was a necromancer, but why.

Why does she want to know that I'm a necromancer? Who is she? Zora thought. If her fiancée had told her about her abilities and Birdie hadn't left her or committed her, then it meant that either Birdie was a human who believed in magic or . . .

Or she herself was a witch, too.

For the second time that night, Zora found herself examining this woman. This time, she wondered if she could sense any power about her. She'd never been able to do it before; she'd never felt comfortable with opening up to her friends about her powers and how she used them. And when she tried to meet witches online, she stumbled across either fakes or witches who still clung to the false belief that necromancy was evil.

Zora shrugged.

"Well, like I said, I'm sorry for your loss but people can't see ghosts because they ain't real."

Again, Birdie looked at her skeptically. She leaned forward and clasped her hands then rested her chin on them.

"C'mon, Zora," Birdie began, her voice goading. "You and I both know that isn't true."

Zora stood and pulled a twenty out of her jeans pocket and tossed it on the table. Her mouth had gone dry and the coffee and chocolate churned in her stomach, sending acid up her throat.

"I don't—"

But then Zora blinked, and Birdie was gone. Zora looked around for the woman, who appeared at her side just as suddenly as she left it, causing Zora to startle.

"Shit!" she blurted out before sighing. Her eyes darted from left to right, checking their surroundings to see if anyone had noticed Birdie's bold display of magic. How could this woman feel so comfortable performing magic on a crowded street filled, most likely, with only humans? Birdie took her seat again and crossed one leg over the other, an air of nonchalance about her that made Zora a little jealous. *What would it be like to have a power I could use freely and without fear?* she thought.

"So, you're a teleportation witch?" Zora asked, her voice low.

"And you're a necromancer," Birdie replied.

Zora nodded and crossed her arms. A lump formed in the back of her throat and her head felt like it was in a vice grip. Her skin tingled as though she was seconds away from crawling out of her skin. Though she inhaled and exhaled slowly, she didn't know how to bring herself down. She'd met witches with all types of powers before, but they'd all turned cold once they discovered

Zora's necromancy. But here was this beautiful woman who seemed to be doing the complete opposite. She seemed to want Zora to open up to her about her abilities, which made a spike of suspicion snake up Zora's spine. Because why would she want Zora to open up? What was her deal? There was only one way to find out.

"Okay, you got me," Zora conceded. "I'm a necromancer. So what?"

"Well, I make it a point to welcome every witch that comes into this city."

Zora scoffed but smiled despite herself. "Who are you, the witchy welcome committee?"

Birdie lifted a shoulder. "You could say that. I know how hard being a witch is in this world, and a Black witch at that."

Zora nodded.

"And so, when I meet a witch who's new in town and planning to make a home here, I always try to make them feel like they have a friend," Birdie said, her lips curling into a smile.

Zora shook her head.

"Oh, I'm not making a home here. Just . . . visiting family."

"Oh? So why are you here at Lulu's alone on a Wednesday night?"

"Because I am," Zora replied, her voice sounding harsher than she'd intended. "My mom's a nurse. She works late nights."

Zora left out the part about her mother practically slamming the door on her when she came to see her.

She didn't even give me a chance, Zora thought. She blinked away the memory and focused on the here and now. She downed the last bit of her coffee then considered her next move. Though Birdie hadn't replied to Zora, she could tell she thought there was more to Zora's story. But Zora didn't respond. She just folded an unfolded the twenty-dollar bill she'd thrown on the table.

"Well, even if you're not planning to be here long—"

"I'm not. I'm a necromancer. Why the hell would I want to stay in one of the most haunted cities in the country?"

Birdie laughed. "Everywhere is haunted, Zora, as I'm sure you know. But if you're going to be in town tomorrow night, I'm having a function and you should come through. Let me give you my number."

As Birdie reached for her phone, Zora shifted in her seat. "I mean, I'm probably going to head back to Memphis. My mom's pretty busy. But I'll think about it."

Birdie gave her a knowing look but remained silent as they exchanged numbers. After hitting the save button, she locked her phone and stood.

"It was great meeting you, Zora. I hope you change your mind and decide to come through," she turned to walk away then stopped and turned back to Zora. "Oh, and don't worry about the cake and coffee. I already paid."

Zora opened her mouth to speak then realized Birdie must've paid the bill when she teleported. She grabbed her phone and purse and walked to her car but not before taking one final glance in Birdie's direction. Just as she suspected, Birdie was nowhere in sight.

As Zora slid into her car, she noticed she wasn't as uneasy as she'd been before Birdie arrived. A slight grin spread on her face as she made her way to her hotel room.

After a long shower, Zora lay in bed, splitting her focus

between some television show about a group of people working in an office and texting her friend Anika. She hadn't told her or anyone else at her dance academy that she was leaving, and she didn't quite know if she was ready to now. She'd left Memphis, left her father, and the only home she'd ever known without much of a plan. While she knew she couldn't bear to stay after what happened, she hadn't counted on her mother not even letting her make it over the threshold.

Zora had left Memphis early that morning before the sun ever came up and arrived in Savannah around midday. After she'd checked into her hotel, she'd showered and dressed then driven to her mother's apartment building and waited outside for the door to open. She told herself that she was just surprising her and that's why she hadn't called ahead of time or asked for the building code. But the truth was, Zora knew if she'd called, her mother wouldn't have wanted to see her. Not after so many years. Not after what happened the day her mother left.

Tears sprang to her eyes as the door opened and she looked at her mother in person for the first time since she was sixteen. Zora saw so much of herself in her: the same round face, brown skin, and wide, dark eyes. Her mother's once long hair was now short and graying. Like Zora, her nose was pierced. But unlike her daughter, Nia McNair did not look pleased.

"What're you doing here?" she questioned.

"I," Zora started, her mouth going dry. "I came to see you."

"Why?"

"Why? Mama, I just missed you. I know we don't talk a lot and—"

"You still foolin' around with that witchcraft?"

The question made Zora blink. "Uh, I mean, I . . ."

"You know how I feel about that. Zora, don't you know your

very soul is at stake?"

"But Mama, I help people," she said. *You didn't help Mr. Lionel.* The thought pushed its way into Zora's mind, unbidden. She shook her head as though she could uproot that thought and send it away.

"I'm sure you think so, but what you do is evil, and I don't want it around me. I'm sorry, Zora, you've got to go."

Before Zora could respond, her mother closed the door. She stood there for a few seconds, frozen in place as hot tears streamed down her face.

She'd spent the rest of the day at Tybee Island, crying as she ate ice cream and listened to old school tunes by Mary J. Blige, Xscape, and TLC, the only things that could soothe her. Then she'd taken a nap and set out for Lulu's, where she'd met Birdie.

It was 11:58 p.m. now as she lounged in her hotel.

Zora got up and opened the mini bar in her room and grabbed a shot of overpriced rum. Then she grabbed the pack of matches she'd purchased from the gas station and walked over to the sliding door and stepped out onto the balcony. She lit a match and stared at her phone, counting down to midnight

Zora's eyes went glassy as midnight struck, as the match went out. She lit another one and looked back at her phone. September 22nd.

"Happy birthday, Zora," she whispered, the bile in the back of her throat making her want to cry. She blew out the match, downed her shot, then stared out at the crowds on River Street, the rum warming her body from the inside out. Growing tired of the humid night air, Zora walked back into her room and lay down, filled with uncertainty for her year ahead.

Chapter 2

"The dead react to necromancers like moths to flames because necromancers straddle the line of life and death. They crave the absolution they can give, but also their light. Their life. There are ways to repel them—most would have you think salt was the strongest way, but I find that, in the face of red brick dusted with wormwood, the specters fade away."

Spell Book of Bonnie Soliloquy, 2004

Z ora woke up the next morning and checked her phone. Dozens of notifications flooded her screen, a barrage of texts, calls, and DMs wishing her a happy 21st birthday. She replied to her brother's text first, a voice message sent at two in the morning.

"Zorrrraaaaaa!" Keith shouted. "It's your muthafuckin' birthday! Yo, I can't believe you legal now. Go turn up and celebrate yourself, and don't let anyone get you down. And if dad tries to get you to take a job today, tell him to give it a rest for the next twenty-four. Love you."

Her stomach clenched at the mention of their father, Ricky McNair. She hadn't told her brother that she'd left home and that she was holed up in a hotel room just across town from their mother. Keith was in college now, and he and Zora had spoken quietly to each other throughout the years despite their mother having taken a scorched earth mentality when she left with Keith in toe, forbidding him to contact Zora and their father. Zora still remembered him as the geeky 14-year-old, wearing glasses too big for his face and reading manga every night before he fell asleep. Now, he was almost 19. He wore contacts and still read manga, but he'd gotten into Clark Atlanta University and was studying to be a journalist. Zora was proud of her little brother, but she was also a little jealous.

Her future had been decided from the time she was a kid when two catastrophic things happened. First, her father lost his job. He'd come home with his things in a box and Zora hadn't quite understood what happened, but she could tell something was wrong by the way he was teary-eyed for the rest of the night by the way her mother barely spoke. He'd been searching and searching and by the summer before Zora's ninth birthday, her father had been out of a job for a year. That summer had been abnormally hot, and on one of those humid nights that felt like trying to breathe through a wet blanket, made more suffocating by the thunderstorm that had rolled in, the second thing happened: Zora saw a ghost.

That night she'd twisted in her bed, first toward her door the her window. As her eyes opened, frustrated from exhaustion and the inability to sleep, she saw it, the briefest outline of a shoulder *I'm dreaming,* she thought, blinking and holding her breath. But each time she opened her eyes, she saw that the thing was still there, silhouetted by the moonlight spilling through her window The thing took one step, two, three. Zora scooted back on her be and drew her covers up. Another step and Zora whimpered. Hot tears sprang in her eyes.

The thing stopped at the foot of her bed

"Zora Mae?" it asked voice sounding hollow like it was passing through a pipe.

Zora recognized the voice and stilled. "Ms. Patrice?"

Lightning sliced through the night, washing the room in white light, and Zora saw its face. Ms. Patrice.

Ms. Patrice, the woman who lived down the street from Zora's house and sometimes watched the neighborhood kids. She stood beside Zora's bed, her body translucent and her nightgown bloody. She stared at her with unblinking eyes, and a cold chill snaked up Zora's spine.

"Are you okay?" Zora whispered. Ms. Patrice didn't answer. "Ms. Patrice?"

Zora wondered how she could've gotten into her room. It was on the second floor, the window facing the street. Someone would've seen her, this woman old enough to be Zora's granny, climbing her way up into Zora's room.

"How did you get in here? Are you okay? I can get my mama to—"

"—was Alex."

Zora knitted her brows. "What?"

"Tell 'em . . . Alex . . . it."

Zora sat up, her heart jackhammering in her chest. Ms. Patrice had begun to look . . . fuzzier, her translucent body blinking in and out like a broken neon sign. *What's happening to her?* Zora thought.

"What are you saying? What's wrong, Ms. Patrice?"

"Was Alex . . ."

Zora sat up on her knees and reached out a hand to the woman. She yelped when her hand passed through what had been Ms. Patrice's arm.

"You're a ghost?" Zora asked.

"Tell . . . Alex . . . it."

Before Zora could respond, Ms. Patrice shimmered away.

Zora sat for a moment, hearing only the storm raging outside and her heartbeat reverberating in her ears. She scooted down into her bed, thinking to use her blankets as protection despite the heat of the night. She pulled her bonnet down over her ears and brought her blanket over her head and cried, unable to comprehend what had just happened but fearing it all the same.

Zora's life had been forever changed by those events. Now, as she typed "Ha! Thanks, Ke, luv ya" to her brother, the memory of Ms. Patrice and her bloody nightgown made the hair on her neck stand up. She exhaled and closed her eyes tightly, attempting to lose the memory. Ms. Patrice was the first but she wasn't the last, and even though seeing her had set in motion Zora's life, she wasn't the scariest ghost she saw or even the most gruesome one.

Tired of lying in bed, Zora walked to the balcony and opened the blinds and sliding door before stepping out onto it. The sun was shining, and the air was already sticky despite it barely being nine in the morning. Zora slid into a chair and propped up her feet as she continued scrolling through her messages and responding. One from her friend Anika, who she'd known forever. A few from her aunt, an uncle, and an ex. Even some of the witches she'd met online, in whose Discord server she sometimes lurked, sent her funny memes or said "May this year bring you abundance. Blessed be."

But there were no messages from her mother or from her father. She'd expected her mother to ghost her; she'd done that last year. But her father? He'd always been there. Had always gotten her something even when they could barely pay rent and keep the lights on. Though Zora had left his house on bad terms, she thought he'd at least say . . . something. He hadn't even called to ask her to reconsider, or to say he was sorry for what happened.

Do you even want to hear from him? she wondered. After all, it'd been her father who had taken the thing that terrified her the most in this world—her ability to see ghosts and to raise the dead—and convinced her to use it to make money. When she told her parents about Ms. Patrice, they dismissed it as a bad dream at first. But when the ghost reappeared and Zora screamed them awake and told them who it was and what she'd said, her parents had two different reactions. Nia held Zora and clasped her hands around hers and told Zora to close her eyes. Then she began praying.

"Lord, we ask you to cover Zora in the blood of the lamb. Cover her in your light and protect her from the bad spirits that haunt her. We know that only through you can we know peace, can we be safe. Lord, we rebuke the spirits that haunt her . . ."

Zora's mind drifted as her mother continued praying. She opened her eyes and looked at her father, who sat at the edge of her bed, fiddling with the edge of his durag, a habit he'd passed down to her. Ricky wasn't praying, though. He was gazing out the window, his mind lost in thought. The next day when he picked Zora and Keith up from school, he pulled up to a cemetery instead of their home.

Her father pulled into an area where a funeral was taking place.

"Dad, what're we doing here?" she asked, her voice wavering. He turned the engine off and sighed.

"Awe, Dad, you turned the song off," Keith whined. Her father wiped a hand across his face and pulled open the glove box, grabbing an iPod and headphones. He leaned back in his seat and placed the headphones over Keith's ears and pressed play. Then, when he was sure her brother could occupy himself, he turned his attention back to Zora.

"Do you remember Ms. Marvelle?" he asked.

Zora nodded. Ms. Marvelle was another neighbor, one who Zora liked much more than Ms. Patrice because she gave the kid candy and told them fantasy stories. Sometimes her husband, Mr. Lionel, told even better stories, ones about dragons and wizards.

"Well, Mr. Lionel told me that she used to use that gift—"

"More like a curse," Zora mumbled.

"No, it's a gift, Zo," he replied, lifting his brows to emphasize his point. "Ms. Marvelle used her gift to help people get information from or about their loved ones, find out things the families needed to know, get justice for people who were killed. And in return, these families were so happy that she was helping them they'd pay her money."

Zora looked from her father to the funeral taking place outside her window. She played with the hem of her shirt, then turned back to her father.

"So . . . is that why we're here?"

Ricky hesitated before speaking. "Yes. Mr. Lionel told me about it and how these families would just help them, give them money and food, help connect them with other people who needed help. Ms. Marvelle was so well known that when she died so many people went to her funeral. Do you remember?"

Zora nodded. She remembered not only the repast and how itchy her gray dress had been but also how sad so many people were. As Zora leaned over the balcony at her hotel, she was once again pulled back into that memory, and her she absentmindedl twisted at the hem of her shirt.

"Well, Mr. Lionel got a call from a family who didn't know sh had died and needed her help. He told me about 'em and said to call them and say I was a referral from her husband and that I knew someone who could help."

"What's a referral?" she asked.

"It's when you tell someone you know someone who can help."

Zora scrunched up her face, her thoughts moving a mile a minute. Images of Ms. Patrice flashed in her mind's eye. *I never want to see a ghost again,* she thought.

"I can't help. I'm only eight." She said.

"Yes, but you're powerful," her father said.

"But I'm scared," she whimpered.

Her father sat quietly for a moment and gazed out of his window. When he looked back, tears welled in his eyes.

"Zora, you know how hard things have been for me since I lost my job. It's like I keep trying but . . ." he blinked away the tears and cleared his throat. "Look, I know it's scary, but you have a gift that can help people, including your family."

She stared at her father through glassy eyes, trying her best to swallow the lump that formed in her throat. She'd seen her father staying up late working on something called a resume. She'd heard him calling places and talking to people, seen him waiting by the phone only for it not to ring again. She'd heard her parents talking about money in hushed tones, seen her mother crying and praying for a miracle. Even though she was terrified of the possibility of seeing another ghost, even though her heart pounded in her chest and all she wanted to do was run away, she knew her father was right. She could help people. She could help her family. She could help her father. And so, Zora took a deep breath, looked at her father, and simply said, "Okay."

For the next twelve years, Zora had spent nearly every day using her powers. She'd learned to affect nonchalance, learned to walk tall, and learned to never show anyone her fear. And she

was afraid. Every time she spoke to a ghost, every time she stare
into the milky eyes of a corpse, heard the snapping sound of its
jaw opening after so much disuse, all she wanted to do was curl
up into a ball, hoping if she made herself small she could hide
and never be found by the dead again.

But her family needed the money. That money paid their bill
paid for her to go to her dance lessons after school, paid for her
used Mustang, paid for her father to lie about all the handyman
work he did around town when he stopped trying to get an office
job after a year of Zora using her powers. And now, on her 21st
birthday, the money paid for her hotel room and it would pay for
her to get her nails done and to take a trip to Sephora.

As Zora took a shower, her mind drifted toward Birdie. She
thought about how she'd clocked her powers right away, and how
she said she made it a point to welcome all the witches who came
to Savannah. The revelation that there were more witches in this
city intrigued Zora. In Memphis, she'd known only a handful
and had never really vibed with them. Perhaps this community
of witches Birdie spoke of so fondly would be more welcoming.
If Birdie's relationship with her necromancer fiancée was any
indication—

Get real, Zora thought. Stay in Savannah? Was she insane?
This place was haunted as shit. Birdie may have been right
about ghosts being everywhere, but Zora had seen more ghosts
in Savannah in twenty-four hours than she had in one week in
Memphis. No. She could barely keep the ghosts out of her room
now. It was only by the virtue of the salt she kept in her purse
and spread in front of the door, balcony, and around her bed that
she was able to sleep that night without being haunted.

The second she'd stepped into the hotel the day before, her
stomach had dropped as she spotted one spirit after another.

She'd been careful not to select The Marshall House or The Planter's Inn or any other relic from the city's past that had made an appearance on one of the myriad of paranormal investigation shows. Yet still, the hotel she'd chosen, a structure built in 2011 that boasted retro furnishings and free soda and popcorn, housed a gaggle of ghosts.

She slipped on a sage green baby doll dress over a white t-shirt. Then she slid into her platform tennis shoes, the ones her father had questioned her about buying.

"You're already an Amazon without them thangs. You'll fuck around and scare off any boy that might take interest in you," he'd warned.

She bought them anyway, saying: "If a man is that intimidated by my height, then he's not the kind of man I'd want to be with anyway."

Of course, that applied to women and non-binary people, too, but she'd never say that aloud to her father. Though he wasn't outwardly homophobic, Zora could tell being around queer people made him uncomfortable. And so, she'd come out to herself long after her classmates did. But once she knew who she was, she never came out to her father.

She sighed as she thought back to Birdie's offer of a party. What could it hurt? She had the room for another two nights, and it wasn't like she had anything else planned. So she pulled out her phone and texted Birdie.

"Hey, it's Zora. I'm free tonight for that function you mentioned. What's the address?"

Before Zora could put her phone down, text bubbles appeared on the screen. She sucked in a breath as she awaited Birdie's response.

Chapter 3

"Witches love their rituals. Any excuse to dress in their finery, commune with each other and the gods, and transcend the woes of life, they will take. But there are a few rituals that are sacrosanct—the midsummer and winter solstices and the vernal and autumnal equinoxes. They are about giving thanks for that which has been received in the past, reveling in the present, and setting intentions for the future."

Spell Book of Dottie Transcendence, 1945

Reminding herself to breathe as she mounted each step, Zora climbed the stairs of a gray, three-story house a block away from Forsyth Park. She could hear the music from the street, could see the shadows of people against the white curtains. She rang the doorbell then stepped back. As she stood, Zora examined herself and tried to ignore the nerves that flooded her stomach and made her heart flutter as fast as hummingbird wings. She wore black booties, the toes pointed and the chunky heels ending in a smaller point. Her dress was lacy, Bohemian, and the color of merlot, the front hitting her midcalf and the back grazing the floor. The top sat off her shoulders, and black and gold chokers were layered on her neck. Her hair was up in two space buns, her edges smoothed and gold filigree tubes intertwined in her tresses.

She ran her hands down her dress just as the door opened.

The tall Black man who answered the door eyed her suspiciously. He held a wine glass in one hand and the door in the other one. Zora wanted to tell him she liked his outfit—it reminded her of what someone might wear to an Afropunk festival. He wore tight black jeans, thigh-high combat boots, a studded belt, and a pink vest that hung open to reveal his bare chest. His nails were painted black and his beard and locs were dusted with gold. A pair of small, round glasses with red lenses completed the look. Zora could see his suspicion of her despite the eyewear.

"Who the fuck are you?" he asked, nodding toward her.

Zora took a deep breath and shifted her shoulders back, tilting her head up slightly. "I'm Zora. Birdie invited me."

He looked her up and down, as though sizing her up. She quirked a brow at him, as if to let him know that his attempt at intimidation wouldn't work.

Seconds later, he stepped aside and let Zora in. She flinched as she stepped over the threshold and stumbled upon the spirit of a man in an old-timey suit and a bullet wound in his right eye. He glared at Zora with his other eye and reached out a hand to her, his fingertips grazing her shoulder. A flash of memory, a woman in a white dress holding a gun while facing him on this very threshold. The bullet sped toward him, and then, darkness. She shuddered and grabbed her purse's chain-link strap and followed the man into the front room on her left, her boot heels clicking against the hardwood floor.

She glanced around the room in awe. Strategically placed photos and artwork covered the black walls. A group photo rested above the fireplace, but Zora couldn't get close enough to see the specifics. Two black couches sat opposite each other, and a wooden table, the top made of what looked like stained glass from a church window, sat in between them.

Instrumental music, heavy on drums and horns, filled the house. So did the people. The room was nearly filled wall to wall with people dressed in all manner of finery. She passed by a woman dressed in a floor-length, black pleather dress, her purple hair big, her lips jet black, and a silver chain connecting her nose ring and the stud in her ear. Beside her stood a man with blue curls and copper skin, who looked like a '50s greaser. They stared at Zora as she passed, and the woman quirked an eyebrow. The man leaned in and whispered in the woman's ear.

Zora could feel the ghost following her, could sense more of them lingering elsewhere in this house.

Ah hell nah, she thought. She looked around, hoping that no one else's eyes were on her. When she saw that no one else was paying her any attention, she pulled a small, velvet pouch out of her purse and opened it, taking a pinch of salt in her fingers and tossing it over her shoulder. It wasn't much but it would force the ghost to keep its distance.

A pang shot through Zora's stomach as she stepped into the dining room and beheld the long, marble table taking up most of the space in the room. *When had she last eaten?* She wondered and remembered with frustration that it had been the oatmeal, banana, and coffee she'd gotten from the Starbucks next to the hotel that morning.

Her hunger increased as she scanned the platters on the table, filled with fresh fruit, cheeses, deli meat, chips, and more. Several bottles of liquor and a large stack of plastic tumblers occupied the other side of the table. Zora stood before the table, thinking to grab something but feeling her cheeks warm. No one else was eating. No one even had a drink in their hand. It would be rude to touch anything on the table when it all was clearly being saved for later in the night.

Something touched her shoulder and the memory from earlier flooded her mind. She fought the fear that snaked up her spine as she turned to see the ghost standing behind her. She looked down at the pouch in her hand.

"Shit," she whispered. It was all gone. She took a deep breath and searched the table for something she could use. Her eyes settled on margarita salt then cut back to the ghost, who was now much closer to her. "I hope this works."

She turned back toward the table and tossed the salt over her left shoulder, holding her breath the entire time. There was silence for a moment, then a chuckle. Zora knitted her brows. She grabbed more salt and launched it at the ghost, who promptly shimmered away.

"Girl, why you in here throwin' salt everywhere?"

Zora startled. She turned to her right to look at the man who sidled up beside her. He had voluminous coils that sat just below his shoulders. He wore fitted, black suit pants, a black corset, and a pink and teal fringe jacket that complimented his golden-brown skin. A pair of long false lashes emphasized his wide-set, brown eyes, and his expertly lined beard showcased his nearly perfect jawline.

"Oh, sorry," Zora said. She smiled and tried to laugh it off. "I'm just superstitious, you know? Throw salt over my shoulder every day to keep the devil away."

She kept her smile on even as he lifted a brow.

"Hmm," was all he replied with. Someone passed behind him and patted him on the shoulder and when his attention was taken, Zora allowed herself to breathe.

"What the fuck," she mouthed. Superstitious? Salt every day keeps the devil away? She sounded like she was seriously on one and she found herself looking at the door, wondering if perhaps she should just leave and save herself the discomfort of tossing salt at ghosts in a crowded room all night. Before she could leave, the man spoke again.

"So, Ms. Superstitious, I've never seen you here before. Where you come from?"

"Around. Birdie invited me." She lifted a shoulder in what she hoped looked like a nonchalant shrug. *Be cool,* she thought. You can do this. He's just a person. No living human is as scary as the dead.

She took another deep breath and felt her heartbeat slow and the lump in her throat relax. The man looked Zora up and down for what felt like forever. Then a look of recognition passed over his face and he smiled, revealing a set of deep dimples and perfect teeth.

"Oh, so you're the necromancer!" he exclaimed, a bit too loud for Zora's liking. "Now I get it, the salt thing."

Zora nodded and slowly exhaled, but not before glancing around the room to see if anyone had heard him.

"I see Birdie's talked about me," Zora said, surprised that the fact made her feel good.

The man shrugged. "She didn't say much, just that you were a necromancer named Zora who may or may not stop by because you may or may not be moving to Savannah."

He tilted his head and pursed his lips; the look made Zora smile. The man returned the gesture and Zora felt herself truly relax in his company.

"Well, that's true, 'cept for the part about me moving here. I don't plan on it."

"Mm-hmm," he replied. "That's what they all say. That's what I said. And here we are, three years later."

Zora laughed. "Yeah, but I'm sure your . . . power?"

She searched his eyes for confirmation. He nodded.

"I'm sure your power don't limit where you want to live. This place is too haunted for me."

"Well, aren't you making assumptions," he said, his tone suddenly serious.

Her eyes widened. "No, I—"

The man leaned his head back and cackled. "Girl, I'm just playin'. I'm a shapeshifter. I could live anywhere. I got no idea what you necromancers gotta deal with and I don't want to know. I'm Taemar, by the way. But you can call me Tae like everyone else."

"Zora."

They shook hands. Zora felt giddy for meeting someone she could potentially kick it with throughout the rest of the . . . what was this, anyway?

"So, what's happenin'? It feels like a party, but no one is drinkin' or eatin'. Everyone's just standin' around."

Taemar knitted his brows. "It's the equinox."

Zora lifted her brows and tilted her head.

Taemar scoffed. "The Autumnal Equinox? As in one of the four most important yearly rituals for witches?"

Zora twisted the strap of her purse in her fingers, her heartbeat quickening again. She hated Taemar's reproachful stare, but what was she supposed to do? Lie? Yes, she'd met other witches and vaguely heard about rituals that took place on certain days. She'd looked up the Celtic wheel of the year and tried to find rules and rituals that Black witches practiced. But she found next to nothing. She'd Googled, YouTubed, and followed witches on social media, but all they focused on were tarot readings. She hated that feeling of being inadequate because she truly wanted to know about her powers and what it meant to be a witch. She tried her best to remember something, anything from her research.

"Well . . . I know the autumnal equinox is one of two days where day and night are equal, and that a lot of cultures think this day is special, and the Celtics—"

Taemar waved his hand at her. "Uh-uh. That's white people shit. No shade to Sabrina The Teenage Witch, but we have our own rituals, our own culture, and our own gods. And we honor them tonight."

Zora bit her lip and nodded, looking down at her shoes, not even thinking to put on her poker face.

"Zora, it's okay. Not all of us are steeped in this from jump. Hell, I grew up with a granny who had the same powers as I do. I know a lot. So as we're doing the ritual tonight, I'll tell you what's up. And if you decide to stick around in Savannah, I can show you even more."

"Not you over here braggin', Tae."

A woman with fawn skin and a wild mane of cherry red curls walked up to them, the silver bangles on her left wrist clinking against each other as she rested her hand on Taemar's arm. The other settled on her hip. Her white satin dress that clung to her ample curves. Her pierced septum sparkled in the light, and her full lips were painted the same color pink as her long nails.

Taemar rolled his eyes but looked down at the woman and smirked.

"Not braggin', just stating facts for the newbie."

The woman turned her attention to Zora.

"Hello, newbie. I'm MK," she said. She looked Zora up and down slowly before adding: "Love the dress."

Zora smiled tightly at MK's comment, unsure if it had been a compliment or a read.

"Thanks. I'm Zora," she replied.

"Zora, pretty name. What brings you?"

"Birdie," Zora and Taemar said at the same time. They looked at each other and Taemar winked. MK glanced between them. She shifted her weight to her other leg and crossed her arms.

"Well, Birdie does have a habit of rollin' out the red carpet for every witch who even steps a foot in this city. But, I think she said you're a necromancer?" she asked, her brows lifting.

Zora simply nodded. She could tell MK was looking for something more—horror stories maybe, or for Zora to feel insecure about the type of power she was given. But she wouldn't give this woman or anyone else the satisfaction. No one needed to know how she felt about her powers. Though most of them wouldn't do more than shrug, something told her MK was the kind of person who would use her fear against her. Zora had dealt with her fair share of that type in school. Girls who thought they were better because they were short, thin, and light-skinned. Zora stood her ground then and, if she had to, she'd stand her ground now.

"Well, that's fascinating. I'd love to hear more. Marquitta always had the best stories," MK said. For just a second, sadness emerged behind her dark eyes. She and Taemar looked at each other and he squeezed her hand in comfort.

Zora crossed her arms. *That must be Birdie's fiancée,* she thought.

"Was Marquitta Birdie's fiancée?" Zora asked.

MK nodded.

"She mentioned her to me. I'm sorry for your loss." Zora looked from MK to Taemar, observing the twin looks of sorrow on their faces.

Taemar cleared his throat. "Thanks. She was everything."

"It's time, y'all!" Someone shouted from the distance. The people around the room began walking past them, several of them whooping and hollering. Taemar grabbed Zora's hand, the sorrow that had shone on his face gone and replaced with excitement.

"C'mon, you're gonna love this."

Zora nodded and allowed herself to be led into the backyard. She gawked at the lights strung along the fence on the left side of the yard and from the gables of the house to the tall trees that dotted the yard in the back and on the right.

She noticed a small fountain sitting just before the fence and a group of witches dressed in more extravagance than even Taemar and MK occupying the three lounge chairs near it. A firepit rested in the center of the yard with its flames dancing high.

Taemar guided Zora to a spot facing the fire pit and the back of the house, while MK settled on the other side of Taemar. Zora heard a whistling sound and the tingling of cymbals, recognizing it as the same type of music that had been playing inside. As the drumbeat dropped slowly and a horn began its distant call, Zora began swaying to the sounds.

"What's happening?" Zora whispered.

"Our House Heads are about to come down those stairs." Taemar pointed to the stairs at the back of the house. "And the ritual will officially begin."

She looked toward the stairs just as two women and a man walked out of the house and stood on the landing at the top, their faces covered. All around her, witches clapped and hollered, including Taemar. Zora gazed at the scene before her, noticing the excitement on everyone's faces.

One by one, the trio descended the stairs and stopped on the second landing before facing the crowd below. The shorter of the two women spoke first. A blushing pink, rose-shaped fascinator nestled on the left side of her expertly curled, raven-black hair. White tulle extended from the fascinator, covering her face. Her dress, the same color as her fascinator, fit her hourglass figure like it was a second skin. The halter top emphasized her cleavage and the crystals that encrusted it made her body shimmer with every step she took. A pair of matching, opera-length gloves completed the ensemble. Zora stood in awe of her as she sashayed down the steps.

"I am Whitley Soliloquy," she spoke, her voice high and absent of any Southern drawl.

"You mean Whitley Neon," someone shouted. Several people chuckled. The woman named Whitley paused until the chuckles died down.

"I am Whitley Soliloquy," she repeated, this time louder and with an edge to her voice. "Head of the House of Soliloquy."

Whitley hiked her dress slightly and sauntered down the remaining steps. She stepped to the right of them and clasped her hands in front of her. The crowd clapped and some of them whooped. Someone whistled, and all the while Zora's heartbeat thumped in time with the music.

"What does she mean by 'house?'" Zora asked.

Taemar leaned toward her, his hair smelling like honey. "There are three magical houses in almost every city. They're our community, and each house has a head. They're there to help guide witches, mentor them, make sure they have a place to stay, a job. They make sure we don't end up on the wrong side of the law, or the gods for that matter."

"Gods?" she asked.

A mischievous grin covered Taemar's face. "Where did you think your powers came from? The Christian god?"

"I . . . never really thought about it."

Taemar chuckled. "Baby, the things you're about to learn." He turned back toward the ritual.

Zora's head was swimming with all that she was learning. She knew there'd be witches, but magical houses? Gods? She bit her lip and fiddled with the lace on her dress, wondering just what she'd gotten herself into.

The man walked next. He was tall, long-limbed. He wore fitted black pants that slung low on his hips and a sequin black jacket that hung open, exposing the brown skin of his bare chest. He wore rings on every finger and a wide-brimmed hat that had a lacy black fabric that covered his face.

"I am Jabari Divinity, Head of the House of Divinity," the man said.

Several people, most of them wearing clothing like Jabari, barked three times. Others clapped. Jabari strode down the steps and stood next to Whitley.

"Why are their faces covered?" Zora whispered.

"It's part of the ritual," MK replied, her tone clipped. "It's their way of honoring the gods that they commune with."

"But then why don't we all have to cover our faces?"

MK sighed. "We just . . . don't."

Zora was left with more questions than answers as the other woman spoke.

"I am Birdie Transcendence, Head of the House of Transcendence." Birdie wore a black cocoon coat, the arms billowy and the waist dropped. Beneath it was a black corset, complete with a garter belt that connected to black thigh highs. A crystal headache band sat on her forehead, and strands of beads hung in front of her face.

Unlike with the other two, everyone in the yard shouted and

clapped.

Birdie, Zora thought. *She must be the favorite.*

Birdie, Jabari, and Whitley stepped toward the fire.

"The autumnal equinox is at hand," Birdie announced. "For only the second time this year, day and night share equal time."

"And so, too, does light and dark," Whitley added.

"And so, too, does good and evil," Jabari added. His voice was deep, and the twang to his voice was undeniable. Birdie and Whitley both turned their heads slightly to look at him as he said the word "evil".

"It is the time to reap the harvests we have sown," Whitley said. "And to give thanks for all we have received."

"Each house will sacrifice something important to them from this last year to show our devotion and love to the gods for all they have done for us, and to ensure their continued blessings as the days begin to grow colder and darker," Birdie continued.

"We sow, we reap, we sacrifice," the crowd began chanting. Zora marveled at their reverence. *What are they going to sacrifice?* she thought. Her heart pounded at the thought of seeing something or even someone be sacrificed.

As Jabari took another step toward the fire, the chanting died down.

"This year has brought us good fortune, and so we give thanks to the gods with our sacrifice." Jabari pulled a set of keys out of his pocket. "The keys to the car that put Obsidian Auto Body on the map and secured our spot as the only place in Savannah for auto care."

He tossed the keys into the fire as the people who'd barked before barked again.

"May the gods keep us and hold us tight through the darkest season," he said.

"May the gods keep you," the crowd replied.

Whitley stepped up beside Jabari. "This year has brought us good fortune, and so we give thanks to the gods with our sacrifice. This is the hair treatment we developed that went viral on TikTok, which led to our entire summer being booked solid."

"Ayyyyeeeee!" the man with the blue hair yelled as Whitley tossed the bottle into the fire.

"May the gods keep us and hold us tight through the winter," Whitley said.

"May the gods keep you." Many of them clapped, but more joined in as Birdie stepped forward.

"This year has brought—" her voice broke. She paused for several seconds and looked down at her hands. Whitley and Jabari turned their heads toward each other. Zora looked over to Taemar and MK, who both stood with their hands over their hearts. Birdie looked up and took a deep breath. "This year has brought us good fortune, and so we give thanks to the gods with our sacrifice. This hundred-dollar bill came from the queen Rihanna herself."

She tossed the money onto the fire.

"May the gods keep us and hold us tight through the loneliest season," she finished. Several people in the group exchanged glances before responding.

"May the gods keep you."

The group began their chant once again. An ornate glass bottle appeared in Whitley's hands in a flurry of pink smoke. She held it out to Jabari, who took a long draw. He spit the drink onto the flames, stoking them. Whitley followed suit then Birdie. She handed the bottle back to Whitley, and the bottle disappeared as quickly as it had appeared.

The three joined hands and chanted three times, "We three

have sown, we three have reaped, we three have sacrificed."

Then there was quiet. Everyone stared at the flames and Zora knitted her brows. Just as she was about to move, the flames turned a deep green before returning to normal. When the fire died back down, the entire group rejoiced. Zora stood with her mouth agape.

"What just happened?" Zora asked, trying to regain her composure. She felt like she wanted to laugh and cry and dance all at the same time. And perhaps more strangely, a part of her felt aroused.

"You just witnessed a proper ritual," Taemar said. He took her hand. "How do you feel?"

"Like everything and nothing all at once," she admitted. When she turned to look at him, her eyes looked glassy and her whole body tingled. She felt like crying and laughing and smiling in the same breath. *Is this what it feels like to commune with gods?* she wondered. Is this what it feels like to have community?

Zora had never been religious. Even as a child when her mother brought her to church, Zora often fell asleep during the sermons, despite the high energy music. But now, as she stood listening to the excitement of the dozens of witches around her, she finally felt like her mother's devotion made sense to her.

Taemar smiled. "The first time is always so transcendent," he replied.

"What happens now?" she asked.

As if on cue, the three House Heads began to speak again.

"Now," Birdie said. One by one, the three House Heads removed their face coverings. "Let's get this party started."

The music started up again, and this time it was a '90s throwback about Rosa Parks. Jabari and Birdie began moving amongst the crowd, giving hugs and stopping to talk to clusters of people, while Whitley lingered by the fire. Both Taemar and MK slipped into the crowd, and Zora stayed in place. She spotted people going inside the house and coming out with plates of food and drinks. Again, her stomach grumbled, and now her feet hurt. She chided herself for wearing new shoes to a function, but she reminded herself she had no idea she'd be standing for the better part of an hour.

I could just leave, Zora thought. After all, hadn't she done what Birdie suggested? She'd come to the function, she'd met a few witches, and she'd learned more about the magical community in this city, which she, admittedly, had wanted. Hadn't that been enough? But even though she knew leaving was an option, something kept her rooted in place. Was she actually feeling guilty?

"Zora!" She looked up to see Taemar looking back at her. He waved her toward him and at that moment, Zora decided she would not leave. Not this party, not now, and perhaps not even Savannah.

I want to see where this goes, she thought, as she crossed the lawn and smiled through the pain in her feet. Taemar stood with a group of people clustered near the firepit. Along with MK and the man with the blue hair she'd seen earlier, another man with a high-top fade and an electric blue, pleather jumpsuit joined them.

"Y'all, this is Zora. She's a necromancer from . . . where did you say you were from again?"

"I didn't," Zora said. "But I'm from Memphis. Just visiting family for a few days."

"Well, Ms. Necromancer from Memphis, you've already met MK. This is Orion," he said, pointing to the man with the fade. Orion nodded toward her and Zora returned the gesture. "This is

Niko."

"Nice to meet you, Zora." Niko smiled and Zora noted the slight gap between his front teeth. Something about his energy was calming, and Zora found herself beaming at him. "Your dre. is everything."

"Thank you, Niko. It's good to meet you, too." Zora nodded.

"So, I hear this is your first ritual," Niko said.

"Yes. To be honest, I had no idea anything like this existed."

MK scoffed. Zora looked over at the woman, who stood smoking a joint.

"Got something to say, MK?" Taemar asked.

Zora surveyed the group. It was obvious that Taemar was their de facto leader. She could see the same disbelief on Orion's face but only MK spoke.

"I mean, I just don't see how a real witch could last this long without trying to find community." MK took a long puff off her joint before exhaling a cloud of smoke. "I know for sure there ar three magical houses in Memphis. My mom was a part of one before she moved to Atlanta."

"Not everyone has the luxury of having magical parents, MK. Niko murmured.

"Especially not bougie ones," Taemar snapped. MK side-eyed him before rolling her eyes.

"Well, I'm just saying. Every witch I know is involved in the Triarchy of their city. Everyone knows the gods, knows the required rituals, and aren't so star-struck by their House Heads.

Zora crossed her arms. "Then I guess you need to get out more."

Niko chuckled. MK narrowed her eyes at Zora and opened he mouth to speak, but Zora turned her attention from her back to Niko and Taemar.

"Anyway, like I was saying. This is all new to me. I'm, I guess what you'd call a solo practitioner."

"Maybe not for much longer?" Taemar asked. "I mean, you did say this was everything."

"I second that."

Zora looked to her left to see Birdie standing on the other side of Taemar. She looked just as gorgeous up close as she did at a distance. Her eyeshadow was a glittery gold and her lips a bright red. She smiled at Zora and strode toward her, then kissed the air beside each of her cheeks.

"Nice to see you again, Birdie," Zora said. She felt giddy in the woman's presence, and she wondered if this was how everyone else felt, too.

"You, too, baby. Though I had no doubt you'd show," she replied.

"Oh?" Zora asked. "And how's that?"

Birdie shrugged. "Call it witch-tuition."

Zora shook her head at the pun. The other two House Heads, Jabari and Whitley, migrated over to the group.

"Jabari," MK squealed, her voice higher pitched than before. She smiled mischievously at him and he responded in kind before pulling her into his arms and kissing her while bringing a hand down to her butt. Zora tried not to laugh at the unamused expressions on nearly everyone's faces.

"Jabari, MK, do you mind?" Birdie questioned. He pulled away from MK and swatted her butt before turning his attention back to Birdie.

"Yes, ma'am," he replied. He made eye contact with Zora and that same mischievous look he'd given MK returned. Zora found her cheeks growing warm again under his gaze. Now that she could see his face, Zora noticed he was even more attractive than she thought. His sleek, elbow-length hair was parted in the middle. His face was long, with high cheekbones, a wide nose, and full lips that were painted black. His eyes were outlined in black, with an expertly drawn wing on both eyes. To Zora, he looked like a work of art, and she could see why he made MK, who'd seemed so cool, act like a little schoolgirl.

"Jabari, Whitley, this is Zora. She's new in town," Birdie said

Jabari took Zora's hand and kissed her knuckles. "Lovely to meet you, beautiful."

Zora smiled, doing her best to maintain her composure.

"You, too, Jabari."

"Hello," Whitley said with a slight wave.

"Hey," Zora responded as she watched the witch closely. Her heart-shaped lips were painted a rosy pink, and her golden-brown skin was dusted with highlighter that shimmered in the light of the fire. Her eyeliner appeared even more expertly drawn than Jabari's, and her eyebrows arched over a pair of oversized, cat-eye glasses. And Zora couldn't take her eyes off her.

"Well, I'm glad I'm not the only newbie anymore."

MK and Orion exchanged a look but neither said anything. It was clear they didn't like her. Had Orion been the one to yell out "Whitley Neon" when she was speaking?

"Where you from?" Zora asked.

"LA," Whitley said. "I was part of the House of Neon but . . . now I'm here."

"Yeah, because your daddy put you on," Orion muttered. MK laughed.

"You better put some respect on the name of a House Head, bruh," Jabari warned.

Orion and MK looked chastened as the smiles disappeared from their faces.

Whitley glared at the pair but said nothing. Zora could tell this was not the first time they had said something about her appointment as House Head, and she made a mental note to ask how someone became the head of a house anyway.

"I've never been to California. Always wanted to go," Zora spoke, shifting her attention back to Whitley.

"Yeah, yeah, enough with the love fest," Taemar said. Birdie sighed but didn't look annoyed by Taemar's interjection. "I'm starving and I'm ready to turn up. Who's got a pre-roll? Jabari?"

"You know I got you, bruh," Jabari replied. He pulled what looked like two pre-rolled blunts and a lighter from his jacket pocket and handed one to Taemar. Jabari lit his blunt and handed the lighter to Taemar, who sparked up and took a long puff. He looked at Zora and lifted the blunt to her in offering. Zora shook her head. He nodded and exhaled.

The group disbanded then, with Birdie and Whitley staying by the fire and Jabari grabbing MK's hand and guiding her back toward the house. Orion slipped his phone out of his pocket and walked toward the edge of the yard, not looking up as he passed people. Niko stole the blunt from between Taemar's fingers and took a puff. Taemar faked annoyance, but Zora could tell it was just for show. He turned toward Zora.

"You hungry? We're gonna head inside if you want to join us."

"Sure," she said. Zora followed Taemar and Niko into the house and marveled at the picked-over platters.

"Damn," Taemar exclaimed. Niko sucked his teeth and shook his head.

They each grabbed a plate and began picking at the food in silence. Most of the people mingled outside, and for the first time that night, Zora felt like she could hear herself think. Despite this realization, her ears rang.

"Now, let's get a drink. Wait, you're twenty-one, right?" he asked, turning to Zora. "And do you drink?"

"Yeah," Zora said, her mouth going dry. "Today's my twenty-first birthday, actually."

Niko paused and Taemar tilted his head. "Really? And you weren't gonna say nothin'?"

Zora laughed. "Kinda felt like the super important magical ritual that only happens twice a year takes precedence over my birthday."

Taemar pursed his lips and gave her a sidelong glance. "Well what do you want?"

"Tequila?"

Niko smiled and nodded. He poured them each a shot of Tequila then raised his glass to his lips.

"Hold on, we gotta do a toast," Taemar interrupted. He grabbed Zora's hand and led her back outside, and Zora's whole body felt like it was tingling.

"Birdie," Taemar called. She turned toward them.

"Today's Zora's birthday."

"For real?" she asked.

"Yeah," Zora replied.

"Girl! We gotta celebrate!" she shouted.

"We need—" Taemar started. Birdie held up a hand. She teleported away and reappeared moments later, a bottle of Tequila and glasses in hand. Once they each had a shot, she handed the bottle to Whitley, and it disappeared in her hands. Zora blinked, dizzy with the amount of magic happening before her eyes.

"Happy birthday, Zora. May this year be full of abundance," Birdie cheered.

"May the gods bless you and keep you," Whitley added.

"Happy birthday!" Taemar and Niko echoed.

Zora nodded then took her shot. She delighted at the warmth of the liquid as it slipped down her throat.

"Thank you," she said. "I appreciate the toast and—"

Birdie turned away and shouted to get the crowd's attention. "Everyone, this is Zora, a witch who's new to Savannah. And . . . today's her twenty-first birthday!"

The witches all turned toward Zora and shouted and cheered.

"Let's give the girl a party she'll never forget!"

"Turn up, Zora!"

More cheering. More witches yelling happy birthday. Someone queued up the Stevie Wonder version of "Happy Birthday" and the crowd erupted into a huge roar. As they each lifted their cups and sang to Zora, tears welled in her eyes and she smiled. For the first time in almost a decade, Zora felt celebrated.

Chapter 4

"Therefore, it is with the power vested to us from the gods that on this day, May 19, 1900, the Savannah Triarchy will come to power, and—following the traditions of every other Triarchy in this nation—shall be responsible for the care, education, and oversight of all witches in the city of Savannah and the oceanside community, Tybee Island. The names and duties of these houses shall be: Divinity, to oversee magical law, Soliloquy, to oversee human law, and Transcendence, to oversee revelry in all that magic offers."

Prelude of Savannah Triarchy charter, 1900

The next morning, Zora woke up in a bed that wasn't hers. Her eyes opened and looked toward a set of double windows that faced out toward a balcony and a tall magnolia tree. Long, white curtains framed the window, the bottoms of them touching the dark wooden floor.

She sat up quickly and immediately regretted it. Her head pounded, both temples throbbing like they were being held in a vice grip. The light from the sun hurt her eyes and as she looked around the room to see just where the hell she was, her stomach bubbled.

"Fuck," she whispered as she clutched her head in her hands.

The room was a stark contrast to what hers had been in Memphis. Where her room had been small, with a queen-size bed pushed against the wall covered in a yellow duvet, this bed had an ornate, white tufted sleigh bed frame and luxurious, white bedding that felt cool to the touch. A desk sat opposite the windows, marble-topped with gold metal legs. A fluffy white office chair was pushed against the desk. Across from the bed stood a tall, white dresser. Above it hung a photo of a Black woman touching her clavicle, gold paint dripping down her face and neck.

Where the hell am I? Zora thought. She looked around for her purse and sighed with relief when she saw it sitting on top of the dresser. She searched through her bag, checking to make sure everything was still there. Thankfully, her phone, wallet, lipstick, makeup blotting sheets, and car keys were all there.

Zora checked her phone, squinting at the screen. It was ten in the morning. Her battery was low, but she noticed she had a handful of belated birthday messages come through. Still, nothing from her parents.

Figures, she thought.

Zora turned to her left and brightened when she noticed a door leading into a bathroom.

It seemed just as opulent as the bedroom, with subway tile, a black clawfoot tub, a set of fresh towels, an unopened bar of soap and mouthwash on the counter. She swished her mouth and washed her face, which helped to lessen her hangover, but she felt the only real thing that would help was food. As she gathered her hair up into a bun at the top of her head, she thought about how much money she still had and where she could go to get a cheap cup of coffee and something to eat when she heard a creak on the wooden floor in the bedroom. The smell of sage and patchouli wafted through the room.

A spike of fear snaked its way up Zora's spine. She took a deep breath and stepped toward the bedroom, where the ghost of a Black woman stood near the desk. Zora stopped short, looking from the woman to her purse, wondering if she had enough time to reach for the container of margarita salt she'd swiped from the party. Just as Zora took a step toward the dresser, the ghost shifted forward. Now, she stood within arm's reach. Zora swallowed the bile at the back of her throat and took a wide step back, her calves now touching the tub. Again, the ghost moved forward, and Zora got a look at her.

The woman's copper coils hovered above her shoulders. Her left arm was covered in an elaborate tattoo arrangement of yellow, pink, and red snapdragons. A plum-colored bruise ringed her neck and red dots made her cheeks and temples look flushed. Her eyes were wide and bloodshot. The woman clasped her hands in front of her olive-green crochet dress.

No, no, no, Zora thought. *Not today. Not right now.*

"Who are you?" Zora questioned. The ghost reached out to touch Zora, to show her through memory rather than words, and Zora recoiled. "Leave me the fuck alone."

"Can't. I need you," the ghost moaned.

Zora blinked repeatedly, surprised that this ghost was able to speak so clearly. Most of the ghosts she'd encountered either didn't speak or sounded like a record skipping, forcing her to piece together what they wanted from mere fragments.

"Of course, you do," Zora said with a sigh. She slowly walked past the ghost, being careful not to turn her back on her. When she stepped into the room, she sighed.

Is this Marquitta? she thought.

"I need you," the ghost repeated.

Don't get sentimental, she told herself. It's just a dead person. She grabbed the container of salt from her purse and ripped the top off, letting it fall to the floor. She grasped a handful of salt, which was all she needed to make the ghost—who was probably Birdie's fiancée—vanish. Her hand hovered in midair as curiosit got the best of her.

"Are you Marquitta?"

The ghost looked surprised by her question, but it quickly nodded. Zora took the woman in again, noting the sadness in her eyes, the gold necklace at her neck that bore her name in cursive. She wondered if it had been a present from Birdie, and the thought made her drop the salt in her hand. A pit formed in Zora's stomach.

She picked up the top of the salt and set the container back c the dresser. She wasn't going to salt the woman, but she wasn't going to let her inject her memories into her, either. Zora slid it back into her purse and slung it over her shoulder.

"Goodbye, Marquitta," Zora said as she walked backward toward the door. The ghost remained rooted in place, still starin at Zora with the same melancholy in her eyes.

"See you," the ghost whispered. Zora's heart jumped at those two words and she quickly scrambled out of the room. She close the door and let out a deep exhale.

Holy fuck, she thought. She stood there for a few minutes doing her best to get her breath under control. When her heart felt like it was back to beating steady again, she took in her surroundings.

The room let out into a narrow hallway with stark white wall Boudoir-type photos of people lined the walls, and a neon sign across from the landing read "We're all mad here."

She descended the wooden stairs, the sound of laughter and clinking glasses growing louder. The front door faced the stairwell. A grand chandelier hung in the entryway and an ornat gold and black carpet sat beneath it.

"The fuck?" she whispered, realizing she was in a different home than the one she entered the night before.

To the right of the stairs emerged a living room, where a large couch faced a television mounted above the fireplace. Gauzy white curtains hung before a set of three windows to the left of the couch, and two black wingback chairs sat before the windows.

Between them rested a marble coffee table, and a single photograph sat upon it. Zora stepped closer to get a good look. She noticed Birdie and Marquitta sitting on what looked to be a set of steps leading into a home. They sat with their thighs touching, each of them holding a coffee cup in their hands. Birdie's head was thrown back and she smiled wide like she was laughing. Marquitta smiled and looked at Birdie. So much love dwelled in her eyes that it took Zora's breath away.

She wondered what it must've been like to love someone like that when she stepped through a long hallway that led to the kitchen. Along the walls of the hall appeared photos of Taemar, Birdie, Marquitta, Orion, MK, and a few other witches Zora didn't recognize. She noticed they all seemed happier than they did now, especially Birdie.

When Zora reached the kitchen, she saw Birdie, Taemar, Orion, and MK seated at a breakfast nook.

They looked up at the sound of Zora's footfalls and smiled.

"Good morning," Birdie said. She gestured toward a chair across from her and Zora slid into it.

"You sleep well, Ms. Necromancer?" Taemar asked. He set a pitcher of orange juice in front of her then a French press halfway filled with coffee. Zora picked up the empty coffee cup to her left and poured herself some coffee, the aroma of the brew awakening her senses and soothing her headache.

"Yeah, thanks. I don't remember getting back here," she said. "Wherever here is."

MK chuckled. "Looks like someone turned up last night."

Zora sipped her coffee. "Yeah, that's what people do on their twenty-first birthday, I'm told." She turned her attention from MK to Birdie who sat neatly cutting a pancake into small square

MK chortled but remained silent.

"You're in the House of Transcendence, baby," Birdie revealed. "You were too out of it to drive, so we brought you back here."

"Thanks for that," Zora said, hoping she didn't embarrass herself the night before. She scanned the spread of food on the table and grabbed a croissant and a few sausage links before scooping some fresh fruit onto her plate.

"So, you got your ritual cherry popped last night," Orion teased.

Zora scrunched her nose at his comment, and when she looked at Birdie and Taemar, who were seated next to each other and wearing matching purple, satin bonnets, they wore similar looks of distaste.

"I guess," Zora shrugged.

"I still can't believe you have no idea about Triarchies or our rituals or our gods. You're so sheltered," MK chimed in.

Zora sighed and Birdie stretched a hand across the table and patted Zora's hand.

"Don't worry. We'll help you along," she assured her.

"Thanks. I don't come from a family of witches," Zora replied directing her comment at MK. "As far as I know, I'm the only one. My mom didn't approve of my witchcraft."

"And your dad?" Taemar asked.

"My dad—"

She stopped herself short. Did she really want to lay out her trauma to these strangers? Did she want to tell them that her father talked her into speaking to ghosts and raising the dead for money? That she told him time and time again that she was scared and he told her she had to push past her fears because her family needed her? That she learned to affect an air of nonchalance at eight, learned how to cry quickly and quietly at nine? No, she would do no such thing.

She didn't know them. She could already feel their judgment for her lack of knowledge of what they believed was common knowledge. Besides, she wasn't planning to stay in Savannah. Why try to cultivate relationships in a place she never planned to visit again? But even as she thought about leaving, a part of her resisted the thought.

Zora took another sip of coffee, trying to cover up her pause. "My dad doesn't care one way or another about my powers." Actually, he cares more about them than he does about me.

"When did you first realize you had them?" Birdie asked.

As she bit into her croissant, Zora could feel them eyeing her, awaiting her answer.

"Eight," she said.

"Young," Taemar replied. "Same with me. I was watching some old school kid's movie 'bout a rooster that lost his singin' voice and was best friends with a basset hound with my mom. By the time she went to the bathroom and came out, I had turned into a rooster. I was so afraid."

"Oh, wow. How did you figure out how to turn back into yourself?" Zora asked.

"Believe it or not, I tried to force my way back, but the change didn't happen until I calmed down and let the fear subside," Taemar explained. "I imagined myself the way I was before that moment and then I was back."

Birdie nodded. "We all start out that way, afraid. That's why having other witches around to guide us is crucial."

"Yeah, but you've only been a witch for a few years." MK rolled her eyes and tilted her head.

Birdie gave the woman a pointed look. "Yeah, but whether your powers come on at eight or twenty-one, you're still a witch. You still need guidance. No one survives in this world without community."

Silence fell over the room. Not wanting to deal with the tension, Zora took a bite of sausage and stood.

"Well, this was all really great, but I've got to get back to my hotel. Gotta check out."

"Oh? Well, let me take you," Birdie said. She slid out of the bench seat and stood.

"No, no, don't go through the trouble. I'll just take an Uber to my car."

Birdie waved a hand at her. "Don't be silly. It's no trouble. Besides, it'll give us a chance to chat."

Shit, Zora thought.

Sounds great," she forced through a smile.

They stepped out of the house and down the steps, which Zora recognized as the same steps in the photo of Birdie and Marquitta. She followed Birdie to a yellow Camaro and slid into the passenger seat. After securing her seatbelt, Zora looked back up to the house she'd just exited.

The House of Transcendence, she thought. It looked every

bit the type of house she'd expect witches to live in—a sweeping Victorian with black shutters and a stark white exterior. The front door consisted of solid wood with a circular window of stained glass. Balconies extended from the second and third floors. In front of the basement window sat a fountain with the sculpture of a trio of women dancing and holding hands. Red snapdragons sprouted along the edge of the iron fence.

"You good?" Birdie asked.

"Yeah, just looking at the house," Zora said. "You do know you can be a witch and not live in such a stereotypical place, right?"

Birdie chuckled as she pulled into the road. "What do you mean?"

"I mean, Transcendence house is beautiful, don't get me wrong, but it looks like it's either haunted or it's home to a coven. Guess one of those things is true."

Birdie sucked her teeth. "'Coven' is such a white, cis-het term. No, we're not a coven. We're a collective. We're a family. And like a lot of families, we have an inheritance. That house? The original founders of the Savannah Triarchy sacrificed a lot to secure it and the other two houses. So show some respect."

"I'm sorry," Zora replied.

She could tell from Birdie's response that this was a subject she was passionate about. As Birdie drove down Gaston Street to Abercorn, she fiddled with the lacy edge of her sleeve.

"That's okay," Birdie said. "You've got a lot to learn, but if you want, I can teach you."

"Why are you so gassed up about teaching me witch shit?" Zora questioned. She'd taken Birdie's first offer as an invitation. But having her and Taemar both offer to teach her Witch 101 and extol the benefits of the Savannah Triarchy over Memphis all within the last twelve hours made her suspicious.

"Because I know what it's like not knowing how to control your powers. Like MK said earlier, my powers came to me so much later in life."

"You were twenty-one?"

"Yes. And I was telling my then long-time boyfriend, who my family all adored, that I didn't want to marry him."

"Whoa, that's heavy," Zora replied. They parked across the street from Divinity house, and Zora looked behind her to see her car still parked where she'd left it the night before.

"Yeah. We'd been together since we were sixteen. I went to Spelman, he to Morehouse. All through college, we were seen as this power couple. And it was just assumed we'd be married."

"Why'd you turn him down?"

"Because I didn't love him anymore. I told them all that, and in the midst of him yelling, I thought about being in my room, and in the blink of an eye, I was there. I didn't fully know what I was doing until I moved here and met Marquitta."

"So, is that why you're trying to help me? To pay it forward or somethin'?" Zora asked.

She surprised herself by not leaving the car. Was she considering Birdie's offer? Was there some part of her that wanted to stay in Savannah? That wanted to learn more about her powers and about being a witch? That wanted to be part of a community? This community?

Birdie frowned. She gripped her steering wheel and turned toward Zora.

"Girl, do you always question people's motives this hard? You know it is possible for people just to want to help you."

Zora lifted a brow. "I get that you want to help me, and I appreciate that. But I feel like there's somethin' you're not tellin' me."

Birdie sighed. She looked over at Divinity house and brought her hand to her face. She sat like that for what seemed like forever before turning her attention back to Zora.

"You know how I told you Marquitta was murdered?"

Zora nodded. Already she felt her heartbeat quicken.

"Well, we still don't know who did it," Birdie admitted.

"Do the police have an idea of what happened?" Zora asked, but even as she did, she already knew the answer. Marquitta was a Black woman, a queer Black woman at that. In the police's mind, she was less dead. In their mind, she got what she deserved for living her "lifestyle". Over the years, Zora had helped plenty of families who the police had abandoned, families who society vilified for not fitting the norm.

Is that why I'm here? Zora thought. Birdie shook her head, confirming Zora's suspicions.

A spark of rage ignited in Zora's heart. She looked at this woman, this perfectly put-together woman, this witch who said she wanted nothing more than to help Zora control her powers. Zora should have known there was a catch. No one just offers their help out of the kindness of their heart. And the worst part? Zora had allowed herself to be lured into this woman's web, had even thought that moving to Savannah wouldn't be so bad because she'd have community.

Suddenly, Zora's thoughts transported her back to that moment when she was eight and her father first posed the idea of her using her powers for money. That funeral had been for a family mourning their son who'd had his skull caved in after a drunken fight at a party. She saw him standing there leaning over his own casket then, the left side of his skull chipped away, revealing the gray matter of his brain. Blood cascaded down the side of his face, outlining his sunken in eye and cheekbone. She heard him shouting, begging to get back into his body, for it all to be a dream and to wake up. When he realized Zora could see him, he ran toward her and she screamed, but not before her father caught her in his arms and held her.

"It's alright, Zo," he soothed. "They can't do nothing to you while I'm around."

He calmed her down as the funeral proceeded but still insisted she try to get a vision of what happened.

"This family is gonna pay us three hundred dollars. You can do this, Zora. For your family," he'd said, his eyes pleading with her.

"Family," Zora whispered. That was the first time she saw the final moments of someone. The first time she knew how brutal the world could be. She'd done all of that to help her family, and she was, at first. But then her mother left and her father got greedy and began seeing her powers as a way to settle his scores. She'd been used as a pawn, and that was why she had to leave Memphis and her father behind. She told herself she'd never use her powers that way again, and yet here she sat with someone who wanted her to do exactly that.

Zora grit her teeth and unbuckled her seatbelt.

"How dare you," Zora spat.

"Pardon me?" she asked.

"Is that why you talked to me at Lulu's? To get me to talk to your dead fiancée and find out who killed her?"

"Zora, I—"

"No, no. You're just like my father. You just want to use me."

Birdie lifted her hands up as if in surrender. "Zora, that's not true. I want to help you. I know what it's like to feel out of control, to have power inside you that feels too big. I can help you."

"How?" Zora threw up her hands. From the corner of her eye, she could see a few passersby glancing over at them but she didn't care. "You're just a teleportation witch. And from what I gathered, no one else in your lil' Triad or whatever is even a medium, let alone a necromancer. You can't help me."

She pushed open the door and stepped out of the car. Birdie reached for her and when Zora looked back at her, tears filled her eyes.

"Zora, please, you're all I got."

Zora pursed her lips and stared at Birdie, feeling the pit in her stomach grow to the size of a basketball. Her sorrow for Birdie's loss had grown, but so had her rage. Zora pushed Birdie's arm off her and stepped fully out of the car.

"You can't help me, and I won't help you. I'm leavin' tomorrow and I think it's best that we don't talk again."

Zora slammed the door behind her and hurried to her car, keeping her head held high. She slid into the driver's seat and started her car. She began sobbing as she drove away, just as she had done when she left Memphis only two days before.

Zora drove around the city before taking the highway out to Tybee Island. She'd gotten food along the way and as she sipped her sweet tea and blasted Flo Milli, Zora's thoughts drifted back to the day her mother left.

She was sixteen and had spent the last eight years talking to ghosts and raising the dead for money. Her mother had been completely in the dark. Whenever she'd raised a question about why Zora had been taken out of school early or why her father would want to spend time only with Zora and not Keith on the weekends, her father would lie.

"Zora's gettin' to be a good handywoman," he'd say. "Might even be able to go into business with me one day."

Her mother would smile as though proud, but Zora could tell she always had her doubts.

It wasn't until her father's friend, JP, had died that their mother realized the truth about her daughter. They'd been at JP's funeral, and though he died of natural causes, his wife had wanted to say goodbye to him one last time. She'd been at her mother's house and had come home to find him dead of a heart attack, lying between the toilet and the shower in their bathroom. Before the viewing, JP's wife had asked Zora to meet her at the funeral parlor and Zora obliged, despite never really liking JP because he always referred to women as "females" and spoke at length about how they were "keeping the Black man down."

As she stood above him, her face stony, her heart pounded and her temples throbbed. Her mouth went dry as she pressed her hands to his shoulders. Instantly, his milky, unfocused eyes popped open. His jaw snapped open with a pop, and a guttural sound rattled in his throat.

His wife wailed and threw herself on him, and Zora steeled herself as she felt his arm move toward her head.

"Tina, you here? I told Pastor Rice I'd get—"

Zora startled at the sound of her mother's voice. All at once, Zora, Tina, and JP snapped their heads to the left to see her standing in the doorway, one hand on the door frame and the other one over her mouth. Tina stood up from her husband's body and his corpse sat up, as though following her movements.

Nia screamed. "Demon! You are not welcome in the house of the Lord! Zora get away from him, you—"

"Mama, it's okay," she replied. When she let go of JP's corpse, it fell back against the cushioned coffin with a thump, his eyes and mouth once again closed. Her mother looked from Zora to the body in the coffin to Tina, as though she were still trying to process what she'd just seen. But then her expression turned from horror to suspicion.

"Zora, why were you touching JP's body like that?" her mother questioned.

"I was helping Ms. Tina . . . she needed to adjust JP in the coffin. His suit was all bunched up," Zora said. Tina looked at her, eyes wide, seemingly surprised at the ease with which Zora had been able to lie. But Zora wasn't. It was another skill she'd picked up from her father. She was so good that she could almost lie to herself.

But Tina was the town gossip. She could never be counted on to keep anything to herself for long, a fact Zora's own mother had bitched about for years. So it wasn't a surprise when she said: "No. No, Zora was helping me talk to my JP."

Nia's lips set in a thin line. She lifted a brow and looked from Zora to Tina and back to Zora again. "What do you mean Zora was helping you talk to JP?"

Tina sighed and looked at Zora as if to say, "I'm sorry." Zora watched with horror as Tina walked toward her mother and grabbed her hand.

"Nia, Zora was helping me talk to JP again. I don't know how she does it, but your daughter, she's a powerful girl, and I—"

"What do you mean, 'she's a powerful girl?'" her mother asked, jerking her hands out of Tina's. "How did you find out she could do . . . whatever it is she's doing in the first place?"

Tina blanched. She twisted her wedding ring on her finger and glanced at Zora once again, and Zora's belly filled with rage as she realized that Tina was more hesitant to tell her mother about her father's involvement than about Zora's abilities. A single tear slid down Zora's cheek and she brushed it off just as quickly as it came.

"From Ricky," Tina confessed.

The wounded look on her mother's face made Zora whimper. Her mother didn't say anything else to Zora or to Tina. She turned on her heel and stormed out of the room and the church. She didn't come back for the funeral, nor was she at Tina's house for the repast. Her absence dominated the conversation at the repast, and though Zora sat with Keith in the living room while most people lingered around in the kitchen or on Tina's closed-in porch, she still could hear fragments of their conversations.

"I always thought Nia knew what was goin' on?"

"I can't believe she'd keep that from her own mother."

"How could Ricky get his own kids to lie to her?"

For his part, Keith sat and held Zora's hand throughout the gossip and reproachful looks. Zora glared back at them all, but her anxiety was mounting so much that by the time they arrived home, she felt like a fish out of water.

All her mother's rage came bursting into the fore the second they walked through the door.

"How could you?" she yelled at Zora's father. "How could you make our own daughter use these powers and what's more, make her and Keith and everyone we know lie to me?"

"I was doin' it to help us, Nia," her father said, his hands up as if in surrender. "We needed the money."

"So get a job! Why force our child to commune with such evil forces just so you could sit at home all day?"

"It wasn't like that and you know that," he argued.

"Then what was it like, huh?"

He looked down at his worn dress shoes and grit his teeth. Zora wanted to say something to diffuse the situation, to come to her father's defense, to tamp down her mother's anger, but she couldn't. She stood, paralyzed in place beside him.

"We needed the money. This gig paid and it paid well. I didn't see you complainin' when I brought home a new TV or when I bought you and the kids new shoes."

A loud pop followed his words then silence. For the first time ever, Zora saw her mother slap her father. Zora startled and she and Keith stared at each other in horror. Their parents argued for what felt like hours before her mother pulled Zora into the room and gave her a choice:

"I don't condone what you did. You used these powers that go against God and everything I've taught you for years and you . . ." her voice broke. "You lied to me."

Zora looked down but her mother cupped her chin in her hand and forced her gaze up. The look of disappointment in her mother's eyes was haunting. "But now's your time to repent. I'm leaving. Tonight, with Keith. And you can either come with me and start a new life away from all of this and without those powers, or you can stay here without me."

Confused, Zora looked from her mother to her father and saw the determination in her eyes and the desperation in his. Could it really be as easy as leaving Memphis? Could she really just start over, a new city, no ghosts?

But . . . no. No, she knew wherever she went her powers would haunt her. And she knew for all his faults, her father couldn't survive alone. She squared her shoulders and made the second choice that would define her life.

"I choose to stay," she decided.

Choices. That was all anyone's life amounted to, really. A

series of choices made with or without knowledge, in good faith or bad. As she sat with the memory of her mother on her mind, on a bench on River Street in Savannah, Zora thought about the choices she could make with the options she had.

Sure, she could return to Memphis and go back to her dad, but he wouldn't apologize for how they left things, and neither would she. But she'd have a roof over her head, she'd have friends and her dance classes, even if it meant she'd have to use her powers for money. Even if it meant trekking to audition after audition to be a dancer.

But here, she'd start fresh. No one would know her as "Ricky lil' girl" or that "lil' witch off Cherry Street." She'd just be Zora. And, she'd be able to do something she'd already done so, so many times before—solve a murder. Yet, there was also the possibility of community. Of befriending people who understood exactly what she was going through, who could teach her how to honor the gods and how not to be so afraid all the time.

Before she fully realized what she was doing, she pulled out her phone and dialed, before putting the phone up to her ear.

"Hello?" the woman answered. Zora could tell she'd been crying.

"What's in it for me?"

"Pardon?"

"If I help solve Marquitta's murder, what's in it for me?"

Suddenly, Birdie appeared on the bench beside Zora. Zora pursed her lips and Birdie smiled and made a show of hitting the end call button before dabbing at her eyes. She turned toward Zora, her hair now done and her curves poured into a black jumpsuit.

"I meant what I said when I told you I could help you control your powers."

Zora folded her arms. "Did Marquitta have control of hers?"

Birdie chuckled then sniffled. "She was amazing. She could get visions without even needing a ghost to be present. She could raise the dead, no matter how far gone, and she could stop the ghosts from talking to her on their terms."

Zora's eyes widened. "You could really show me how to do that?"

Birdie smiled wistfully and nodded. Zora returned the gesture then frowned

Get a grip, Zora, she thought.

"But I need more than that. I can't just help you for free."

"Well, do you know how to make a drink?" Birdie asked.

"I could figure it out." Zora shrugged. "Why?"

"You see that building across the street?" Birdie gestured to a three-story building nestled on the corner of the Lincoln Street Ramp, where cobblestones still lined the steep road up to Bay Street. The building seemed out of character for the area—for one, it was the only one painted gold. For another, instead of the antiquated door overhangs that hung over nearly every shop on the street, it displayed a large neon sign that read "Nightingale's". Long, flat steps led to the entrance on the side of the building, and still more steps led to another entrance where a small patio sat.

"Yeah," Zora said.

"That's my club, Nightingale's. Patrons from all over the state come to the club, get a taste of our drinks, and see my girls dance."

Zora lifted a brow. "You own a strip club?"

Birdie rolled her eyes and scoffed. "Not a strip club, a burlesque club. Big difference. You can find beautiful, naked bodies at any ol' strip club, but Nightingale's specializes in the art

of the tease. My dancers don't just strip; they seduce. Anyway, w
need another bartender. You could start today if you wanted."

Zora considered this thought for a moment. "No," she
responded.

"Wha—"

"I'm a dancer. I've been training since I was six."

Birdie chuckled. "Baby, burlesque is a lot different than the
things they teach you in dance classes."

"How would you know?" Zora questioned.

Birdie cocked her head. "Because I've been around dancers
for years and because I run this mothafuckin' club. We've had
dancers come in before thinking they had it in the bag, but then
they were about as sexy as a kick in the head."

Am I really gonna do this? Zora thought. Zora closed her eye
and exhaled before turning toward Birdie and looking the woma
in the eyes.

"The last thing I want to do is use my powers. But I know I've
got to figure them out if I'm gonna survive. So if you can help
me control 'em, I'll help you solve Marquitta's murder on two
conditions."

Birdie gestured to Zora to keep talking.

"You help me find a place to stay, and you let me dance at
your club."

"The room you stayed in last night is vacant, so it's yours
now if you want it. But Zora, I can't just let you dance," Birdie
said. "My dancers are known for being the best, and that means
we only accept the best. You can audition, and if you can bring
the technique and the sex appeal, then you should have no
problems."

"Fine. But I think you'll end up hirin' me anyhow," Zora
boasted. Then she stood and strutted to her car.

Chapter 5

"We settled on Nightingale's, as callin' the club Birdie's would have been too much. On opening night, there were lines out the door with witches and humans alike wantin' to get in and see us dance."

Spell Book of Marquitta Transcendence, 2019

That evening, Zora pulled into the parking lot across the street from Nightingale's, which shimmered in the glow of the sunset. She'd gotten Birdie's text giving her the full details about the audition—she was to show up at six with a song in mind and dressed in something she could easily remove. Having a burlesque costume beneath was optional; she knew Zora was living out of her suitcase, so she advised her to wear a matching bra and panty set she wouldn't be ashamed to show people. And there would be people. While Zora auditioned for Birdie, the other dancers who worked at Nightingale's, including MK, would be there to watch as well.

"I'm not a dancer by trade; that was Marquitta's gig. But these dancers are pros, so if you've been talkin' big shit and can't deliver, they'll clock it," Birdie had texted.

Zora wasn't nervous about having more people there to watch her audition. She knew what she was capable of, and soon, they would, too. She'd taken the time between talking to Birdie and showing up for her audition to buy a lingerie set that, while not necessarily fit for a Vegas stage, would do for a three-minute song on a Savannah one.

As she peered into her rearview mirror, Zora applied her lipstick, a bright red that matched her lingerie set—a pair of lacy panties that exposed the bottom of her butt cheeks, a matching corset that cinched her in and emphasized her waist, and a lacy bra that showed off her ample breasts. She fluffed her hair with her pick and sprayed herself with perfume before leaving her car. She strode across the street, her heels clicking against the cobblestones, and walked into the club. She climbed three steps then opened a red curtain, immediately taken aback by the opulence of the club.

Red and gold filigree wallpaper that stretched from the dark hardwood floors to the crimson ceiling covered the walls. Instead of chandeliers, gilded birdcages hung from the ceiling with clusters of candles in them. The windows along the right side of the room, facing the river, flaunted long, blood-red curtains that hung before them. Though the curtains were now drawn, the windows didn't offer much light.

Rather than standard tables and chairs, Nightingale's employed chaise lounges, wingback chairs, and plush, L-shaped couches in shades of red and gold. Zora noticed small, black tables placed strategically near clusters of seats, and atop them all a single red candle in a black candle holder.

The stage seemed modest but boasted a catwalk that protruded toward the crowd. Zora nodded at Birdie, who stood on stage with MK and several other witches she recognized from the night before. Across from the stage was the bar, embellished with black wood and a red and gold marble top. Behind the bar was a large mirror shaped in a half-circle, and small stage lights extended out from it like sunrays. A neon sign that read "Nightingale's Est. 2019" in swirling, vintage-looking font was attached to the center of the mirror. Zora hoisted herself onto a black barstool. As she sat, she marveled at the fact that there were no ghosts in the room at all. Her shoulders relaxed and she took a deep breath.

So this is what it feels like to be normal, she thought.

Taemar eased over to her from the other side of the bar. He wore a shimmering gold, silk shirt unbuttoned to his navel and tucked into black pants. Strands of pearls and a gold chain adorned his neck, and his dark hair was down and wild.

"So, what was that about you absolutely, positively not moving to Savannah?" Taemar smirked at her. Zora couldn't help the smile that crept across her face.

"I don't remember saying that at all," she joked.

Taemar scoffed. He set the cloth he was using to wipe glasses down on the bar and crossed his arms.

"Uh-huh. Birdie tells me you 'bout to audition?" He grabbed a bottle of water from a small refrigerator beneath him and Zora accepted it gratefully. She unscrewed the top and took a sip, careful not to mess up her lipstick.

"Yeah. I've been dancin' since I was six. Figured if I was staying to help Birdie, might as well do somethin' I love."

Taemar cocked his head. "What'll you be helpin' Birdie with?"

As Zora opened her mouth to respond, Birdie called out to her, "We're ready for you, girl."

Zora shrugged at Taemar and strode toward the stage. He smiled and shook his head then busied himself with the bar.

"Okay, ladies," Birdie said as Zora stepped onto the stage. "This is Zora. Some of you met her last night, but just to reintroduce you, you know MK."

Birdie gestured to the petite woman who stood with a hand on her hip and an impassive look on her face. She smiled curtly and

Zora returned the gesture.

"This is Tanisha, Chansi, Raheem, Deja, Safi, and Livia," Birdie continued, gesturing to each dancer as she introduced them. They all smiled and welcomed her, though she could tell Deja and Livia, both perfectly toned Black women, were taking her in with some skepticism. They'd probably never seen or paid attention to a dancer who looked like her, who wore size 14 jeans and who towered over everyone else with or without heels.

It didn't matter, though. Zora was going to show them what they'd been missing.

"Nice to meet y'all," she said, waving.

"Did you happen to pick a song to dance to?" Birdie asked.

"Harlem Nocturne," she replied. Birdie gestured to the left of the stage, where Orion stood behind a DJ booth. With one hand he queued up the track, clutching his phone tightly in the other. Birdie and the other dancers cleared off the stage and Zora began to dance.

When the saxophone blared, she stepped forward and swayed, bringing first her left shoulder back then her right. When the music paused, she unzipped her yellow top and pulled it off in time with the music, revealing her red, lacy bra. As the music switched tempo, she made use of the stage, gliding from the right to the left and twisting out of her black skirt. Then she stood in her lingerie set and wound down to the floor before stretching a leg out and doing the splits.

The air was cool but sweat streamed down her stomach and her temples as she stood. Her heartbeat raced and she smiled in anticipation as she bent backward and glanced at the group standing to watch her dance. She winked at Birdie before bringing herself back up and unclipping her bra.

Zora turned as the song wound down and let her bra slip into her hands, revealing cherry-shaped pasties covering her nipples.

When the song ended, she exhaled. A smile covered her face as she clasped her bra. Birdie, Taemar, and most of the dancers clapped and hooted at her. Only MK and Deja stood with their faces screwed up. Zora slipped her skirt back on and shrugged back into her top before stepping off the stage.

"Girl, you killed that! I'd never know that was your first time doing burlesque," Birdie grinned.

"It was cute or whatever," MK added.

Zora rolled her eyes, but she didn't reply. When it came to witchery, Zora knew she needed help. But when it came to dancing? To moving her body? Zora was an expert. So she looked at Birdie, who stood looking between Zora and the rest of the dancers.

"Me and the dancers here are gonna deliberate. Tae, can you take Zora outside and keep her company?" Birdie said.

Taemar nodded and walked over to the bar to collect two waters and a golden cigarette case off the top of the bar.

Zora began walking toward Taemar and the patio, but she cast one last look at Birdie and the other dancers, many of whom eyed her with curiosity.

Zora stood on the small patio outside of Nightingale's with Taemar and leaned over the railing, watching as the crowds increased on River Street. Looming off to the side of the cobblestone steps several feet away hovered a group of ghosts, young men dressed in baseball jackets with backwards hats. Some of them were missing limbs, while others had caved in faces. Zora could tell they noticed her and, like all ghosts around a necromancer, had at first clamored toward her wanting to show her their last moments. But it seemed whatever was special about Nightingale's protected her even on the patio, and Zora had never felt more at ease despite their scowls.

She listened intently as Taemar told her about the history of the building and how Birdie and Marquitta founded it.

"This used to be a factory back in the 1800s but then some big wig bought it and turned it into a cabaret in the '20s," he said. "Marquitta told me it changed hands for decades before becoming Bon Temps, a strip club.

"She worked here then, started just out of high school apparently. Became close to Mr. Bouchard, the old owner of the place. He helped her get into community college and she started teachin' dance classes on the side. Let Marquitta tell it, he thought of her like his own daughter, so when he went tits up in 2018, he left this place to her."

Zora turned around and leaned against the railing, gazing up at the building.

"So, how'd it become Nightingale's?" Zora asked.

"Marquitta wanted to move away from strippin' and do somethin' else. She and Birdie met not too long after she took over this place. She had a mind for dancin' and promotin', but Birdie was the businesswoman. They met and soon after Birdie became her partner in business and in life."

Zora listened as Taemar told her how they'd kept the dancers who were willing to change their style, even the ones who wanted to work behind the bar instead, and helped the others find jobs elsewhere. Many of the dancers who stayed, like Chansi, Raheem and Safi, were witches.

"Now what I want to know is, what made you come here from

Memphis? You know Savannah's haunted, right?"

Zora grimaced.

Taemar gave her a comforting look. "Girl, look, I know we don't know each other like that but seems like you got a lot of trauma surroundin' your situation you got to work through. And one of the best ways to do that is to talk about it and say exactly how you feelin' about it."

"Okay, Iyanla," Zora said, rolling her eyes.

Taemar sucked his teeth. "Uh-uh, don't compare me to her. She's a life coach. I'm going to be a therapist."

"Oh, I stand corrected."

"That's okay, baby. You never met no one like me anyway. My plan is to get my PhD and start a practice where I can treat witches, 'specially queer Black witches."

"I see. Does that make me your first patient, Mr.?"

Taemar extended his hand for a handshake. "Doctor Fitzgerald. But those in the know will just call me Dr. Taemar Transcendence."

"So, what is it with the naming thing? Do you like—"

"Uh-huh, don't change the subject."

Zora rolled her eyes again and pursed her lips.

"We take on the name of the house we are invited to join. There's a ritual and everything. Now spill."

"Is there some kind of test you need to pass to be invited?"

Taemar exhaled and tilted his head. "Miss thing? You really don't like talkin' about yourself, do you?"

"I already said I'm not very interesting," Zora shrugged.

Taemar shook his head and began walking toward the door.

"Wait—" Zora's mind raced and her palms were clammy. How had it come to this? Why did she feel so anxious about sharing her story with someone? About letting someone in?

Taemar stopped and looked at her.

"I . . . I used to talk to ghosts and raise the dead for money," Zora admitted. She surprised herself with how easily the statement rolled off her tongue despite never having told anyone before. "And I left Memphis because I got someone put in the hospital."

Taemar's eyes widened but he sat and listened intently as Zora told him the truth.

Last week, their neighbor, Mr. Lionel, called Zora and her father over for breakfast. Over coffee and pancakes, he told them about how his nephew, Anthony, had been murdered while working at the Quick Stop in Buckingham Farms. He asked Zora to help him and before she could respond, her father insisted she would. Mr. Lionel had been the one to put them on, the one who set them up with this gig after all. She tried her best to connect with Anthony at the home but he wasn't there. So she drove to the Quick Stop and saw him standing by pump 9, still holding a squeegee despite the bullet holes in his stomach and the blood dripping from his mouth.

He'd been killed by a local, small time dealer and hustler called Saint Louie. Zora had grown up with him—Louie had been the quiet kid with hand-me-down clothes before he dropped out and started dealing. Anthony had been having an affair with his girlfriend, and Saint Louie settled the score then made it look like a robbery gone bad. Zora told her father all of this and he thanked her for helping Mr. Lionel. Before she could call Mr. Lionel to tell him, her father had insisted he do it being that they "go way back."

Zora hadn't thought much of it, but the next day as she was driving home from dance lessons, she saw a group of men at the park and recognized her father, Mr. Lionel, and several of their other friends. Mr. Lionel stood with a bat in his hands.

Her stomach dropped as she parked haphazardly across two parking spaces and leapt out the car. A crowd had gathered to watch the display.

"What's goin' on?" she asked someone in the crowd.

"Lionel gettin' his revenge," a woman responded. "Found out Fiz shot Anthony and robbed the store."

Zora gasped as she saw Mr. Lionel swing the bat at Fiz, a hustler with an even bigger reputation than Saint Louie.

That's the wrong man, Zora thought. She shrieked as the bat connected with Fiz's arm. He yelled out in pain. Holy shit, he's gonna kill him!

Zora pushed through the crowd and hurried to her father. As she pulled him aside, he tried to jerk out of her grip, but Zora held firm.

"Dad, you know this isn't the one who did it," Zora whispered. The crowd was so loud, yelling and hyping Mr. Lionel up, that she had to repeat herself. When she did, her father just looked at her and shrugged.

"Dad—"

Mr. Lionel landed another blow. A sickening crack echoed through the air as Fiz's forearm seemed to shatter. The man cried out and kept pleading for Mr. Lionel to stop, to just listen to him.

"Dad, please, this isn't right," Zora begged. The crowd pushed her and her father closer toward the scene, the onlookers eager to see more as Mr. Lionel landed blow after blow.

"You killed my nephew, you sick mothafucka!" he yelled.

"Dad!"

"Zora, shut up. We told Mr. Lionel we'd handle it, and so we did. And now he's getting his justice."

The look in her father's eyes sent a spike of rage up her spine and into the base of her skull.

"This isn't right!"

Ricky pushed his daughter and turned back toward the fight. Mr. Lionel handed him the bat and Zora turned away before she could see what happened next.

She found out later they'd shattered his forearm and broken his collar bone, legs, and jaw, which had to be wired shut. That night as she cleaned the kitchen to ease her anxiety, Zora discovered why her father had lied to Mr. Lionel.

She stumbled upon a note in the trash from Fiz. In big, block letters it read, "RUN ME MY MONEY BY MONDAY OR ELSE."

Zora sat down on the couch, trying to process her discovery. She'd known her father was in pain after falling off a ladder and injuring his back during his short-lived stint as a maintenance man for an apartment complex. He hadn't broken anything, but he'd been in tremendous pain ever since. He didn't have health insurance, so he'd been unable to get any pain meds that weren't over the counter.

At least, that's what Zora had thought. She knew Fiz sold percs and other medical grade shit—had her father started buying and been unable to pay?

Instantly, thoughts rushed through her brain as she considered how many times her father had spoken for her in recent months. How many times he'd made her feel voiceless and powerless. Their meeting with Mr. Lionel wasn't the first time.

I can't do this anymore. The thought hit her like a ton of bricks. She glanced around the small home and suddenly felt like she was crawling out of her skin. Before she knew it, she was up and striding into her room. She grabbed her suitcases and packed all the belongings she could fit into two duffle bags and a backpack, including pictures of her and Keith when they were younger. Then, she turned off the lights and closed and locked the windows, and she left the only home she'd ever known.

Chapter 6

"Birdie knew we were going to use magic in our acts despite all the non-magical customers. So we came up with our signature cocktail, the Savannah Serenade—3 parts peach juice, 2 parts pineapple juice, 2 parts bourbon, 1 part ginger beer. Mix in the magic erasure potion, add a splash of grenadine, and garnish with lemon. For the non-drinkin' honeys, replace the 2 parts bourbon with extra ginger beer."

Spell Book of Marquitta Transcendence, 2019

Laughter and shouts from the excited crowds on River Street filled the night, but the one person Zora wanted to hear from, needed to hear from, stood silent. Taemar's dark eyes took her in, and his mouth was set in a grim line. Her stomach was doing flips and her mouth was dry. Her temples throbbed and she just wanted him to say something, anything. Even if it was to tell her she was a shitty person who deserved all the bad she'd endured.

She clenched her jaw as Taemar sucked in a breath. Instead of speaking, Taemar strode back toward her and wrapped her in his arms. Her eyes widened and she blinked away tears.

"I—" Zora started.

"Shh," he soothed. "Thank you for trusting me with your secret, your story. I know how hard that must've been. You're very brave, Zora."

He pulled away from her enough to look down and smile at her.

Zora's eyelashes fluttered, the warmth of Taemar's smile overtaking her. His sincerity surprised her. She'd expected him to judge her, to be repulsed by her actions and to push her away But he hadn't done any of those things. He'd sincerely wanted to get to know her and to hear her story and instead of judgement, he offered her comfort. Zora's heart swelled and for the first tim in her life, she truly felt like she could be her total self.

"I've never talked to anyone about how I've used my powers before," Zora said, sniffling.

"Why not?"

"Most people think magic isn't real or it's a sin. And witches are no different when it comes to necromancy. Even the most progressive of 'em turned into purists when I told them I communed with the dead. You really think I'd be able to say I di it for money?" Zora scoffed.

Taemar nodded. "Well, you got nothin' to be ashamed of, baby. We all gotta do what we gotta do to survive at one point or another in this life."

Zora cringed. "I'm not sure that's entirely true. I mean, if I had just caught on to my dad's game earlier or if I'd called Lione myself . . ."

Taemar waved his hand. "Ain't no sense in beatin' yourself up over someone else's actions. You were tryin' to help and your father played you. It was horrible, and he put that man in dange not you, you hear me? Not you."

Zora choked back tears as she nodded. "Okay," she replied. "Okay."

"Alright, good." Taemar looked her up and down. "Now let's talk about how you learned to do that backbend because I need tutorial."

Zora chuckled and dabbed at her eyes. The door to the club opened and Birdie stepped out, her hands in the pockets of her satin jumpsuit. Zora and Taemar turned toward her.

Birdie stood there expressionless for three seconds, each second causing Zora's heart to beat faster.

"I spoke with the dancers. We think you'll be a great fit! Welcome to Nightingale's, Zora. You're hired."

Zora smiled widely, fighting the urge to jump up and dance. She was finally going to be able to make money doing something she loved instead of something she feared.

"Thank you so much!" she exclaimed.

Taemar clapped and nodded. "I know that's right! You're goin' to do so well."

"Thank you."

"I knew you weren't done with Savannah just yet." Birdie smiled.

"Guess you were right," Zora said.

"I often am." Birdie glanced at Taemar and winked. He returned the gesture with a knowing smile.

"So, when do I start?" Zora asked eagerly.

"Tonight," Birdie replied.

Zora's breath caught in surprise then she looked down at her clothes. "Well, I guess that means I'm going to need something a bit fancier."

Birdie laughed. "Don't you worry about that. I've got the perfect thing in mind."

The opulence of Nightingale's had captivated Zora during the day, but at night when the candles were lit, music blared and customers buzzed around the room, the club seemed even more beautiful. Even more magical. The night was still young bu already customers lined up at the bar, either mingling with thei friends or flirting with the club's patrons.

Zora sat at the end of the bar, wearing a dress she borrowed from Birdie, an emerald green mini dress with a corset top and tulle bottom. Zora had touched up her makeup and gathered he hair into a bun mohawk. She watched as Taemar mixed a layere drink that looked like a peach ring.

"What's that?" Zora asked.

"Nightingale's signature drink, the Savannah Serenade," he replied. "Peach juice, OJ, bourbon, and sweet tea."

He slid the drink across the bar toward a petite Asian woma who smiled widely and left him a hefty tip. Taemar thanked her and slipped the cash into his jacket pocket.

"That sounds good. I'll take one," she said.

There was a break in customers, and Taemar looked around before leaning over the bar. "The Serenade's just for our non-magical customers. There's a little somethin' extra mixed with the peach juice so they don't remember the magic of the place, just all the other razzle dazzle."

Zora knitted her brows. "What, like a magical mickey?"

"Girl, no!" Taemar snapped before leaning in closer to her.

"We can't have humans knowin' about magic but we also got bills to pay. This potion just ensures that their brains process what they see on stage differently, so if a dancer used a potion that made them disappear or if a witch creates a fire ball in thei hand, they just remember that the witch left the stage quickly and that the fire ball was from a candle or some shit."

Zora nodded, still not quite understanding the mechanics. "Wouldn't it be easier just to ward the place?"

"Only if you wanted to erase their memories completely," he replied. When he noticed Zora's expression hadn't changed, he tried a different tactic. "Wards are a lot more literal than spells and potions. You put up a ward on your building so patrons forget what they've seen and it's just that—they forget everything, the magic and the non-magical shit. But a spell, a potion, allows you to be more exact."

Zora nodded, once again feeling inadequate in her magical knowledge. Taemar turned toward a cluster of people all asking for the Savannah Serenade and he made animated conversation with them as he mixed their drinks.

Just as the doubts began flooding Zora's mind, a velvety voice interrupted her thoughts.

"Green's a good color on you." Zora turned to see Jabari standing beside her. Instantly, her cheeks warmed. He slid atop the barstool beside her, his movements as graceful as a panther. Zora caught a whiff of his cologne, a heady scent with notes of coffee and almond and rum, and her heartbeat raced.

"Thanks," she said, keeping her voice and her expression nonchalant. She looked him over. His black jacket shimmered like an oil slick, matching the darkness of his pants. His pointed black boots had two rows of silver buckles on them. His hair was perfectly blown out and spilled down his back. His high cheekbones shimmered in the dim light. Taemar stepped over toward them and he and Jabari dabbed fists.

"What can I get you?" Taemar asked.

"The usual. And, of course, get the lady whatever she wants," Jabari replied, greedily drinking in the view.

Taemar nodded toward Zora.

"I'll take . . . Crown and Coke?" Taemar busied himself with fixing their drinks. As he did, Zora caught Jabari observing her out of the corner of her eye. She grounded herself against the barstool, fighting hard to keep still.

"So, I hear you're Nightingale's newest dancer?" he asked.

"Yeah, well. How often does one get the chance to dance at a magical burlesque club?"

He chuckled, releasing a deep, smooth sound that made Zora want to keep saying things to make him laugh.

"Not very often, I imagine." Jabari paused, holding his stare. "I look forward to seeing you on that stage."

Zora fought the urge to smile, thankful that Taemar slid their drinks before them.

"Thank you, Tae," Jabari said. He turned to Zora and lifted h glass. "To you. May your time in Savannah be full of abundance, discovery, and passion."

As their glasses clinked together, their knuckles brushed against each other and Zora felt a throbbing between her thighs. She sipped her drink and looked toward the crowd, not sure how to respond to such a statement.

Crowds of people clustered together on the L-shaped couches and on the love seats. Many of them laughed and some cast excited glances at the stage, awaiting the show. Seated at a table farther from the stage was Whitley. She sat alone and stared at her phone, as other people, other witches from the other night, clustered together in kinship. Zora couldn't help but be curious as to why the head of Soliloquy house was being seemingly ignored.

"Does she normally sit by herself?" Zora asked. Jabari looked over at Whitley and for a brief second, he grimaced.

Jabari shrugged.

"Is that by choice?"

"She's new. And quiet as it's kept, not exactly well liked."

Zora remembered how less people had clapped for her during the ritual, how someone had shouted "Whitley Neon," and how when she'd told Zora she'd gotten a referral for the House Head role from her father, MK and Orion had shaded her. Was she being dogged because she was an outsider? Because her father had gotten her into the Triarchy? Or was there something more?

"She seemed nice to me," Zora responded.

Jabari waved a hand. "She's fine. But enough about her. I want to know more about you."

Zora looked at Jabari as he leaned closer. Despite the undeniable attraction she felt toward him, she stood.

"And maybe I'll tell you. But, some other time." She faced the bar. "Taemar, can you get me . . . whatever Whitley normally drinks?"

Taemar nodded. He uncorked a bottle of champagne and pulled out a champagne flute. He poured a glass then slid it across the counter to Zora. She thanked him and as she turned to leave, she observed the annoyance on Jabari's face. But she didn't care. She wasn't going to spill her guts to him in the middle of a crowded club, no matter how fine he was.

Taking a page out of Birdie's book, Zora walked toward Whitley and asked if the empty seat across from her was taken. Whitley shook her head and Zora set their glasses down on the table before sitting.

"Thank you," Whitley said, seemingly surprised. Her dark hair was styled like Bettie Page, and Zora thought her peacock blue, off shoulder dress and red lipstick looked radiant on her. She smelled like jasmine, and the heady scent made Zora want to sit closer to her.

She's so beautiful, Zora thought.

"You're welcome. Hope I'm not intruding. Saw you on your own and I thought—"

Whitley sipped her champagne and inspected Zora with a confused expression on her face. "I always sit by myself."

"Why don't you go join the others?" Zora asked.

"I've tried, believe me. But I'm an outsider. To them, I'm just some saditty LA bitch who's only the House Head because my aunt was the former Head."

"I'm sorry they treatin' you like that."

Whitley looked unfazed. "I don't exactly want to be here, anyway. I'd rather be in LA. The beaches and the night life are better, the people aren't so passive aggressive, and the summers don't make me feel like I'm gonna die from boiling in my own sweat."

Zora lifted her brows. As though sensing her discomfort, Whitley added: ". . . but at least the food's better here."

Zora laughed despite herself, and Whitley joined in. Zora sipped her Crown and Coke and looked out at the club, surprised to see that the two of them sitting together was drawing attention. Whitley seemed to notice it, too, and rolled her eyes.

"So, I hear you're a necromancer."

Zora nodded.

"Yet, you've decided to stay in this haunted-ass city. What made you decide that?"

Whitley's abruptness took Zora aback. The woman examined her with dark eyes, and there was an air about her that made Zora feel as if this woman truly didn't care one way or the other whether Zora responded or decided to stay seated with her. It was relaxing, in a way, to not feel like she had to fill the space between them with words. And somehow, it made Zora want to keep being near her and talking to her all the more.

"I got a job here and a room at Birdie's."

"That a better set up than where you came from?"

"Yeah," Zora replied, bracing herself for more questions.

Whitley simply nodded. "Well, I'm glad. Almost everyone deserves a fresh start."

Zora tilted her head at Whitley's comment. *What does she mean by almost?*

Before she could respond, the lights dimmed and Birdie appeared on stage, dressed in wide-leg, high-waisted pants and a studded, black bustier. She wore a leather choker around her neck, and her plum-colored lip gloss glistened in the light. A large chorus of claps arose, and Birdie smiled at the attention. She stepped toward the edge of the stage, lifting her hands, prodding the guests to keep going.

Damn, she looks good, Zora thought.

"You're looking so good tonight, Birdie!" someone shouted from the crowd as if reading her mind.

"Thank you. Thank you. Welcome to Nightingale's, where the drinks are good, the dancers are hot, and the night is always," she said with a sly smile. "Magical!"

More whoops erupted from the crowd, and as Birdie joked around with them, Jabari walked over and sat on the love seat behind Zora and Whitley. Accompanying him was the man who'd let Zora into Divinity house the night before. Jabari lifted his glass in greeting and leaned back into the seat as the man leaned against him. Zora nodded in response and turned back to Whitley, who gave Jabari a side-long glance, her lips pursed.

"You know, you don't have a good poker face," Zora said.

Whitley raised her eyebrows and scoffed. "That's because I don't bother hiding my emotions. Why should I try to be polite and pretend when I'm annoyed or happy or turned on?"

Zora's heart skipped a beat at her last words, and she wondered if Whitley knew how attracted to her she felt, and whether Whitley felt the same.

Birdie's voice pulled Zora out of her thoughts. "Now, who's ready for our first performance?"

"Yes!" the crowd shouted.

"Put your hands together for Nightingale's Dolls!" Birdie shouted before the lights turned completely out and spotlights shone on the stage.

The slow strum of a guitar sounded before the bass kicked in. Zora recognized the song as "Idlewild Blue" from OutKast. The dancers Zora had met before sauntered onto the stage, arms bent and wrists slack in front of them. Their hips popped to the beat, and when Andre 3000 began singing, the dancers leaned back and gyrated their midsections like belly dancers before twisting and removing their skirts. Raheem and Safi pulled their shorts off with the same flourish. They clapped and danced in a circle, each dancer shimming their chest when they were the ones facing the crowd.

When Andre 3000 finished the second verse, begging Sally not to worry about him, the dancers all twirled, clapped, and removed their tops. They strode to the back of the stage and turned, linking arms. Then they shimmied their hips, working their nipple tassels, as they danced to the front of the stage. They broke their line, and each of them received a moment to shimmy and to do their dance center stage.

MK danced last, and though Zora expected the woman to show off in some way, what she did made Zora gasp. She seemed to clone herself and danced on both ends of the stage, each version of her bumping her hips and twirling her nipple tassels as the song ended. When it finished, both versions of MK blew kisses to the crowd before joining back together.

The crowd exploded in applause. The dancers smiled and bowed and blew kisses to the crowd before gathering their belongings and sauntering off the stage. Then Birdie reappeared, clapping and asking the crowd what they thought of the routine.

"Encore!" someone yelled.

"We want more!" someone else called.

"Don't you worry, baby. There's more where that came from," Birdie announced.

The audience clapped, some of them barking in anticipation.

"Coming back to the stage is Nightingale's resident firecracker."

The crowd celebrated before Birdie even finished her words.

"You know her for her big hair, multiple piercings, and uncanny ability to appear in multiple places at once. Let's give it up for MK!"

The fanfare was real. Everyone in the room stood, even Whitley and Jabari. Zora glanced around and followed suit. MK strutted onto the stage, dressed in a long, white, halter top dress, matching gloves, and pleasers. Birdie teleported off the stage and MK's set began.

"Diamonds are forever," Shirley Bassey crooned. But the song was remixed, the bass heightened. MK lip synced the song as she danced. First, she removed her gloves then pulled out the hair clip securing her coils. Once released, they tumbled down onto her shoulders. She turned her back to the crowd and unhooked her dress before twisting back to the group.

By the second verse, MK had taken off the dress and stood on stage in silver bikini bottoms and diamond pasties. From her bottoms, she pulled a small potion jar and downed it just as

Shirley Bassey sang the bridge.

The lights went out and the song stopped. Zora looked around, wondering what was to come, but everyone seemed to be staring at the stage in rapt attention.

Seconds later, the song continued, and now three MK's stood on stage. As the song reached a crescendo, with Shirley singing "diamonds are forever," MK seemed to step into the air. She lifted one foot and then the other, and suddenly she floated high above the stage, above them all, twirling and dancing to the song which Orion had extended. Zora gasped, eyes and mouth wide as she watched MK sashay through the air. She wondered how she could accomplish not only cloning herself but also walking and dancing on air.

Zora stood in awe of MK as she finished her routine and pranced off stage, waving at the crowd, a smile plastered on her face.

"She's incredible," Zora said, breathless.

"Yes, she is," Whitley said stoically. She lifted her glass to her lips. "Just don't let her know you think that. Bitch is full of herself as it is."

Zora snorted. Whitley wasn't wrong, but the venom in the witch's reply made Zora wonder if she'd done more to the woman than just say a few bitchy comments. As Raheem took the stage, Birdie appeared beside Zora.

"How're you liking it?" she asked.

"It's everything," Zora replied, feeling giddy. "I didn't know magic could be used like that."

"Then what do you know about magic?"

Zora closed her eyes, mentally preparing herself for MK's presence.

The smell of cotton candy wafted through the air and Zora

turned in her seat as MK sauntered over to the love seat Jabari sat on. Immediately, the man he'd been sitting with backed away from him, picked up his drink, and walked away.

"MK," Birdie warned.

"I'm just askin'," the redhead replied, her voice fake-sweet and mocking.

Zora had known this woman for less than forty-eight hours and already she wanted to beat her ass. She took another sip of her drink and watched MK with narrowed eyes, knowing she wasn't quite done with her insult.

"I mean, at this point, I'm wonderin' if Zora's a witch at all."

"And I'm wondering if you're capable of adding value to a conversation instead of just getting off on the sound of your own voice, but I guess we'll both be left with questions tonight, won't we?" Zora smirked.

MK snorted and rolled her eyes. Jabari rubbed one of MK's shoulders and kissed the other one, his eyes locked on Zora.

Zora shook her head then finished her drink and stood. "I'm gonna get some air," she announced to Whitley, who shrugged and nodded.

As she stepped outside, Zora inhaled the fresh air. She sighed with relief when she saw that only Taemar and Niko were there, sitting at the table on the far end of the patio.

"Not into the show?" Zora asked. Niko blew a cloud of smoke and rolled his eyes, which were accentuated by blue eyeliner the same color as his hair.

"I saw the routines while they rehearsed," Taemar said. "I'm not spendin' my break watchin' it again."

Zora shrugged and sat beside them. She crossed her arms against the slight chill in the air.

"So, is Nightingale's everything you expected it to be?" Niko asked. He snaked an arm around Taemar, who leaned in to him and planted a kiss on his neck before turning back to Zora.

"I've never seen witches do this stuff, like MK doin' that who walkin' on air bit?"

"Yeah, she got that shit from Marquitta," Taemar said, unimpressed.

"Hmm. Well, they're all so talented, and I hate to admit it, even MK."

"As talented as she is bitchy," Niko quipped. Taemar and Nik laughed.

"Yeah, I've gotten some of her smoke. She like that all the time?"

Taemar sucked his teeth. "That's what happens when you unsettled in your spirit. Start lashin' out at folks for no damn reason."

"She seems to have a distaste for Whitley, too, least from wh I saw at the ritual last night."

Niko and Taemar glanced at each other.

"What?" she asked.

Niko lifted his hands up as if in surrender. "Don't look at me She's my House Head, and my boss at the salon. I like her fine, but we ain't close. Not like how Tae and Birdie are."

"Not everyone is blessed to have a friend like me," Taemar replied, lifting his head and fluttering his eye lashes dramaticall Niko groaned and peeled his arm from around his shoulder and resumed smoking his joint.

"Anyway, some people think she don't really belong here," Niko said.

"Why's that?" Zora asked, though she already knew the answer. She was an outsider, coming into a position of power because she had the right connections. Zora couldn't help but wonder if they'd all feel the same way about her.

"'Whitley Soliloquy' is originally Whitley Neon," Taemar started. "She comes from a house in LA where her parents been runnin' the House of Neon, which is just like Transcendence, since the '90s. We don't know exactly what happened, but somehow she left there to come here and be with her aunt Bonnie, who had been the former Head of Soliloquy."

"So, she moved houses. Is that frowned upon or somethin'?"

"Not at all, a lot of witches move around. Hell, Jabari's been in more houses than anyone here," Taemar replied.

"So, what's the issue?"

Taemar sighed. "Like I said, no one knows why she left Neon. While some think she just knew her aunt was havin' health troubles and she wanted to be closer to her, others wonder if maybe . . ." He shrugged. "Maybe she did something bad and instead of her family stripping her powers and exiling her from the community, they shipped her down South to her aunt."

Zora's mind wandered. Though she didn't know her at all, Whitley had seemed nice enough, quiet. But she also seemed like someone who wasn't afraid to let the world know exactly what she felt and thought, and she seemed to have much disdain for her situation. What, then, could this witch have done to make her community, her own flesh and blood, want to push her out?

"So, is that why y'all feel a way about her? Because you're scared?"

"I wouldn't say scared. Just . . . cautious," Niko explained.

"It just don't sit right that this girl who we don't even know, who was likely kicked out of her own house was made Head, and took over managing Bonnie's salon, Bob-A-Lula's. Mind you, Niko and several other witches have been in the house for a while," Taemar added.

"Is MK the only one who felt a way about this?"

Taemar snorted. "Baby, most of us gave Whitley the side-eye for months, even Birdie."

"Even Marquitta?" Zora asked, before realizing it.

Taemar hesitated before speaking. "Marquitta was the sweetest woman, took a lot to make her mad, but Whitley just wanted to come in and change things. Make things like how they were in L.A. When Marquitta, who'd been Transcendence for nearly a decade, tried to talk to Whitley, she all but said the Southern way was backward. That really pissed Marquitta off. They never really fucked with each other after that."

"More than that," Niko added. "They fought damn near every time they were around each other. Birdie had to play mediator."

"Which was shit for their relationship, lemme tell you," Taemar interjected.

Zora nodded. Whitley hadn't seemed happy here, so, of course, there was a part of her that would want to make things like how they were back home. And that was a sure-fire way to piss people off. If Niko and Taemar were right, then Whitley was a powerful witch who no one liked, especially Marquitta. Could the conflict with Marquitta and possible resentment from being sent away from home have made Whitley snap? Could she have had something to do with Marquitta's death?

"But, I don't think Whitley had anything to do with Marquitta's death," Niko said, staring at Zora.

"Why would I be thinkin' that?" Zora asked, hoping her facial expression didn't expose her thoughts.

Taemar and Niko looked at each other, and Taemar's lips peeled back into a grimace.

"Because you're helpin' Birdie try to find out what happened to Marquitta."

Zora lifted a brow. "Why you say that?"

"The police ain't doin' shit despite Birdie stayin' on they ass," Taemar began. "And then suddenly a necromancer comes to town and she brings you in like that?" he snapped.

"I see how you'd think that. But really, it's all a coincidence," she said, crossing her arms tighter.

"Okay, okay. I get it. Zora the Necromancer is on the case, so you don't want to give it away and you've got to consider everyone a suspect." Taemar took a long puff before stubbing out the roach of the joint. He continued, holding in the smoke as he said: "But, for the record, I am glad you're here."

"Me, too," Niko said sweetly.

"Course." Zora shrugged a shoulder. "Havin' a necromancer would come in handy to try and solve a murder, if that's what was happenin'."

"Look, if you are helpin' Birdie find out who killed Marquitta, then I'm happy. She was like a sister to me, and it's killin' me seein' Birdie so devastated. But I also mean, I'm happy you, Zora, are here."

"Why?" Zora asked, blinking repeatedly.

"Because I think you've got a lot to learn. But I also think you've got a lot offer, more than just your ability to raise the dead."

With that, Taemar stood and kissed Niko before nodding to Zora and heading back inside. Zora bit her lip Niko turned in her direction.

Chapter 7

"Booker, Titus, and I knew we couldn't live forever despite trying to craft a spell for immortality. Other witches will have to take over for us when we journey to the afterworld, so we decided that future House Heads will be elected in one of two ways. Either the existing Head will elect a witch who they believe will fill their shoes the best, or, if Geddemin has come to call for them before they've chosen a successor, the house will vote as a collective."

Spell Book of Mobley Divinity, 1902

Gazing out the window in her hotel room, Zora replayed yesterday's events in her mind. So much had happened in such little time that she hardly had time to process it all. Thoughts swarmed around her mind all night, keeping her awake even as the darkness faded from the sky. Even though she barely slept, Zora arose with a smile on her face. That same smile reappeared as she turned toward the door where her packed bags were ready and waiting. After glancing at her phone, Zora scooped up her bags and hurried toward the door. Her new home awaited her.

Taemar and Birdie met her at the door of the Transcendence house, both smiling and seemingly excited to have her around. After she set her belongings in her room—the one she'd woken up in—Birdie gave her a tour of the house. The bathroom attached to her room was one she'd now share with Taemar. His room was a study in purple; the walls, his bedding, and most of the decor featured various shades of the royal color. Some shades Zora struggled to name. When she looked at Taemar, eyes wide, he simply shrugged and said: "What? Purple is my signature color."

Across from Zora's room was Birdie's room. It was the master, and the one that had three windows facing the street, offering a view of the beautiful oak trees that surrounded it. Next to Birdie's room was MK's and at the far end, Orion's. Nothing special captured Zora's attention about their rooms. Each one looked like a carbon copy of the photos commonly seen on a social media influencer's Instagram account. A final bedroom sat vacant across from Orion's room. Zora wondered who the next lucky houseguest would be to fill it.

A front room and a living room sat adjacent to each other. The living room boasted a mounted television, a plush, black couch, and matching chairs. MK and Orion lounged on the couch watching YouTube, and when Orion's video popped up on the screen, MK squealed.

"Not your video having over two thousand views in just an hour!"

Zora rolled her eyes. Neither MK nor Orion said more than a half-hearted "What's good?" to Zora when she arrived.

"What's your channel about?" Zora asked.

Orion looked back at her briefly. "Pop culture."

Zora glanced at Taemar, who shook his head and strolled into the kitchen, where the long, marble island led to the breakfast nook at the far end of the room. Large windows illuminated the space and paintings like the ones in the hallway, portraits of people dressed in corsets and lingerie, were placed strategically on the gold-painted walls.

They walked through a set of French doors and into a formal

dining room. An ebony table filled most of the space, and behind it a large black and white photo of the Transcendence house decorated the wall. On the frame, inscribed in gold lettering, were the words "House Transcendence, Established 1900." In the foreground of the photo stood two Black men and one Black woman. The men wore suits with long coat tails and the woman an elaborate skirt and suit jacket. Each wore a hat with a flower pinned to the side of it.

"This is beautiful," Zora gushed. Birdie stood beside her.

"These are the founding members of the Savannah Triarchy," Birdie began. "Titus Soliloquy, Booker Transcendence, and Mobley Divinity."

Zora stared at the trio for a long while, wondering what they endured to reach the moment captured in the portrait.

When Birdie turned to walk up the stairs again, Zora and Taemar followed. They walked up two flights of stairs and opened a door to the attic. A round, ebony table sat in the middle of the room atop a black carpet with a symbol painted in gold. On the table laid two notebooks that looked similar to the ones on the squat bookcase beneath the large, arched window. Atop the bookcase rested a record player, and a carton of records sat on either side of it. Zora chuckled.

"What's so funny?" Taemar asked.

"Nah, it's just . . ." she gestured around the room. "An attic? I didn't realize I was in an episode of Charmed."

"In the old days, a lot of rituals had to be performed in the attic to prevent humans from catching on to witches doing witchy things. Couldn't exactly get caught with this spellbook in their kitchen if a cop came by, could they?" Birdie asked, picking up one of the books on the table. "After a while it just became a tradition to have one's altar be in the attic or in some cases the basement."

Zora watched as Birdie walked around the room and tidied. "What do you do if you don't have either and you have a lot of humans around?"

Birdie laughed. "Well, then I suppose you'd better hope you've got a walk-in closet or a pantry."

She glanced around the room once more before gesturing to the stairs. Zora turned on her heel and walked down to the second story. Her growling stomach caught Birdie's attention.

"Wanna grab lunch?" Birdie asked.

"Sure," Zora responded.

She sat in the backseat of Birdie's Camaro in awe of Savannah's beauty as the magnolia trees zipped by. The historic district of downtown Savannah lived up to its name, appearing as if it had been frozen in time, its ghosts as well. The specters lingered near two and three-story brick buildings wearing clothe from every decade, each of them frozen at various stages of their life.

Taemar occupied the passenger seat and Orion and MK sat on the opposite side of Zora in the backseat. Though Zora had preferred to sit in the front with Birdie, she figured she could survive the ride, but only if MK kept her mouth shut. Mercifully, the woman spent the whole ride scrolling on her phone.

The group carpooled to a soul food restaurant in downtown Savannah. Located on the corner of a quiet street, the restaurant burst with personality from the bright coneflowers near the entrance to the faux, brick fireplace that embellished the back wall. As soon as they entered the restaurant, the smell of shrimp and grits and chicken and waffles made Zora's stomach to growl once more. Luckily, the music, a mashup of classic hits from the '50s, '60s, and '70s, drowned out the sound.

Despite the pleasant atmosphere and delicious food, lunch was awkward. Birdie either praised the restaurant's service or commented on a news story every few minutes, trying her best to spark up a conversation. Besides the occasional head nods and one-word responses, conversation remained at a minimum.

MK and Orion sat on their phones and barely acknowledged Taemar, Zora, or Birdie's presence. The only time either of them said anything was when Zora made fun of Taemar for liking Texas barbeque more than Memphis'.

"You clearly don't know the good stuff," Zora quipped. "Memphis barbeque is the best in the country."

"If you love it so much, why don't you go back there?" MK questioned.

"Girl, I'm not goin' anywhere. You might wanna stop spinnin' your wheels."

Zora prepared her next comeback, ready for the woman to clap back, but instead she just stared at Zora in disgust before turning back to her phone.

Even though Birdie offered Zora a reassuring glance, as if telling her not to worry, Zora struggled to shake the uneasy feeling MK gave her. *Why's she so determined to hate me?* Zora thought.

When they returned to Transcendence house, Orion and MK retreated to the living room, while Zora and Taemar sat outside with a couple of iced coffees and split a bag of M&Ms. Though they asked Birdie to join them, she declined, choosing instead to spend the afternoon at the altar. Though Zora didn't know what

Amanda Ross

Birdie was doing, she heard the sound of neo-soul spilling out of the open window.

"So, are things always this tense with witches?" Zora asked.

Taemar smirked.

"Oh this? Nah. That's just the warmup," he chuckled before taking a sip of his coffee. When he set his cup down, a thoughtful expression covered his face. "To be honest, things weren't always like this. Since Marquitta died, everyone's been on edge."

"Even MK? 'Cause from what you said the other night, she's always been stank."

"Absolutely. But somehow . . . it's like Marquitta's death put a battery in her back. Now, it seems like she's just looking for a fight."

"It sounds like Marquitta's death has been hard on everyone," Zora began. "And grief can twist people into knots. I helped a family once who'd lost their father out the blue. This was apparently a close-knit family, but when I tell you it felt like a turf war or somethin' when I talked to them. Mom against kids, kids against aunties and uncles. Everyone felt like their hurt was the biggest and deserved the most space and time."

Taemar snorted. "Yeah, that kinda happened here, too. See, most of us been in the Triarchy for years, and for MK, Orion, and Jabari, they knew Marquitta way before Birdie came on the scene. Jabari knew her especially well, if you get me."

Zora knitted her brows. "Wait, they were together?"

"For a few years, almost moved in together and everything."

Zora sat back in her chair, stunned at the revelation.

"Anyway, when she died last month, everyone wanted to do something, use magic to find her killer, plan the funeral, the whole shebang. But Birdie wouldn't let nobody do a thing.

100

Marquitta was buried, there was no repast, and even though she told folks she didn't want to use magic to find the killer, she went and found a necromancer." Taemar tilted his head to the side briefly, as if to punctuate the end of his sentence.

Zora groaned. "I'm sensin' that whatever type of investigation I do in to Marquitta's murder won't exactly be a secret."

Taemar laughed. "In this city? With these witches? Girl, good luck."

Later that night, Zora fell asleep almost as soon as her head hit the pillow. Thoughts of her conversation with Taemar drifted in and out of her consciousness until she entered a deep slumber. That night she dreamed about Nightingale's, about magic and rituals and the moon, cast in bronze light.

The hunter's moon.

She turned toward her window, briefly waking up before falling back into a different set of dreams. Whereas the first part had been ritualistic, almost prophetic, these dreams were violent. In one of them, she saw the woman from the photograph of the Savannah Triarchy founders, Mobley Divinity, falling to her death. The sound of her head cracking against the pavement made Zora's eyes snap open.

There's someone in my room, she thought. But the room was pitch black and she couldn't see a thing. As she began waking up, she felt pressure on her legs. She stretched a hand out, searching for her phone in the dark. When her hand landed on it, she gripped it tight and instantly brought it up to her face and turned the light on. Zora twisted slightly in her bed when the light on her phone screen revealed Mobley's ghost sitting on the edge of the bed with her hand around Zora's legs. Though Zora knew this was a founder of the Triarchy and should be treated with respect, Zora jerked her legs back and crawled out of bed, her feet hitting the floor with a thud.

"Oh, hell no," she yelled. She ran toward her purse atop the dresser when she felt herself being pulled back into Mobley's memory. This time Zora saw her mere seconds before she was pushed out the window. Mobley turned and looked at her killer directly in the eye, a young witch with light skin and a thick mustache. He eyed Mobley with malice before pushing her out the window. Again, the cracking sound of the witch's skull made Zora spasm and she fell to the floor before she could reach the dresser.

Mobley knelt over her, her bloodshot eyes assessing Zora. Though she lifted herself up, Zora's knee ached and her left shoulder blade screamed at her.

"Please, no," Zora begged. She clawed her way across the floor as Mobley loomed over her.

"Help me. Help me," the ghost whispered over and over. Zora could feel the ghost above her, knew she was so close to laying a hand on her. The helplessness she felt in the moment sent her crashing back to the night when she first saw Ms. Patrice.

The lights clicked on and Zora squinted as a set of furry slippers came into view.

"Zora!"

Zora recognized the voice as Birdie's, but all she could think about was her aching body.

"Salt, purse," Zora said, pointing to the dresser. But Birdie didn't move, and seconds later, the ghost disappeared. Birdie extended a hand down to Zora and helped her up, and a sharp pain shot through Zora's knee as she stood.

"What was that? How'd you get rid of her?" she asked, leaning on Birdie for support.

Birdie's brows knitted. "C'mon. Let's get you some tea."

They sat at the breakfast nook in the kitchen, Zora extending one leg out and resting an ice pack on her knee. She winced as she adjusted herself to a more comfortable position.

"You sure there's no potion or spell to heal this?"

Birdie chuckled. "Sure, there is. But we can't use magic for everything. After a while, you start to rely on it too much, and you lose sight of those experiences that make you human."

"Sounds like a way to make people suffer," Zora grumbled.

Birdie shook her head. "Drink your tea, you'll feel better."

Zora took a sip and waited for the tea to calm her. She closed her eyes and released a deep breath.

"What's in it?" she asked, opening her eyes. "And what's that stuff you used on the ghost?"

"That 'stuff' is red brick dust mixed with wormwood. As for the tea, I don't totally know," Birdie replied, picking up the jar of loose-leaf tea. "Chamomile, ginger, cannabis, I think? Probably more shit but I can't remember. It was Marquitta's." Birdie stared at the jar in her hand.

"You miss her a lot, don't you?" Zora asked.

Birdie nodded and dabbed at her eyes before clearing her throat. "I'm sorry. I shouldn't be doin' this. You've just had a traumatic experience from the sounds of it. We should be—"

"But, everyone's got to feel their feelings at some point," Zora replied.

Birdie sighed. "There's only so much feelings I can feel."

"What do you mean?"

"Well, I know it was Mobley Divinity you saw earlier. As

unfortunate as it is, her death has always served as a cautionary tale to the magical community. She was killed by a member of Soliloquy house who wanted to take over as head of Divinity."

Zora's eyes widened. "But how could it be that easy? Isn't there some kind of election or somethin'?"

"Not in those days," Birdie said. "Witches just took control. But Mobley's death after thirty years as one of the best House Heads the community ever had made not just Savannah but witches around the country take notice. So the Mobley Treaty was passed, stating that House Heads must be elected by their house or chosen by the existing head, something that she and th other house heads were actively planning when she was killed. Any witch who violates the treaty will be exiled from their city and branded an insurrectionist. Probably have their powers stripped."

"That sounds democratic enough," Zora said, her mouth hovering over her cup. She sipped her tea as Birdie spoke.

"It hasn't stopped witches from trying to overthrow House Heads. They may not be able to overtly murder but we're witche . . . that doesn't stop anyone of us from trying some slick shit lik poisoning or curses to get their way."

Zora's stomach tightened when Birdie mentioned the word "curses." Had one been placed on Marquitta?

She blinked the thought from her mind. "Well, you ain't got worry about me'. I'm still a novice. I wouldn't know the first thir about curses or poison. Hell, I spend most of my time afraid of my powers."

Birdie took Zora's hand in hers and smiled. "You will get there. Now, given what happened tonight, I say we get your magical training started now."

"Like, right now?" Zora asked, swallowing a gulp of air.

Birdie laughed heartily. "After you finish your tea, baby."

Chapter 8

"Aside from their powers, a witch's greatest asset is their spell book. There they keep the spells and potions they invent or copy, and write about their days and nights in hopes that what's written will help their future self or future generations of witches."

Spell Book of Titus Soliloquy, 1909

"**T**ell me what happens when you see the dead?" Birdie asked.

"I tense up," Zora started. "My heart races, and all I want to do is look away or make myself small so they don't come after me. If I'm in public, I try to ignore it. Doesn't always go so well, though."

Zora thought back to the ghost that haunted her at school. She first saw the woman, with her singed, pastel yellow dress and her face covered in burn marks, as she walked between gym class to English. She'd tried to ignore her when she paced by the door, but when the woman appeared near Zora's desk, she couldn't help how startled she was, how her knee hit her desk.

"Shh," her teacher said, scowling at Zora. Her classmates pointed and giggled.

Zora slid down in her seat and buried her face in her book as she clenched her teeth, keeping her face a mask of indifference.

She kept it there even as she felt the dead woman's gaze bore down on her.

Even as the dead woman knelt down in front of Zora, her eye so pale that they looked almost completely white, save for the pupil.

Even as the ghost stretched out a hand and placed it on Zora arm.

Flames danced in front of Zora's eyes as she saw the memory of this woman's last moments—a fire in this very classroom, and she'd succumbed as she tried to save her students. Zora's heart pounded and she blinked away tears as the ghost stared at her, silently demanding her attention.

The bell ringing forced Zora out of the woman's memory. She didn't even bother to slide her books into her backpack. She slid them off her desk and grabbed her bag. Out of the room she ran not caring about the whispers of her classmates or the quizzical look on her teacher's face.

Zora blinked away the memory. In the present, she sighed and took a sip of the coffee Birdie had brewed for their late nigh training session. They sat with the full pot between them, and a leather-bound notebook sat in front of Birdie.

"I don't mean your reaction, baby. I mean what happens to you, magically."

"Oh." She laughed nervously. "You know that feeling you get when a part of your body falls asleep?"

Birdie nodded.

"It feels like that, only throughout my entire body."

"And how does it feel when you touch the dead?"

Zora's stomach dropped, and Mobley's death flashed through her mind.

"It feels like what's inside of me, what makes me who I am, has been pushed out and replaced by what they want me to see. Then when it's over, it's like I'm coming up for air after being submerged for what feels like forever."

Birdie nodded. "I remember Marquitta used to feel that way sometimes. Said it felt like she was- breathless, watching something she couldn't control."

"So what can I do? If Marquitta felt that way—"

"Don't compare yourself to Marquitta," Birdie snapped.

Zora's brows shot up. She twisted the edge of her shirt around her finger, unsure of how to respond.

"I'm sorry. I just meant, you're your own person. You're powerful in your own right. But first you have to accept who you are. You're a witch, a necromancer. You have the power to speak to the dead in all their forms. That's a very powerful thing."

A powerful thing, Zora thought. But being able to see the dead was the thing that made her feel the least powerful. As she had for years, she found herself wondering why she wasn't gifted with the power of telekinesis or empathy or even premonition.

"Most people who hear about my powers think they're evil. My whole life people felt that way, my mom, other witches."

Birdie clucked her tongue. "They're just stuck in the past."

"But how can I disagree when this power makes me feel so afraid?" Zora asked. She shuffled in her seat, feeling so uncomfortable yet relieved as she shared her feelings about her powers.

"You just don't know how to use it yet. But that's why we're here. And that's why this is yours now."

Birdie slid the notebook across the table toward Zora. She grabbed it and began examining it. On the inside of the notebook, Zora found Marquitta's name on the first page. As she flipped through it, she noticed that each page had something written on it. Some of the writing appeared to be spells, while others appeared to be diary entries.

This must be a spell book, Zora thought. She'd heard other witches talk about their spell books before. Zora never had one; she wasn't versed in spells or potions or anything that required something to be written down.

Zora's eyes widened as she looked through the pages of this woman's life whose ghost lingered in this house. She stopped on an entry to summon a ghost.

"I didn't know I could do that," Zora said, pointing at the entry. Birdie looked at it and nodded. "They always just appeare whether I wanted 'em to or not."

"Let's try it." Birdie looked at the spell and began reading ou the steps.

Zora tensed at the thought.

"First, close your eyes and clear your mind."

Zora took a deep breath and exhaled. She pulled her shoulders back and tried to do what Birdie told her. After a few seconds, her body relaxed and her head slumped down, her chin resting on her chest.

"Now, picture in your mind's eye the being you want to summon. Think about their features, the way they looked when they last appeared to you."

Zora thought about Marquitta as she'd looked when she stoo in her room—the olive-green crochet dress, golden bracelets on her wrists, perfectly coiffed afro, and the deep purple mark that ringed her neck.

Suddenly, she smelled something that hadn't been in the room before. The intoxicating mixture smelled like bergamot an earl gray, with a hint of some type of citrus. When Zora opened her eyes, Marquitta stood on the other side of the table, her wide eyes staring at Birdie. Zora startled then winced as her bruised leg fell off the seat and her foot touched the ground.

"What is it, Zora?" Birdie asked.

Zora fought to steady her breath as she so often did when a ghost appeared before her. She twisted her shirt around her finger with one hand and clenched the other one into fist.

"It's Marquitta," she whispered.

Birdie whipped around in her seat, as if she could sense where her lover stood.

"What do I do now?" Zora managed in between short breaths. Marquitta stood stock still, but now her gaze shifted toward Zora. She stepped toward Zora. Zora closed her eyes and clenched her teeth. "Birdie?"

"Sorry," Birdie apologized, returning her attention to the task at hand. She looked back down at the spell book. "You have to temper your fear."

"How the hell do I do that? She's standin' right here, starin' right through me."

Birdie reached out a hand as though she could touch her lover's body. When she realized all she touched was air, Birdie sighed and brought the hand to the gold bird charm around her neck.

"It's your fear that's blocking your ability to truly tap into your powers," she explained.

"Are you kidding me?" Zora questioned. *How the fuck am I supposed to stop being afraid of ghosts?* she thought. But when Birdie didn't respond, Zora took several deep breaths and tried to slow down her heart. After a few seconds, she examined her hands. They appeared steady. Her mind even felt a bit clearer. Maybe I can do this, she assured herself.

"What now?" Zora asked.

"Now, you've got to state your intentions for her," Birdie instructed.

"My intentions?"

"Yes. What do you want from her? Remember, you're the one alive here. . ." Birdie's voice trailed off.

"Marquitta, I want to know who killed you," Zora stated.

Within seconds, the room grew cold. Zora had felt this before. When the dead were overwhelmed with emotions, sadness or rage or even happiness, they displaced so much energy that they affected the temperature around them, turning it hot or cold. Birdie shivered and brushed her hands up and down her arms. Marquitta closed the gap between her and Zora and once she stood beside her, Zora shivered.

"She's really sad right now," Zora explained, the emotion heavy in her voice.

Birdie pursed her lips and gripped her lover's spell book in her hands. "Is she saying anything?"

Zora looked up at Marquitta and whispered: "Tell me who killed you. I want to help."

"I—" Marquitta began. Her brows knitted and she tried to speak again, but no words came out. *Hadn't she spoken to me the other day?* Zora thought. But even as Marquitta's mouth moved, no words came out.

Zora decided to switch tactics. "What's your name?" she asked.

Right away, the ghost responded, "Marquitta Transcendence.

"Marquitta, tell me who killed you."

Again, Marquitta's ghost seemed paralyzed.

Zora's mouth dropped. "It's almost like she's blocked when I ask her who killed her. Like she can't say anything."

"Well, get her to show you."

Zora gulped. "Marquitta, can you—"

The ghost touched Zora's arm, and she tensed as she prepared herself to see this woman's last moments. But something else flashed before Zora's mind. Instead of seeing Marquitta dying, Zora saw her living.

Marquitta was standing in front of a mirror wearing the same dress she wore in death. She was singing along to an R&B song playing from her phone as she applied makeup. Now humming, she sipped tea from a tall coffee mug and went back to applying mascara. She looked happy. Like a woman taking solace in a moment for herself. She sprayed her makeup with setting spray before reaching for her perfume. Then she turned to the side and checked herself out in the mirror before walking out of the bathroom. And then there was darkness.

Zora knitted her brows as she emerged from Marquitta's memory.

"Did you see?" Birdie asked. "Did you see who it was?"

"No."

"No?"

"No," Zora replied. "I didn't see anyone, only Marquitta."

Birdie furrowed her brows. "That doesn't make sense."

"How did Marquitta die?" Zora asked.

Birdie bit her lip before disappearing and reappearing with a manila folder. She slid it across the table and Zora's mouth dried up and her whole body warmed as she skimmed the crime scene photos of Marquitta's death.

In them Marquitta lay face up on the floor of what Zora assumed was her bedroom. She wore the same dress Zora saw in her memory, meaning the memory Zora saw happened not too long before her death. Her eyes and mouth were wide, and her hands rested at her clavicle. The ring around her neck somehow appeared uglier under the flash of the camera, and Zora could see that the redness on her cheeks and face resulted from blood vessels. One sandal balanced on her left toes and the other one lay on the floor beside her. Her feet pointed toward the bedroom door, and Zora wondered if she'd been facing the hall when her attacker struck. No other bruising was present, and the room showed no signs of a struggle.

Zora read that the cause of death was strangulation. She winced at that fact, at how brutal and terrifying it would be to die that way. The coroner's report stated the time of death was estimated between one and four in the afternoon.

"I didn't see this happen," Zora said.

Birdie tilted her head. "What?"

Zora looked up from the documents. "Usually when I touch the dead, I see their last moments first, and the longer I hold on to them, the more memories I see."

Birdie nodded. "Yeah, that's how it worked for Marquitta, too."

"But when I touched her, I saw her alive. She was doin' her makeup and singin' in the bathroom. Then when she walked out of the bathroom, it all went black so abruptly."

"Isn't that what normally happens? The fade to black, I mean."

Zora nodded. She poured more coffee into her cup and walked to the refrigerator for more creamer. Birdie's eyes followed her.

"Yeah, but in this case, it happened like that." Zora snapped her fingers. "Like when a frame of a movie is cut or somethin' ju blacks out."

Zora slid back onto the bench and held her coffee in both hands, tapping her cup as she thought.

"I don't remember Marquitta experiencing them like that," Birdie replied as she flipped feverishly around her lover's spell book.

"Could it be . . . like, a spell or somethin'?" Zora asked.

"Maybe. But I've never heard of anything like this. Usually a spell will break when a person dies."

"Why?"

"Because death is the ultimate spell breaker. It's a reset button." Birdie said. "But for this to still be in place after death, and for a necromancer to not even be able to get around it. . .This is some powerful stuff."

Birdie flipped through the pages of Marquitta's spell book again and when she didn't find anything, she heaved a sigh of exasperation. She walked into the dining room and grabbed three more books and handed one to Zora. The name "Dottie Transcendence" was written on the inside cover in scrawling cursive.

Zora flipped through the book, reviewing spells for love, potions for glamouring one's appearance, and instructions for how to be a canticle witch, someone who used songs to enchant listeners.

But there was nothing about memory spells or death spells in Dottie's book. And from the way Birdie tossed her spell books onto the table and clenched her fists, there was nothing in the two she reviewed, either. Not for the first time since she came to Savannah, Zora felt extremely out of her depth.

"What was Marquitta able to do again?" Zora asked.

Birdie leaned her head against her hand. "She could summon the dead and raise them, and she could speak with ghosts. She could see their memories, speak with them, help them move on. Toward the end, she was able to control them, and she could suppress them when she didn't want to see them."

Zora's heart leapt at the possibility of never having to see a ghost again, unless she wanted to. And she was quite certain she didn't want to.

"How do I do that?" she asked, leaning her body forward.

Birdie shook her head slowly. "In time, baby. In time."

By the time Zora dressed for her first official night at Nightingale's, the pain in her knee had subsided. She was grateful there wasn't a huge bruise, but the fear she felt when she'd been inside Mobley's memory, and inside Marquitta's memory, still lingered.

While Zora waited backstage for her name to be called, her heart felt like it would jackhammer straight out of her chest. She could hear it pounding in her ears and for a second, it felt like the ground would rise up to meet her.

She took deep breaths and practiced grounding techniques she'd seen on a YouTube video once. As she thought about all the things she could see, feel, and hear, MK appeared by Zora's side.

"Good luck out there, new booty," she purred. Zora rolled her eyes but didn't engage, knowing MK was only trying to knock her off her game.

Just be cool. You can do this, Zora thought.

"I don't need luck," Zora said. "I've got this. But thanks for the well wishes, MK."

As MK opened her mouth to speak, Birdie's voice interrupted her.

"It's my great pleasure to introduce you to our newest dancer Zora!"

Without a second glance toward MK, Zora walked out on stage, her left hand in the air and a smile on her face.

The crowd clapped and hooted and hollered as she graced the stage, her entire body buzzing with anticipation. She took in the sound of her heels clicking against the stage, the warmth of the spotlight and its reflection on her gold fringe dress. She'd picked it out especially for her first dance, wanting to make the best first impression.

She chose a slow song, one that reminded her of something a snake charmer would play back in the day. As the drums began at the top of the song, Zora moved her hips in a circle. She slithered across the stage, using up every part as she undulated and moved her shoulders back. In that moment, the rest of the world fell away as it often did when she danced. She felt powerful as she stuck out a leg and slowly brought it back in toward herself.

Zora unbuttoned the side of the dress as the piano became more prevalent, revealing a hot pink bra and matching panties. She slinked to the front of the stage and hit the backbend she'd done in the audition, only this time she stayed there for longer and removed her bra as she did so, showing off glittery gold tassels.

The crowd went wild. Zora could see Jabari and several other witches staring at her in rapt attention.

Eat your hearts out, she thought. She stood up slowly and slunk to the back of the stage, circling her hips and moving her belly in and out as though belly dancing before she turned to the front again and shimmied down to the ground. She ended the number on her knees, hands covering her nipples after she stealthily removed the pasties on the last beat of the song.

The crowd rose to their feet clapping and hollering and clamoring for more. She reapplied her pasties and stood then waved at the crowd. She made eye contact again with Jabari, who looked like he wanted to leap on the stage and take Zora right in that moment. She shifted her gaze to Whitley. As before Whitley was seated alone, and she raised her glass of champagne toward Zora in salute. And she'd been right before when she said she didn't hide her emotions—Zora could tell by the look on her face she was just as turned on as Jabari. This notion made Zora's cheeks and chest grow warm.

Zora delicately grabbed her costume before waving to the crowd one last time and prancing off stage.

"Whoa, girl, you did great!" Safi shouted. Raheem and Chans nodded enthusiastically.

"Thanks," Zora said. Her body and her soul were on fire as she walked into the dressing room. In the small but organized room, lockers flanked the far wall and the one to its right, and a table piled high with makeup and mirrors and costumes occupie its center. To the left of the door was a vanity, a large mirror covering half the wall. MK, Deja, Tanisha, and Livia stood there touching up their makeup.

"Girl, how you do that backbend?" Tanisha asked, turning to face Zora.

Zora smirked. "I learned it in my dance classes. I could teach you if you want."

"For real?" she replied.

Zora nodded and Tanisha snapped her fingers before turning back to the mirror.

"Your routine was so good," Raheem said. "I never seen people give a newbie a standin' ovation."

"Me neither. Guess we've got ourselves a new favorite dancer," Livia quipped.

Even though Zora shook her head, she couldn't help but smirk.

"Oh, please. I get a standing O on my worst night," MK said, snapping her head in Livia's direction. "This bitch does a backbend like she's the fuckin' demon in the Exorcist and suddenly she's the shit?" She turned toward Zora. "No, baby. You may have gotten people's attention this time, but it's not what happens that first night when you're new. It's what happens the next time when you've gone from new booty to a regular."

"Ooooh," one of the dancers said. They looked from MK to Zora.

"What's the matter, MK? Afraid you'll lose standing as the sexiest witch in Savannah?" Livia teased.

MK scoffed. "She could never."

"Mmm. Well, if the way Jabari looked at me while I was on stage tonight was any indication, you might be on shaky ground," Zora sassed.

MK glared at her as the other dancers laughed and looked between them in delight. Zora shrugged and grabbed her purse before leaving the room, hearing MK say "that bitch" as she did so.

A sly grin spread across Zora's face as she thought to herself, *"That bitch" is right, and she's not going anywhere.*

Chapter 9

"When it comes to joining a magical house, the thing I know to be true is—you don't choose your house. The house chooses you."

Spell Book of Frankie Neon, 2009

Who would want to kill Marquitta Transcendence? That's the question Zora kept asking herself the next night as she danced another ensemble routine and performed not one but two sets. With each flip and turn, she scanned the crowd, wondering if Marquitta's killer could be hiding in plain sight.

After yet another standing ovation, Zora strolled toward the bar, maneuvering through a sea of club goers who fawned over her and complimented her on her body, her dancing skills, and her sex appeal. Once she'd answered them and sent them on their way, she found Niko and Whitley standing together but not talking. They both smiled at Zora as she approached. She made her way to Whitley, who sat not alone but with Niko this time.

"Girl, you killed it," Niko gushed.

"You looked sexy as hell up there," Whitley added.

"I know. Thank you," she replied. Whitley quirked a brow and nodded in approval of Zora's confidence. Zora noticed the same sparkle in Whitley's eyes that she had when Zora had been on stage, and it excited her in more ways than one.

Zora shifted her attention to Taemar, who stood at the other end of the bar surrounded by a crowd of people waiting for their drinks.

"Get you anything?" asked the other bartender, a tall, stocky person named Iris.

"Coke?" Zora asked.

Iris nodded. Seconds later, they slid a Coca Cola across the bar toward Zora, who dropped a few singles into the tip jar and thanked them. She cracked the can open and sipped it, thankful for the quickness with which the caffeine went to work.

As the next act took the stage, a duet between Safi and Livia, Zora's mind drifted.

Who would want to kill Marquitta Transcendence? she thought. Now that she'd seen the gruesome crime scene photos, and read the police and autopsy report that Birdie had stolen the morning for them to review, Zora felt in her gut that the murder had to be personal.

There was no forced entry. Nothing seemed to be missing. And from the autopsy, it seemed as though Marquitta had been strangled from behind, with some kind of rope or scarf.

She kept wondering who could've hated Marquitta that much. In Zora's experience with death, most of the time it was a loved one, particularly the spouse or partner, who committed the murder. So often it happened in a moment of passion, which would explain why there was nothing missing and no signs of forced entry, and why it happened from behind.

Zora wondered if it could've been Birdie. She was her fiancée after all, and isn't the partner often guilty? But then why would Birdie try so hard to bring her into the fold and get her to help? Had she been the one to kill her lover and then curse her and was now after Zora's help to ensure the curse was powerful enough to stay in place? So that no one would know about her crime?

She took another sip of her drink. It seemed like a stretch, treating Birdie as a suspect, but she couldn't rule her out, either. Nor could she rule out Whitley, the woman standing to her right, who stood so close that her bare arms and thigh brushed against Zora's. Her skin was so soft, so warm. And her perfume still had a hold on Zora. She gazed at Whitley, who wore red cigarette pants, a black, cherry-printed crop top, and a high ponytail, and she wondered.

Whitley was obviously a powerful witch, and one who disliked the community she was forced into. But what had she done to get herself kicked out? And could what she did be one of the reasons why Marquitta didn't like her? Could Whitley, upset about being in Savannah and her treatment from Marquitta, have killed Marquitta then cursed her? But if she had, wouldn't she be acting weird, knowing that Zora was a necromancer? Wouldn't she be worried she'd be discovered?

"Zora?"

She shook her head, shaking lose the reverie she'd been stuck in and looked at Whitley, who'd been trying to talk to her.

"Sorry," Zora said. "Just zoned out."

"You good?" she asked.

Zora nodded. "Yeah, just tired. What were you sayin'?"

"I was asking if you're ready for tonight? Being initiated into Transcendence."

Zora nodded slowly. A part of her felt like it was all happening so fast. Did she even want to be a Transcendence? What if she was supposed to be a Soliloquy? How did one even decide who belonged in what house?

But then again, Birdie had been so kind to her. She'd given her a job and a roof over her head. And aside from MK and Orion's foolishness, she enjoyed Birdie and Taemar's company.

"I am. But I was wonderin'—who decides who belongs to which house?" she asked.

"We draw straws," Niko quipped. Zora shook her head.

"My dad used to say, 'The house chooses you.' Usually whichever witch approaches you first and talks to you is often th one whose house you join," Whitley commented.

Jabari eased over then, an aura of lust surrounding him. He took Zora's hand and, as he'd done before, kissed her knuckles, not bothering to apologize for interrupting their conversation.

"You were a revelation up there," he said. Objectively, Zora knew the line was just that. A line he'd probably told half the dancers, including MK. But deep down, Zora felt her desire stir.

Damn, he looks good tonight, she thought. He looked down at her and gave her the same look he had when she'd been dancing.

"Thanks," she replied coyly.

"It's my pleasure, really," he leaned against the bar. "So, I wanted to see if I could take you up on that offer of yours?"

Zora lifted a brow. "Offer?"

"Yes, to learn more about you. I'd love to take you out soon."

Zora could hear Whitley suck in a breath beside her. She looked over at the woman, who rolled her eyes hard but said nothing. Niko looked from Whitley to Jabari, his lips pursed.

Zora bit her lip, her face and neck suddenly warm.

"Uh, sure. Just text me," Zora replied.

They exchanged numbers and Jabari sauntered away, a group of witches following in his wake.

When he left, it seemed as if the air shifted. The witches sipped their drinks quietly with no mention of their previous conversation. Whitley spoke first, breaking the silence.

"Well, I think that's my cue." She turned to Zora.

"What? You're leavin'?"

"I came to see you."

Zora's heart leapt.

"Now that I have, I'm gonna head home for a bit, get ready for your initiation."

Though unable to place it at first, Zora realized the pang in her stomach was one of disappointment. She didn't want Whitley to go. She wanted to get to know her, both because she had to make sure she wasn't the one who'd killed Marquitta, and because . . .

Because she was incredibly, deeply attracted to her.

"If all this is too much, we can go outside?" Zora asked, hoping to steal away with Whitley, even if only for a minute.

Whitley squeezed Zora's shoulder. But still, she grabbed a ten-dollar bill from her pocket and left it on the bar. "You're sweet. But I really just want to be alone for a while."

"Oh," Zora said, her shoulders drooping.

"I meant what I said. You were very sexy up there. I'll see you later," Whitley said. She fist bumped Niko before grabbing her purse and strutting out of the club.

Zora slid onto the barstool next to Niko and nursed her soda. Taemar, finally out of the weeds, walked over.

"Man, Jabari's such a ho," he said.

Zora couldn't help but laugh, both at the lateness of his comment and at the statement itself. "What?"

"He's been with most of the witches here, including MK," he responded.

"And Raheem," Niko added.

"And Orion," said Taemar.

"And Marquitta," Niko said.

"Yeah," Taemar replied. "Pure disaster bi energy. So . . . if you do go out with him, just be careful. He can be flighty and I don't want you gettin' your feelin's hurt."

Zora nodded.

"Good," he replied, before being swarmed by another crowd of thirsty customers.

Zora lifted her head just as a thought popped into her mind. With Taemar busy filling drink orders, she turned toward Niko.

"You and Tae mentioned Jabari had been with Marquitta before. How long were they together?" Zora asked.

"I'm not sure, honestly," Niko said. "But I think it was a few years. Tae would know more than me."

"Huh," Zora replied. As the next dancer came on stage and the lights dimmed again, Zora wondered why Birdie hadn't ever mentioned that Jabari and Marquitta had been an item. Who would have more of a motive than a jilted lover? But he seemed like someone who was only looking for something casual, and he had his fair share of witches looking for the same. So why would he, after all this time that Marquitta and Birdie had been together, suddenly want his former lover dead?

She scowled as the lights dimmed and the next dancer began their routine, her list of suspects increasing.

After being met with mixed responses from the crowd following her announcement, Birdie closed the club early that night. The whole Savannah Triarchy met at Transcendence house, as they had at Divinity house for the autumnal equinox. Yet again, everyone was dressed in their best avant garde finery, and Zora was in awe of the community's creativity.

Zora borrowed another dress from Birdie. This one a lavende

color with tulle sleeves and an A-line tulle bottom that grazed the floor. She wore her hair down and parted down the middle, with crystal clips on either side of her part. Though she felt like a princess in waiting, she wondered if anyone would ever tell the story of a queer Black princess solving a murder mystery.

She was uncertain of what to expect as the group gathered on the patio. Instead of a bonfire, this ritual would take place around a large basin of water. Only Birdie stood by the water basin, the other House Heads stood with their house members.

Last time, Zora could blend in with the crowd. This time, all the attention fell on her. She wanted to say she'd changed her mind, that maybe she'd moved too fast. She wanted to jump into her car and make a run for it. She wanted to be anywhere but there.

When Birdie spoke, however, Zora felt the tension ease from her shoulders.

"Thank you all for being here this evening," she said. "Before we begin the ceremony, I'd just like to say something."

The crowd watched her intently, as did Zora.

"It's hard being one of us, isn't it?" Birdie began, looking from left to right at the witches who stood in a semi-circle around her. "And I don't just mean magical, and I don't just mean Black. And hell, I don't just mean queer because most of us here are that, too."

Zora looked out at the group, many of them nodding and glancing at each other.

"But I mean all three of those things. We exist at the intersection of demonization and marginalization and yet we all . . . you all somehow still manage to push through. And why is that?"

She paused for dramatic effect. Dozens of curious eyes stared back at her.

"I'd like to think it's because of this right here. This community, these three houses, dedicated to protecting our own," Birdie continued. Some of the witches snapped their fingers while others nodded and said things like "I know that's right" and "speak on it."

"House Divinity, there to ensure we follow the rites and rituals of our magic to appease the gods and ensure our power everlasting. House Soliloquy, to hold us accountable to the human laws and ensure we maintain our anonymity, which is sacrosanct. And House Transcendence, to ensure we revel in ou power and all that magic has to offer.

"We have all been saved by this community, been extended lifelines. For some, it yanked us out of the depths of our shitty, mundane human lives and thrust us into our power. For others, it helped us get on our feet at a time when we didn't have two nickels to rub together. And now, I'd like to extend that lifeline t someone else," Birdie turned toward her. "To Zora."

Zora nodded as the witches around them applauded, surprised by the emotion building inside of her.

When the circle grew silent again, Birdie picked up a small knife from the patio table and pricked her finger. She held it alof as blood trickled down the finger and said: "Zora, tonight we welcome you into the House of Transcendence. This house will be your advocates, your educators, your friends, and your family As our blood mixes with water, our lives now intertwine."

She pressed her nail into her finger and droplets of blood fell into the water. Taemar walked up next and pricked his finger an repeated Birdie's final line. He smiled at Zora so sincerely before he turned back toward the group that Zora's heart felt like it would burst.

MK and Orion followed suit, their movements stiff and robotic. They reluctantly recited the words of the ritual, not even looking at Zora before returning to the group.

Why are they like this? Zora wondered.

She shook the thought from her head as the blood and water mixed. Then the substance began to congeal and solidify. After it formed into a jagged crystal, Birdie scooped it out and pierced it before sliding it on to a gold chain. Then held the necklace out to Zora with both hands.

"Welcome to the House of Transcendence, Zora."

Zora took the necklace and placed it around her neck. The witches showed their jubilation with some clapping and others using their powers in celebration. Birdie then turned back to the table and grabbed a yellow leather-bound book.

"And I present to you your first spell book. May it be your best friend in your times of joy and sorrow." Birdie held the notebook out and Zora grasped it slowly. She ran a hand over the smoothness of it before pressing the empty spell book to her chest and biting her lip.

As it had the night of the ritual, music began to play. Witch after witch approached Zora and offered their congratulations. She looked at them all and smiled and nodded before her eyes landed on Whitley. Whitley raised her glass to Zora, congratulating her from a distance. Zora motioned toward her, only to be stopped by a new group of witches. While waiting for the crowd to disperse, Zora's gaze drifted up to her room and she noticed a light shining from the bedroom window. Marquitta stood in the window, staring down at the scene, and possibly at her killer.

Chapter 10

"Like all magic, curses aren't inherently good or evil. Sometimes they're the only justice a witch can get. And other times, they're their only revenge."

Spell Book of Sabrina Bounty, 2014

Zora had never had an issue seeing the memory of the dead. But yesterday, as she was sucked into Marquitta's memory, all she'd seen was a beautiful woman getting ready for the day. She thought about the position she was in and chuckled mirthlessly. A few days ago, she was actively avoiding ghosts and their emotional baggage. And now, she sat in the middle of her bed with her legs crossed, about to summon Marquitta's ghost and invite her into her head. Because Zora knew in order to solve her murder, she'd have to sit with Marquitta's ghost longer, and try to recover the memory of her death. And if she couldn't, she'd have to search more of her memories for clues about the perpetrator.

She cleared her thoughts and pictured Marquitta in her mind's eye. Almost immediately, the air shifted. Zora heard the hardwood floor creak, felt a weight on the bed beside her. She took more deep breaths and tried to steady her heart, tried to combat the dread that made her stomach clench. She opened her eyes and Marquitta was there, beautiful and tragic, and staring at Zora expectantly.

"Hello, Marquitta," Zora said. The woman nodded.

"Okay, well, let's just . . ." Zora held out her hands for Marquitta to take. Seconds later, Zora found herself consumed by Marquitta's memories. She no longer saw Marquitta getting ready. Now, she saw the woman eating lunch on the patio. Birdi sat across from her, and she looked so different. Gone were the black clothes and dark circles beneath her eyes. She looked lighter and she smiled at Marquitta as the pair flirted and kissec Then Birdie said she was leaving to run errands before going to the club and interviewing for a new bartender. She urged Marquitta to stay and relax.

"You're the talent, after all," Birdie said sweetly. "I just get tc kiki on stage for a moment. You're the one who's actually gotta work tonight."

They kissed then walked into the house. Birdie turned as she opened the front door. "I'll see you later, baby. I love you."

Marquitta stood on the stairs as she called out to Birdie, "I love you, too."

And just as Zora was expecting to see more of the memory, it went black. She pulled away and scowled at Marquitta, who stared at Zora with an unreadable expression. Zora took the ghost's hand again and this time, she saw Marquitta making coffee, still dressed in a robe.

Zora gasped. She jumped out of her bed and darted across th hall to Birdie's room. She banged on the door and Birdie opened seconds later. Her eyes widened as she saw Zora and stepped aside to let her in.

"What's wrong?"

"I think . . . I think there's something really, really wrong wit Marquitta's memory."

"What do you mean?"

"When I first tried to see her last moments, I saw her getting ready, right? But just now, I saw what must've been an hour or so before that, you two eating lunch."

Birdie sat on the window seat and crossed her arms. Zora began to pace.

"And I tried again, and then I saw her in a pink robe, her bonnet on, making coffee."

"So you saw her that morning, too? This is good, you're going back through—"

"No, I mean, the memories after the ones I see are gone. When I saw you two having lunch, everything went to black after you left to run errands. There was nothing after, and the same thing happened when I saw her making coffee. It's like . . . the more I try to see her memories and dig, the more things get . . . deleted."

"Deleted?" Birdie asked flatly. Zora rolled her eyes.

"You know what I mean. It's like some kind of virus going through and getting rid of her memories so now I can't go back to those memories to try to see what happened."

Birdie shook her head. "Well, this isn't a virus. It's probably some kind of curse. Like I said last night, whoever did this is powerful. We've got to do some research on this, find out what kind of magic this is. If we do, maybe we can find out who killed Marquitta."

"How would that help?" Zora asked quizzically.

"Because whoever cast this had to have done some serious curse work before. This isn't the work of a newbie—and they probably had to have found the curse in a spell book somewhere. I'll look around."

"Fine. I'll start handling this the old fashion way." Zora plopped down beside Birdie. "Tell me where you were when Marquitta was killed."

Birdie scoffed. "You're kidding, right?"

"I need to know." Zora shrugged.

"Why would I ask for your help solving Marquitta's murder if I was the one who killed her?"

"It wouldn't be the first time I've had a murderer ask for help," Zora replied.

She recounted the time when she was hired by a white man to raise his wife from the dead. He wanted to know who killed her—and the combination of her family's safe. The woman had been shot by their gardener, at his behest. When Zora told her father what happened, he talked her out of doing anything about it.

"What do you think is gonna happen when you call them, huh? How you gonna justify the knowledge you got? You think the police will believe a Black girl who said she discovered who killed that rich white woman by raising her corpse? Just drop it, Zora. That man got what he needed and so did we."

In the present, Zora stared at Birdie and waited for her to respond.

Birdie tightened her jaw then relaxed it. "I was at the club doing inventory with Taemar, then I had an interview with an applicant for the bartender position, the one I'd hoped you'd fill before you decided to be a dancer," Birdie said.

"I'll ask Taemar," Zora started, ignoring Birdie's comment about her choosing to dance over slinging drinks. "Are there cameras that can corroborate you were there the whole time?"

"So, you're a detective now?" Birdie quipped.

"Let's not forget who put me on the case," Zora retorted.

Birdie's fists clenched. "Yes, Zora. I'll get you whatever you need so you can stop grilling me."

"Birdie, listen—you were her fiancée and you're the only witch who has the power to teleport. I'm sorry this hurts, but I have to be sure."

She sighed. "Fine. Taemar should be at the club after his classes around three. You can talk to him then."

"Great. There's someone else I can talk to in the meantime."

Birdie stared at Zora, as if asking who was next on her list of suspects. Zora studied Birdie's eyes for a moment then stood, saying nothing as she exited the room.

Zora looked at her phone. Nine a.m.

Bob-A-Lula's, a hair salon in a shotgun style house in Yamacraw Village, just opened for the day. Though the house had been abandoned in the '80s, it had been converted into a business in the '90s. The window featured a painting of a black woman with a bob, one hand on her neck and her head tilted back. The shop name was written above her in flowery cursive.

Zora felt like she was stepping back into the '50s as soon as she stepped into the shop. Subway tiles covered the floors. A jukebox sat to the right of the door, and four rows of pink and leather barber chairs occupied both sides of the room. Before each of the chairs stood a pink vanity with an arched mirror attached, and lightbulbs ringed the mirror. The room smelled like peppermint, and as Whitley walked from the back of the salon, Zora's heart leapt.

"Hey, girl," Whitley said as she approached. Her hair was tied back in a head scarf, the same color pink as her smock. Now that she was wearing flats, Zora could see that Whitley was several inches shorter than her, a fact that made Zora like her even more.

"Hi. I brought you coffee," Zora said, holding out the cafe au lait she'd gotten for Whitley on the way to the salon. She figured if she was going to put someone on the spot, the least she could do was bring them a bougie coffee.

This is the second time you've brought me a drink," Whitley commented as she took the coffee. "I'm going to have to repay th favor some time."

Zora sipped her coffee, her attempt to cover the smile that played at the edges of her lips. *Focus, Zora, focus,* she thought.

"So . . . what brings you?"

"I need a cut. It's been forever." *And I need to know where you were when Marquitta died,* she thought.

"Well, good thing for you, my chair's open." Whitley gestured toward the first chair on the right. Zora sat and Whitley unfurled a black cape and pinned it behind Zora's neck. She gently pulled her hair from under the cape and removed the scrunchie Zora had used to pull her coils up into a bun. Zora noted how soft, how gentle her hands felt.

"So, what're we doing?" Whitley asked.

"I'm thinkin' bangs," Zora said, glancing at herself in the mirror. Because she typically wore her hair back, or at least had the front part braided, Zora never thought about bangs. But she figured, why not? New job, new city, new hair.

"You'd be so cute with bangs," Whitley remarked. Zora met her eyes in the mirror. "I'll cut them then add some layers aroun your face to blend it all together, then maybe some long layers in the back. And I think your ends just need a slight trim. Sound good?"

Zora nodded, her stomach in knots. Whitley smiled.

"C'mon, let's wash you first."

Whitley guided Zora to the washing station and helped her lower her head back into the wash basin.

"Let me know if the water's too hot," she said. She pumped product into her hand and began washing Zora's hair, her stiletto-shaped nails feeling good against her scalp.

"It's good," Zora replied.

"Great. So, how's your day going?"

"Uh," Zora cleared her throat. "Just starting my magical trainin' with Birdie."

Whitley rinsed the shampoo and applied conditioner.

"Cool. Glad you're getting acclimated. I'm sure it must be overwhelming, but if you ever need help—"

"Yeah, I do, actually," Zora said.

"Shoot."

Zora startled as the water turned off. Whitley sat Zora up and patted her hair with a microfiber towel. She guided Zora back to her chair and began applying product to her hair as she sectioned it off. When she finished the last section, she guided Zora to a row of overhead dryers. Zora sat beneath one and crossed her legs as Whitley set the timer.

"Well, I'm practicin' how to summon a ghost," Zora began, competing with the noise of the dryer. "And I summoned Marquitta, for Birdie."

She looked at Whitley, searching for some kind of reaction to Marquitta's name but there was none.

"That's nice of you. I bet it was tough for Birdie."

"Yeah, it was. And I'm readin' her spell book and hearin' so much about her, I'm startin' to feel like I know her."

Whitley nodded as she walked back to her station and took a sip of coffee.

"So, I just keep wonderin' what could've happened to her," Zora asked.

"You're not the only one."

"You, too?" Zora asked, surprised.

Whitley shrugged a shoulder. She pulled her phone from the pocket in her smock and her brows knitted. She set her coffee down and her nails tapped furiously over the screen before she slid her phone back into the pocket.

"Sorry, client question. Anyway, I mean, just because we didn't fuck with each other like that doesn't mean I didn't care. She meant a lot to so many people; it's been hard watching their grief."

"I'm sure. It's hard not knowing what happened. Who could done somethin' like that? I mean in the middle of the day? Who have time?"

Whitley snorted. "You'd be surprised what people can do."

Zora furrowed her brows, deciding to switch tactics.

"Did the police even try to find out who did anything? Did they talk to everyone?"

"Girl, you know the cops won't dig too deeply into the murder of a Black woman. But, they spoke with pretty much everyone in the community."

"And we see how well that's gone," Niko chimed in. He walked in from the rear of the salon and began cleaning what must've been his station.

"Well, it's only been a month," Whitley said. "Maybe they aren't scratching their asses too much."

"I've never had to talk to the cops. What'd they even ask you? Zora asked as Whitley lifted the dryer. Zora followed her back to the chair and waited as Whitley grabbed her sheers and began cutting her hair.

"Shit. Everything. Literally everything. Who I was to her, where I'm from, why'd I move from LA to Savannah. Where I was that day."

"And what'd you say?"

Whitley paused. Zora looked up at her and tried to keep her face blank, but inside she was thinking, Please, please don't be the killer.

"The truth," Whitley said, an edge to her voice now. "That I was handling my regular customers, and that there was video footage to prove it. And that it's no one's business why I moved from LA to here."

"Video footage, that's good," Zora said. Whitley frowned, and Zora realized she was losing her. Even Niko turned and lifted a brow.

"So, I get what Jabari does, the magical law thing," Zora began, hoping that if she shifted topics, things would stop feeling so awkward. "And Birdie is like, I guess balance and partyin'. But I'm not quite sure how you oversee human law. I mean as a salon owner and everything?"

Whitley stared down at Zora with annoyance written all over her face.

"You know those regulars I mentioned when you were grilling me about Marquitta's death?"

"I wasn't—"

"I know an interrogation when I see one, Zora. You're obviously looking into Marquitta's murder and I suppose I'd be a suspect, seeing as how Marquitta and I didn't get along."

Whitley finished cutting Zora's bangs and turned her back toward the mirror before setting her sheers down on the vanity. Zora's heartbeat quickened.

"But I was here, like I said. So you'll have to move on to your next suspect."

"I'm sorry, I—"

"And about those regulars, one of them is Judge Earline

Creighton. And the woman Niko is waiting for is Detective Tiffa
Poe. I may only be a 'salon owner,' but the truth is, people trust
their hair stylists more than almost any other relationship,
including their partners or therapists. We keep their secrets, and
they help us when we need it."

"I didn't mean—"

"And to think, I honestly thought the coffee was just an
innocent gesture, your way of continuing our conversation from
the other night." Whitley set her scissors down on her vanity.

"Whitley, wait. I'd still like to—"

"Niko, can you come and finish Zora off, please? I need a
minute."

Without another word, Whitley stormed to the back of the
salon, leaving her coffee on the vanity. Zora looked down at the
ground, wishing it would swallow her up.

"That went well," Niko said flatly.

"Yeah, I'm a real fuckin' gum shoe," Zora replied.

"No kiddin.'" Niko sectioned off her hair and began adding
layers to blend in her bangs. Zora sat in silence, ruminating over
her conversation with Whitley and wondering how she could've
said everything differently.

Zora fanned herself, suddenly feeling warm.

"It hot in here to you?" She asked.

"uh-uh," Niko replied as he put the finishing touches on her
hair. "You havin' a hot flash or somethin'?"

Zora sucked her teeth and shook her head. Why had it gotten
so warm all of a sudden? She looked around the room, trying to
find the source of the sudden temperature change and spotted a
ghost dressed in an old timey suit shuffling down the steps. His
hair was close cropped, his beard expertly lined. To the average
eye, nothing about him seemed off, except for the sunken eyes,

the sweet smell of almonds, and the discoloration of the front of his shirt, which looked like this man's last meal.

The ghost took another step down.

You gotta be fuckin' kiddin' me, Zora thought.

Zora gripped the arm rests of the barber's chair and her eyes widened. Try as she might, she couldn't tear her gaze from the stairs. Acid churned in her belly. Her temples and the tips of her ears throbbed, and sweat collected on her upper lip.

Niko rolled his sleeves up, now feeling the shift in temperature.

"Now you mention it, it has gotten warmer in here."

Zora nodded toward the stairs.

"Oh, hell nah, is there a ghost in here?"

"Man, on the stairs. Suit, messed up shirt, smells like almonds. Looking at me like he wants to kill me."

"All I wanted was a hot meal, woman," the ghost grumbled, its voice coming out strained, a trail of white foam oozing from its mouth.

"I thought ghosts turned the air cold?"

"Ghosts can make it hot, too, 'specially if they mad," Zora said slowly.

"What can I do?" Niko asked, but Zora had already snapped out of her surprise and slid out of the chair. She dug through her bag for the red brick dust and wormwood Birdie had given her but found only the tin of margarita salt from the ritual.

How could I have left it at home? Zora thought.

She grabbed the tin and stood and her purse dropped to the floor. Zora peeled the lid off and turned toward Niko.

"Unless you know how to get rid of a ghost, you can't—"

"Get rid of me? Woman, you could never," the ghost rasped. In the blink of an eye, the ghost had traveled from the stairs to where Zora stood. Its hands wrapped around Zora's neck and Zora was surprised at how real they felt. But she didn't have much time to do so because the ghost's hands were close to crushing her windpipe. Zora grabbed the tin of salt just as the ghost slammed her into the vanity mirror. A cracking sound echoed through the room and Zora hoped it was the mirror and not her skull.

"What the fuck?" Whitley said as she ran in from the rear of the salon. Whitley rushed over to Zora and Niko scrambled to lock the door and slide the blinds down.

"Zora, you got more salt?" Niko implored.

"Salt? She should have red brick and wormwood. It's stronger," Whitley said.

She knelt down to pick up a handful of salt and tossed it at the ghost. As the ghost muttered obscenities, it disappeared. Zora breathed deeply before bending over.

"You didn't tell me this place had ghosts," she rasped, her chest rising and falling quickly.

"Baby, this is Savannah," Niko said. "Everywhere has ghosts."

"That's why there are spells to get rid of them for good. There should be one in Marquitta's spell book. Have you studied that one yet?" Whitley asked.

Zora shook her head, momentarily unable to focus through the searing pain emanating from the back of her head. The ghost reappeared on the other side of the salon, and the temperature raised even more..

"Not in great detail," Zora said, eyeing the disgruntled ghost. "Do you have one in yours?"

"Do I look like a necromancer?" Whitley sassed. "No. But I can get Marquitta's book for you."

She pressed her hands together and closed her eyes. When

she opened her hands, Marquitta's spell book appeared within a flurry of pink smoke.

Before Zora could brace herself, the ghost rushed toward her, pushing her back against the vanity. She wheezed as he wrapped his hands around her neck again, flooding Zora's mind with his last moments.

Him, sitting at dinner, the same mean expression on his face. He grabbed his utensils and clutched them in his hands.

"Woman, where in the hell is my supper?" he questioned.

"Coming, Charlie," sounded a gentle voice. Charlie grumbled and ground the edge of his knife into the table.

"Better not be cold," he shouted. Seconds later, the woman walked into the room, her dress swishing around her as she set a casserole in front of him.

Without another word, Charlie dug into the casserole directly, not caring about how hot it was, only about feeding himself. Zora watched him shovel food in his mouth. Halfway through, he stopped and clutched his stomach. He fell out of his chair and writhed, reaching for his wife, who stepped back and away from his touch. Then he began foaming at the mouth and he seized for minutes on end, and his mind went black.

"You've shown me your story. Now let me go," Zora rasped.

"I want your warmth," he said through gritted teeth. Someone tossed salt on the ghost and Zora could breathe again.

"Okay, Zora, I've got it," Whitley shouted. She passed Marquitta's spell book to her, opened on a page for permanently banishing souls.

Zora grabbed the book just as the ghost reappeared. "I call upon Zephyrym, the god of wind and change. I call upon Yamala, goddess of rebirth and first breath, and I call upon Geddemin, the god of death themself."

The ghost stopped short and gasped, his body shimmering.

"With the strength of the gods within me, I cast the specter before me away from this place, away from this world, away from life itself," Zora looked at the ghost, who now writhed on the floor, face contorted in agony, just as it had been before he died. Already she could see his spirit disintegrating into the air. "I cast you to the gates of the afterworld where you will meet Geddemir firsthand. May they judge you harshly."

The spirit exploded into a fine mist as she finished the spell, but not before crying out one last time. The shop grew quiet for a moment, and Zora sank into Whitley's chair. Her lungs still ached and her head throbbed. She could feel the tension settling in at her neck and shoulders. Pressure started to build up behind her eyes, making her feel like they were being carved out by a melon baller.

"Zora, are you okay?" Whitley asked.

"I did it," Zora exclaimed. "I banished a ghost. I banished a fuckin' ghost!"

And then, Zora's vision went black.

Chapter 11

"A witch can worship the gods anywhere of course.
But their altar is the only place where they can truly
commune with them. Every magical house has an altar,
like every witch has a spell book."

Spell Book of Guillermo Prudencia, 2017

Zora's eyes snapped open. Her gaze settled on a ceiling of wooden slats, and her brows knitted. *Am I still in Bob-A-Lula's?* She wondered. As her brain started to refocus, the pain she'd experienced at Bob-A-Lula's returned. The back of her head throbbed and her shoulders and neck ached. She tried to sit up from the chaise lounge she lay on, but a pair of strong hands stopped her.

"You're not quite healed yet, Zora," Jabari said. She met his gaze as he stood over her. It seemed odd seeing him without his finery. He wore black sweatpants and a black graphic t-shirt that read "Warning." His durag shimmered in the dim light of the room. He held two metal rods and waved them over Zora; the sound they made reminded her of someone running a wet finger along the edge of a glass. "Where am I?" she rasped. She cleared her throat, the lump of bile there refusing to dislodge. With his eyes closed, Jabari continued waving the wands over her.

"You're in the House of Divinity," he replied. Zora looked around as much as she could, taking in the space she was in. The room smelled like dragon's blood incense and espresso. The lounge she was on was firm but not uncomfortable, the fabric velvety.

An altar sat against the wall at the foot of the chaise lounge. purple cloth lay on it and so, too, did a litany of candles, crystals and a golden statue of two hands pressed together at the base of their palms. A blood-rest holster and the hilt of a dagger rested across the statue's palms.

Above the altar hung a painting of a Black man, a close-up of his torso and face with his head tilted to the right. A black snake coiled around his neck and rested its head on the man's forehead, its golden eyes staring down at the viewer. Zora had only ever seen a handful of altars but none were anywhere near as elaborate as this one. And though she didn't know who was in the painting above the altar, he somehow felt familiar to her. As she continued scanning the room, Zora noticed two large bookshelves stacked with spell books and dusty paperbacks on either side of the altar.

Across from the chaise, she spotted a set of stairs and a wooden door directly at the foot of it.

I must be in the basement, Zora thought, realizing why she didn't recognize this room even though she'd been in Divinity house not three days before. Zora looked back up at the witch standing above her as he emitted a low, steady growl. Suddenly, everything that had hurt before no longer did. Jabari stepped back and set the rods on a small side table beside the chaise.

"You should be good now," he said as he smiled. *Lord, this man is fine,* she thought, before forcing herself to look away. "Tr standing; let's see how you feel."

Jabari held out a hand and Zora took it. He was right. She felt better, perhaps even more so than she had before she'd been attacked by an angry ghost.

"I do feel better. Thank you." She adjusted her shirt and fluffed out the hair in the back of her head, hoping Jabari hadn't noticed her flattened coils.

"You've had quite the time since you've been in Savannah, haven't you?" He asked.

"Nah. Takin' part in rituals, fightin' with magical burlesque dancers, and gettin' attacked by ghosts from the '50s is par for the course for me," she joked.

"You got jokes, huh?" Jabari chuckled. "Good. You'll need 'em with the kind of powers you have."

"What do you mean?" Zora asked, her eyes curious.

Jabari sighed. "I've never met a necromancer who wasn't constantly at odds with their powers. Always thought what a pity it is to be afraid of one's own magic, to feel so consumed by it." He looked at Zora and it felt like he was looking straight through her, reading her whole life with his words and his gaze. "Got me thinkin' not all magic is a gift, you feel me? Maybe some of it's a curse."

"All magic is a gift," Zora said before realizing it. *Birdie's rubbing off on me,* she thought.

"If you say so," Jabari replied, though Zora could tell he didn't believe her. He walked over to the last of the basement steps and flicked the light switch; Zora winced at the harsh overhead lighting. Then Jabari walked over to the altar and began blowing out the candles.

"But, I thought Marquitta had mastered hers?"

Jabari paused, hovering over the last candle before blowing it out. "Not a hundred percent. There were good and bad moments, but ultimately, she was always on edge, overwhelmed. She talked once about binding her powers, but between you and me, I don't think Birdie would've let her."

"Oh? Why's that?" Zora asked. She kept her face blank, trying not to show how much she doubted Jabari's statement.

"Birdie always means well, sometimes to the detriment of those around her," he said. "She has a habit of pushing people past their limits, even when those people have told her very directly what they want."

Zora's stomach clenched. Birdie didn't seem like the type of person who'd force someone to keep their powers if they were that much of an issue. Then again, wasn't she insisting Zora use her powers to help her? Powers she knew Zora was afraid of? And didn't she push Zora to keep trying to recover Marquitta's memories the night before, even though she'd been traumatized by the ghost of a House Head?

"Don't get me wrong, Birdie's my good sis. Never met a more competent and respected House Head, aside from myself, of course. But her hustle can make her so focused that she don't think about what might happen as a result."

He walked toward Zora and placed a hand against her cheek. Zora had to stop herself from leaning into him. "Just . . . be careful. I don't want to see anythin' bad happen to you."

Zora nodded, unsure of what to say. Jabari pulled his hand away and glided up the steps, not waiting to see if she was following him. She glanced around the room once more then hurried behind him.

As they emerged from the basement and entered the living room, Zora spotted Birdie and Whitley sitting on the couch. In the corner by the window sat Taemar and Niko, his hand resting on Taemar's leg.

When they saw Zora, they all stood. Birdie rushed toward her with Whitley on her feet just as fast.

"Thank the gods you're okay," Birdie said as she wrapped

her arms around Zora. She pulled away and before Zora knew it, Whitley was hugging her now. Zora relaxed in her arms.

"I was worried," Whitley whispered.

"I'm okay, thanks to you," she replied. When Whitley pulled away, Zora wished she hadn't.

Zora turned back to Jabari. "Thanks again for healin' me. What was it you used?"

"Dousing rods," he said. He sauntered over to the couch and sat. "They're usually used for finding ley lines, but most don't know they can be used to heal, too, in the right hands."

"Jabari uses metal and sound waves to heal," Whitley explained. "He saved me a visit to a chiropractor just last month."

Zora nodded. She'd never met a witch with that kind of power. Most healing witches she knew just healed with the touch of their hand, or they were nature witches who used plants and herbs on wounds and broken bones to heal them. Just as she wondered what else Jabari could do, she glimpsed the other witches in the room.

For a moment, everyone stared at Zora, as though expecting her to combust. She rolled her eyes but couldn't help the smile that crept over her face at having so many people genuinely concerned about her.

"Okay, y'all. Perk up. I'm not dead, so let's keep this day pushin.'"

"Right," Birdie agreed. She stood and walked toward the door. "I'll take you to your car."

"I'll meet y'all back at the house," Taemar said, joining Birdie by the door.

"Well, I'm going back to the salon. Got a few regulars I need to attend to. I'm glad you're okay." Whitley took Zora's hand and squeezed it. "Niko?"

Niko nodded. "I'm glad you didn't get killed by that ghost. It would've been a real fuckin' bummer," he said as he stood befor Zora. Taemar swatted his arm. "What?"

"Whatchu mean, 'what?' Why would you even say that? What's wrong with you?" Taemar chastised, but the look on his face told Zora he was teasing him, and based on Niko's smile, Zora could tell he didn't mind at all.

"Zora, I'm sorry."

Zora laughed. "Nah, you good. Thank you, Niko. I'm glad I didn't get killed either. I wouldn't want 'death by angry, arsenic poisoned ghost' on my tombstone."

They all laughed. Niko and Whitley said their last goodbyes t Jabari, Birdie, and Zora before departing.

"Well, Jabari, I'm grateful for your help today," Birdie said.

Jabari waved a hand at her. "Ain't no thing, Birdie. That's what we do; we take care of each other."

Birdie smiled tightly. "Yes. Well, we'd best be going as well. Now that Zora's all healed, we've got to get to the club for rehearsals."

"Excellent, I'll see you tonight then," Jabari said. Finally, he stood and walked toward them. He wrapped Birdie in a tight embrace before doing the same to Zora.

When he wrapped his arms around her, he spoke firmly: "Ma the gods keep you."

And, in a lower voice, he said, "And remember what I said. B careful."

Zora nodded and followed Birdie out to her car. She slid into the passenger seat and after she clicked her seatbelt on, she looked in the mirror at her new haircut and smiled.

"Looks like Whitley hooked you up, girl," Birdie commented as they pulled out of the driveway.

Zora smiled again, but it faded as soon as Birdie looked away.

By the time they arrived at Nightingale's, all the dancers had heard about Zora's encounter at the salon. Many of them wanted the gory details of what it was like to see a ghost, and some of them asked what it felt like when they imparted their memories upon her.

"What did it feel like when it was choking you?" Livia asked, her eyes wide.

"Like I was being deprived of oxygen," Zora said tersely.

"Too bad you can't press charges," Deja snickered.

The whole time, MK and Orion sat at the bar on their phones, ignoring the conversation. After a while Birdie stepped in and broke up the inquisition. "Last I checked, we had a show to prep for tonight. Y'all can bump your gums later."

The dancers grumbled with annoyance as they hit their marks, and Zora mouthed "thank you" to Birdie as she took her place at stage left. MK and Raheem choreographed their newest routine, an ensemble number to "Desperado" by Rihanna.

After rehearsing the routine a few times, the dancers began running through their individual choreography. Zora figured she may as well take Birdie up on her offer to look at the video footage from the day of Marquitta's murder while she waited. Taemar led her upstairs to a large office just above the stage. There sat two desks, one in front of the window across from the door and the other to its right, where Taemar slid into the office chair.

"So, how do you have access to all this?" Zora asked.

Taemar logged into the computer and clicked through a set of files. "Well, I guess you could say I'm a manager now. After Marquitta died, Birdie kinda promoted me. Mostly because she needed the help, but she don't have the bandwidth to do everything on her own."

As Zora sat with that thought, Taemar pulled up footage from inside the office on the day of Marquitta's murder. It showed Birdie sitting in the same chair Taemar sat in, typing on the computer and making phone calls. She popped in and out of the office.

Zora crossed her arms and her lips set in a grim line as she felt a knot form in her stomach.

Birdie walked out of the office around three, and the camera in the hall showed her walking down the stairs to the stage. Then she watched the dancers practice their routines.

She looked at her phone as though checking the time, but then MK and Orion spoke to her. Taemar fast forwarded the tape, pausing only to show that for the next half hour, Birdie watched MK rehearse, while Orion stood beyond the DJ booth on his phone. Then, Birdie checked her phone and made a call. She hung up the phone again, then dialed once more. She typed on her phone then turned her attention to the bar, where Taemar sat reading a book. They spoke for several minutes before Birdie made a call again.

She's calling Marquitta, Zora realized. Suddenly her mouth dried up. She gripped the back of Taemar's chair because she knew what came next. In the video, Birdie teleported. She fell to her knees when she reappeared on the stage and screamed. Taemar and all the dancers rushed to her, including Orion and MK. Taemar stopped the footage as Taemar wrapped an arm around Birdie and gestured at the other dancers.

Neither Zora nor Taemar spoke as the gravity of the footage set in. Minutes later, it was Taemar who broke the silence.

"God, I didn't want to relive this," he said, his voice trembling.

"I figured Birdie had been the one to find her, but I didn't realize . . ." Zora's voice trailed off.

"I had to drive her back to the house and she never let anyone drive her car, not even Marquitta. But she couldn't she was so... devastated. Then the cops came, the rest of the houses showed up. I'll never forget them carryin' her body out in a bag like she was just . . ." a tear streaked down his face. Taemar sniffled and looked down at his hands. "Like she was just nothin.'"

Now it was Zora's turn to comfort him. She leaned down and pulled him out of the chair and held him as he sobbed.

"I'm going to solve this," she vowed. "I'm going to find out who killed her."

I just hope the truth doesn't kill me, Zora thought as she squeezed Taemar tighter.

That night, the dancers all wore matching lacy, red ensembles, that complemented each shade of melanin that graced the stage. When they used MK's trick of using a potion to complete their routine in air, the crowd collectively erupted. The patrons roared so loudly that they nearly drowned out the music. Luckily, the Dolls made it to the end of their routine without missing a beat.

After a brief intermission, each dancer returned to the stage to perform an individual routine. Zora danced second to last, and she added some more acrobatics to her set. As she twirled on stage to a throwback burlesque track, the crowd's energy fueled her. When she finished on her knees at the edge of the stage, a feathery fan in hand, not one person remained seated in the audience. Everyone stood on their feet, their applause and cheer growing louder each second. Zora danced and smiled and played the part, but inside she felt emotionally drained.

She stood and blew kisses to the crowd then collected her items before walking off stage.

"You betta watch where you going," MK warned as Zora rushed backstage, accidentally bumping into MK.

Zora glared at the woman but chose to keep the peace as Birdie welcomed MK to the stage. Once Zora entered the dressing room, she changed into a fuchsia, satin jumpsuit and walked into the main room while MK closed out the show.

She spotted Jabari holding court on a long, L-shaped couch to the left of the stage. All the Divinities surrounded him, each one dressed in black, many of them wearing either leather or lacy body suits and corsets. For his part, Jabari looked sleek in tight, black pants, a corset, and a sheer, black button up top, his hair braided in two His eyes drifted toward her and he smiled as she perched on the edge of the couch next to Teague, the witch who she'd first encountered when she arrived at Divinity house for the equinox ritual. He nodded at her in greeting but turned his attention back to the stage.

When MK finished her set, the lights brightened. Most nights the club remained full for at least an hour after the last set. Birdie took to the stage one last time to thank everyone for coming. Once Birdie walked off stage, music began pumping through the speakers.

Zora searched the crowd for Whitley, but she wasn't there. Once again, Zora found herself disappointed. She pulled out her phone to text her but paused when she heard Jabari call her name.

"Yes?" she said, looking up at him.

"You keep amazin' me every time you take the stage." He looked at her like he was undressing her with his eyes, and Zora couldn't fight the smile that spread across her face.

"Thank you," she replied.

"If Birdie was smart, she'd give you the chance to choreograph somethin'."

"I'd love that, but I've only been here a few days. Let the dancers get used to me first before I start doin' somethin' like that."

Jabari shrugged. "Or you could just do it. Everyone sees how talented you are, so why not ask for forgiveness instead of permission?"

Zora marveled at Jabari's words, at his nonchalance, at the way he spoke to her as though no one else was around.

"That your life motto or somethin'?" Zora asked.

Jabari laughed.

"Perhaps. For real, I think you'd kill that shit," he began. He glanced at his watch then back at Zora. "But we can talk about your aspirin' career as a choreographer later. Right now, I want to get to know you. So how 'bout it? Can I buy you a cup of coffee?"

Zora's heartbeat quickened as she thought about being alone with him. While she knew he likely envisioned only one outcome of their conversation, Zora thought it would be a good chance for her to interview him and to figure out whether he could've murdered Marquitta or not.

Sure," she said. She cast a look over at Taemar before taking Jabari's arm and stepping into the night.

Twenty minutes later, Zora and Jabari sat at a dimly lit coffee shop. With a mixture of coffees, teas, cocktails, and spiked drinks featured on the menu, the coffee shop seemed perfect either for date night or for a late-night rendezvous.

Zora sipped her latte and marveled at Jabari as he savored a double espresso.

"Do you plan on sleepin' at all tonight?" she asked.

His lips curled around his petite cup. "Depends. Do you plan on keepin' me company?"

Zora fiddled with the strap of her purse and smiled tightly. She knew where his mind was, and she'd be lying to herself if she said she wasn't thinking about the same thing. But she wouldn't become another situationship for him, so she took a deep breath and changed the subject.

"So, how long you been a House Head?"

He stared at her for a long while before responding. "Four years. But I've been a member of one house or another for much longer."

"Where you from, originally?"

"Houston."

"So, you were in that Triarchy there?"

He shook his head. "I moved around a lot as a kid. So by the time I was a teen, I was used to gettin' up and goin' every few years. Moved to New Orleans after high school, then Little Rock, then Miami before settlin' here."

"Wow. What made you come to Savannah?"

"Had an uncle who could hook me up with a job at his shop. I've been obsessed with cars and fixin' 'em up since I was a kid, so once I got tired of blowin' in the wind, I decided I needed a change. Hell, I was twenty-two then and I'd lived damn near everywhere in the south."

"And now you own the shop?" Zora asked. She wrapped her hands around her coffee mug, delighting in its warmth.

He nodded and sipped his coffee. "I took my uncle's shop over when he died earlier this year, hired many of the witches that are in Divinity."

Zora dropped her head slightly then lifted it. "Sorry for your loss."

Jabari nodded.

"I'm just amazed at you, Birdie, and Whitley. All ownin' your own businesses before you're even close to thirty. My whole life, all I've ever wanted to do was dance."

A tender smile broke out over his face. "You sound like Marquitta."

Zora felt a pang in her stomach at the mention of Marquitta. Now was the time to start asking him questions about her death. *Here we go,* she thought.

"From everything I've heard, sounds like she and I had a lot in common."

"You do. Beautiful, confident, talented dancers."

"I heard you two used to date."

Jabari's eyes darkened. He sniffed and leaned back in his chair. "We did. And I loved her. But then she met Birdie and I just knew."

"Knew what?"

"That I was never gonna be it for her. From the second them two laid eyes on each other, it was obvious they wanted to be together. And though it hurt like a bitch when she broke up with me . . ." he heaved a sigh. "They were soul mates. Fuckin' end game."

"That must've been tough, though, havin' to look after this whole community of witches with the woman she left you for."

"Oh, the way I wanted to curse the fuck out of them for the first few months. Just ruin 'em. But then I got my mind right." H shrugged. "We were cool. Even went on double dates, trips to tł beach. There was no ill will on my part."

Zora smiled tightly, but inside her stomach roiled. Jabari didn't sound like someone who'd been hurt and had transcende the pain. He sounded like the hurt was still front and center for him. And more than that, he sounded angry.

She sipped her coffee and thought about how she'd ask him what she really needed to know.

"Still must've hurt when she was killed," she said, her heart beating wildly.

His lip curled slightly, and his brows knitted. He finished the rest of his espresso in one gulp before he set the cup down and cleared his throat.

"It still does. But you didn't agree to come to coffee with me just to talk about me and Marquitta, did you?"

That's exactly why I agreed, she thought. "Course not. I just wanted to say I'm sorry for your loss. You love her, and it's always hard losin' someone you love."

"Loved," he corrected.

"Loved," Zora emphasized, though she didn't believe his affection for her existed solely in the past.

She shifted in her seat. "Anyway, there's not much to me: I'm 21, from Memphis, a Virgo, a necromancer, a dancer, and my favorite color is yellow."

"What would you do if you weren't a witch?" he asked, tracin the rim of his empty cup with his index finger.

The question caught Zora off guard. She'd never thought about not being a witch, only wondered what it would feel to never see the dead again.

"I've never thought about it," she admitted.

"Sure, you have."

"No. I've thought about how much easier life would be if I had telekinesis or could control fire, but . . . I'd never want a world without magic."

Jabari titled his head to the side, considering Zora's thoughts. "I suppose that makes sense. If not for magic, you wouldn't be here. And I wouldn't be able to get to know how wonderful you are."

Her eyes fluttered uncontrollably. "Have you always been such a sweet talker?"

"It's the only way I know how to be."

"And how often does it work on the person you're trying to sweet talk?" she asked, resting her chin on the base of her palm.

"You tell me? It workin' on you?"

Zora kept herself calm as she gazed into his dark eyes, eyes that looked at her as before, like he wanted to undress her.

"I think you'd better take me to my car."

He shrugged and stood, extending a hand to help her up. They walked the block and a half back to Nightingale's in silence, her arm threaded with his, and Zora contemplated how she was going to find out where he was the day Marquitta had been killed.

"So, Taemar told me that there was never a funeral for Marquitta."

"No. Birdie said she didn't feel ready," Jabari spoke, keeping his gaze forward. "We all gave her space since that was her fiancée."

"I can see that. 'Specially since it happened out the blue. I can't imagine what it must've been like for everyone," Zora said. They reached her car and she leaned against it and looked at Jabari, who dug his hands into his pockets. "I mean, how did it feel, getting a call like that at work? You were probably helpin' a customer or somethin.'"

"I was off that day," he replied. "So I was at the gym, mid bench press, actually."

"That's good . . . that you didn't have to tough it out at work, I mean."

He stepped closer to her, his face mere inches from hers. He placed a hand on her hip and the other beneath her chin, tilting her head up toward him. "You seem obsessed with my grief. Why?"

Her heart pounded in her chest, so loud that her ears throbbed. *Be cool, be cool,* she thought.

"Because I've spent my life surrounded by it," Zora started, knowing she needed to tell him at least a little of her truth to prevent suspicion. "I used to use my gifts for money, partly to help grieving loved ones get closure, but mostly to keep a roof over my and my father's heads. I've seen how grief can eat someone up, and I don't want that for you."

"You continue to amaze me, Zora," he said. Despite the sweetness of his words, there was an edge to his voice. He planted a kiss on her forehead before stepping back. "Get home safe."

He turned on his heel and walked back into the club, the music spilling out into the street as he opened the door.

Zora watched Jabari disappear then hopped into her car. As she leaned against the headrest, she considered her dilemma. She appeared no closer to uncovering the mystery of Marquitta's killer than she had before, even after her own brush with death. Furthermore, she dreaded identifying Marquitta's killer because it would alter her relationship with one of the witches in this community she was beginning to love, forever. She sighed, and drove out of the parking lot, crestfallen as she sped toward Transcendence house.

Chapter 12

"Necromancers beware—Bonaventure Cemetery is haunted as shit."

Spell Book of Marquitta Transcendence, 2010

After seeing Birdie and Taemar's grief fully realized, Zora was more determined to solve Marquitta's murder than she had been in the last few days. She devised a plan— all three of the House Heads were suspects, and all three were powerful witches who could teach Zora everything she needed to know about magic. So instead of training only with Birdie, Zora decided she'd also ask Jabari and Whitley for help. Not only would she learn more about magic, but she'd also learn enough from them to either break the curse on Marquitta so that she could see who her killer was, or she'd learn enough about them to be able to determine who the guilty party was for herself.

In the first few days, Zora mastered the art of summoning ghosts. Ghosts were naturally drawn to necromancers—they straddled the line of life and death, according to Birdie. When it came to summoning the ghosts of people she knew, Zora simply centered herself and focused all her intention on them. When she sought to find ghosts she didn't know, Zora focused her intention on casting her energy out into the world around her and, like moths to a flame, the ghosts came readily. Though it became easier to summon them, she feared them no less, these specters who looked at Zora with so much wanting.

She was relieved when Birdie showed her how to mix red brick dust and wormwood, something that subdued ghosts for a much longer duration than mere salt.

"The red brick is for your protection and the wormwood is what sends the ghosts back to the veil between here and the afterworld," Birdie told her.

Zora made sure to place the mixture in the velvet pouch she kept in her purse. Though she'd asked Birdie to ward the house just as Nightingale's was warded, she knew they couldn't, not yet. Not until they knew what happened to Marquitta. Therefore she sprinkled the red brick and wormwood on her windowsill and at her doorframe every night. Once she did, Zora slept more peacefully than she ever had in her life.

Exactly a week after Zora first arrived in Savannah, Birdie gave her a day off from Nightingale's. Zora knew exactly how she would spend it—she texted Whitley and asked if she'd be willing to help her boost her magical knowledge.

"Sure. Meet me at Soliloquy house at three," Whitley had replied.

Zora pulled up to a yellow, three-story house with a Tiffany Blue door. The living room was just to the right of the door, marked by two white pillars on either side of the opening. Across from the door was a steep set of stairs.

Whitley, dressed in a simple, pale pink baby doll dress, her hair up in a daisy-patterned silk scarf, gave Zora a hug when she opened the door.

"Good to see you. Love that color on you," she said as she pulled back to look at Zora, her arms still wrapped around her. Zora looked down at her yellow cropped sweater.

"Thank you, it's my favorite color." Zora replied, her cheeks warming.

Whitley smiled brightly before pulling away and ushering her into the living room. The walls painted pea green and the furniture looking straight out of a 1950's movie.

"I see where you get your style inspiration from," Zora teased.

Whitley laughed, and Zora noticed the dimple in her right cheek, the way she tilted her head back slightly when she laughed, and how the sound was so melodic that it made Zora want to revel in it.

As in the Transcendence house, a photo of the Savannah Triarchy founders hung on one wall. A photo of the Soliloquy house members, including Whitley and the woman Zora thought must've been Bonnie, as they posed on the front steps of the house hung on another. Photos of individual witches and of Savannah itself adorned the walls in beautiful composition, giving the room a chic, editorial feel. Potted plants rested by the windows, and on the round, white marble coffee table sat a pile of spell books.

Zora thumbed through them as Whitley made them coffee. She smiled at Zora as she returned with two steaming cups of coffee, a small pot of cream, and another one of sugar on a tray. After Zora added cream and sugar to her coffee, she sat back on the couch and basked in the aroma of the coffee and the sweet smell of the fresh cut roses that sat in vases on both side tables. After several minutes, Zora realized she hadn't seen a ghost in the house at all.

"Have I stumbled into the only house in the city that isn't haunted?" she asked.

Whitley laughed. "No. I warded it when I knew you were coming over."

Zora's eyes widened. "Really?"

"Yeah, I didn't want you to be uncomfortable. There's a lot I want to show you, and we didn't need some annoying ghost of a former Soliloquy witch interrupting us."

Whitley turned her attention back to the open spell book on her lap, but all Zora kept thinking about was what she had done for her.

"I didn't want you to be uncomfortable," she'd said. Her words played in Zora's mind as they spoke about the history of the Triarchy system.

"Witches have always existed in collectives, clusters of witche coming together to support and protect each other. But after the Salem Witch trials, they began to split off into smaller groups, thinking they could avoid suspicion if they did so. But they also realized that to truly protect each other, they still needed to be connected and stay in touch. And, because people have always been scheming and dreaming up visions of grandeur, there was always in-fighting, witches trying to figure out who'd be the 'Hea Witch in Charge,'" Whitley began.

"After years of fighting and bloodshed, they split into two houses. Each house would have a Head who would care for the witches within their own home and then the broader witch community. These two House Heads would come together to make decisions for the whole community. They broke up responsibilities to further make the situation feel communal: on house would guide and be responsible for helping the communit to adhere to human law and the other for magical law.

"As America became larger and people moved, this system was adopted all around the nation, but they still kept the balance of human law and magical law even if there were different name But the houses were not integrated; white people thought that Black and Brown people were inferior even in their magic and so we did what we always do—we built our own thing and made it better."

She sipped her coffee and crossed one leg over the other, toward Zora.

"We added the third house, the one to help witches revel in their powers, and to help make decisions a majority vote. And in our Triarchies, as we call them, House Heads are less like dictators and more like mentors."

"And these houses, are they only in certain areas?" Zora asked.

Whitley chuckled. "Girl, they're all over the country."

As Whitley spoke about her time in Neon house, Zora found herself wanting to be closer to her. She wanted to lean into her, run a hand up her toned, smooth legs. She wanted to feel her body pressed against hers as it had been when the hugged minutes ago.

How could she have killed Marquitta? Zora thought. She's just so . . .

But then Zora took a deep breath. *Focus,* she thought. *Focus.*

That first day, Whitley showed her a few basic spells—one for illuminating a dark space, another for using a glamor to cover up a skin issue or to change hair color for a day. After an hour, they took a break over more coffee and some lemon pound cake, She took a bite of the pound cake and delighted in the tart lemon flavor.

"This is good," she said.

Whitley's cheeks flushed. "Thank you. I made it myself."

Zora nodded and took another bite. As their conversation lulled, she knew she had to try asking Whitley more serious questions. "So, why'd you leave LA?" Whitley lifted a brow.

"Why did you leave Memphis?" Whitley shot back.

"I . . . it's complicated," Zora replied.

"And have you ever thought my past might be the same?"

Zora sighed. She knew she would have to divulge some of her truth to be able to get anything out of the woman.

"If I tell you something from my past, will you tell me?"

Whitley examined Zora, and as the sunlight caught her brown eyes in its rays, illuminating the richness of them, the flecks of gold within them, Zora wanted nothing more than to kiss her.

"Fine. Why didn't you join the Memphis Triarchy?"

"I didn't know any of this existed until last week. I'd met witches before, but they soured real quick when I told them I was a necromancer. I never had a witch community before now, hence me needin' so much magical help."

"And your parents? I'm assuming they aren't magical?"

"No." Zora replied, knowing their agreement had been for Zora to tell her one thing only. But perhaps the more she spilled the more comfortable Whitley would be. "How did they feel about your powers?"

"One thought I was a sinner who was choosing the left-hand path, and the other talked me into using my powers for money."

Whitley placed a hand on Zora's thigh.

"I'm sorry to hear that." Had her hand lingered any longer, Zora's body would've convulsed.

"Yeah, it sucked," Zora began. "But I've answered multiple questions, and now it's your turn."

Whitley groaned.

"I only want to know why you left LA."

Whitley grit her teeth as a multitude of emotions passed over her face.

"Fine. I left LA because I was kicked out of the House of Neon. I did something that . . . well, it's hard to come back from. So instead of stripping my powers and exiling me, my mom begged my dad to send me here to be with my Auntie Bonnie. She was sick with some kind of illness and needed help running the salon."

"Why didn't she use magic to heal herself?" Zora asked, thinking back to Whitley's comment about Jabari saving her a trip to the chiropractor.

"Because we're witches, not gods, Zora," Whitley replied. "There are things even we're not capable of stopping."

Zora hesitated. "Whatever you did, you are one of those people who deserve a fresh start."

Whitley pressed her lips together. "I need a refill. You want some more?" she asked abruptly.

Zora nodded, and Whitley picked their cups off the coffee table and hurried into the kitchen. Zora looked after her as she disappeared then turned her attention to Whitley's spell book. She stared at the open book that sat on the coffee table in front of them. She grabbed it and placed a finger to mark their place and flipped through the front part of the book. She paused when she saw an entry on December 21, 2021.

"Fight with YN. Found a spell that could help."

Zora took a photo of the entry before scrolling back through the pages. Dated a month later, another entry read: "YN resolved. But Dad found out. Whole house pissed. They're gonna make me go to Savannah to be with Auntie Bonnie."

She snapped a picture of the second entry and set the book back where she'd found it just as she heard Whitley's sandals against the hardwood floor of the hallway. She flipped the camera to selfie mode, pretending to use the camera as a mirror.

"You know there are mirrors all over this house, right? You don't have to use your phone," Whitley mentioned as she set their drinks on the table.

"Oh, I just needed to do a quick fluff," Zora said as she locked her phone screen.

"Your hair looks great, Zora . . . and so do you." Whitley gazed at Zora and sipped her coffee slowly.

Zora smiled and savored her coffee, grateful for the distraction.

The next time Zora sat with Whitley at the Soliloquy house, Whitley showed her a curse from her father's spell book. When Zora saw it, a spike of suspicion shot up her spine. It was a curse that caused the recipient's bones to become as fragile as glass. Could Whitley have used this on this YN? Is that why she was kicked out of her house?

Zora flipped to another curse in the book, one for making the recipient invisible until the curse caster broke it.

"Theoretically, could this spell be used on the dead?"

Whitley scowled. "I don't know why you'd try to do that. Generally, spells and curses break once a person dies because—"

"Death is the final spell breaker, I know, I know. But say you had a ghost and they were cursed and you wanted to uncurse them. Could you do that?"

Whitley thought about it for a long while. "I guess, theoretically, you could."

"Could I get a copy of this?"

"Why?"

"I just need it for practice. That's what you're helpin' me with right?"

Zora could tell Whitley was skeptical, but she made a copy anyway.

When Whitley handed the spell to Zora, she held on to it tightly. "Be careful with this, Zora. You don't want to do something you might regret."

Whitley loosened her grasp as Zora nodded, unsure of whether to take heed to Whitley's warning or to view it as a threat.

Every House Head had their own way of teaching, and Jabari was no different. He was open to sharing information but often became exasperated easier than Zora would've thought. When she sat with him in the basement of Divinity house, she asked about the painting of the man above the altar.

"That is Geddemin. I guess you'd say they'd be your patron saint if that was a thing with our gods." He pulled the picture off the wall and handed it to her. "They're the god who guides spirits to the afterworld and presides over its entrance. They decide when it's time for a person to die, and often they're the one who dictates whether a spirit is ready to enter the afterworld."

"Why would a spirit not be ready for the afterworld? Isn't it like hell or somethin'?"

Jabari shook his head and rolled his eyes.

"For us, there is no heaven and there is no hell. Good and evil exist on earth and within all of us. Every spirit goes to the afterworld. What they see when they get there is a different story."

He explained how spirits saw that which they sowed in life. A person who sowed chaos would only know the same in the afterworld. But it wasn't an all or nothing thing; because people are complex, often their afterlife reflected that.

"Someone who spends their life wantin' more and not celebratin' what they already have could spend their afterlife

forced to be seated at a lavish dinner and eat and eat and eat onl
for the food to taste like shit, according to my pops. And a perso
who spent their life helpin' others often spends their afterlife in
complete peace."

"Geddemin sounds like a powerful god," Zora said.

"They all are. Here." He handed her an ancient-looking book
whose pages looked so delicate that a deep exhale would destroy
them. Within was a list of the gods and their descriptions. Her
eyes turned big and round as saucers, amazed at the extent of
what the gods could do.

That same day, she found a spell for how to stop a heart.

It came from the spell book of a witch named Guillermo
Prudencia, which she found on one of the shelves next to the
altar, along with spell books from other witches: Sabrina Bounty
Celeste Eerie, and Tyrell Hypnotic. As she scanned the pages,
a nagging feeling overtook her. Guillermo's spell book looked
relatively new, with dates ending in 2018. From what she'd
learned about spell books, they were passed along to other
witches only when the original owner died. And even then, they
were supposed to be kept within their own house, or their own
Triarchy.

So why did Jabari have these books?

"I would've thought something like this would be classified
as a curse," she said, holding open the spell book so that Jabari
could see the spell in question. A look of anger passed over his
face.

"Don't be touchin' stuff that that ain't yours," he snapped. He
snatched the book from her hands and put it back on the shelf.

Zora held her hands up and took a step back. "I'm sorry. I jus
thought all of this was stuff I could access to learn."

"Well, you were wrong. You need to ask first before you touch anythin' in here. This is a sacred space and you're lucky I'm lettin' you access it, given that you're not even a Divinity."

She stood, mouth agape, wondering if what she'd done was so bad that it warranted his reaction. He adjusted his silk robe and brushed a hand through his beard.

"I'm sorry," he said, taking her hand. "These things are fragile and important to me. I was lucky enough to be gifted these things from the houses I was in and I'd hate to lose them."

Zora nodded. "I understand. I didn't mean nothin' by it. I'll put it back." Before she did, she looked at the spell again, doing her best to memorize what it said in a short period of time. She slipped the spell book back onto the shelf and they continued their training.

The rest of the day was spent with him teaching her how to set up an altar and how to properly pray to and worship the gods. Though Zora tried to focus, her mind drifted back to the spell books, wondering what else they held inside.

When she wasn't training with the House Heads, Zora was spending time with Taemar and Niko or practicing her routines. Though she hadn't been at Nightingale's very long, she was already gaining quite the following, much to MK's chagrin. Zora noticed the woman's scowl deepen every time someone complimented her or whenever she received more applause.

Despite the fact that she was perpetually annoyed by MK, she couldn't help but wonder why the woman had instantly been antagonistic toward her. And as the weeks progressed, her attitude only soured. When Zora caught MK sitting by the window in the front room, looking at a picture of Marquitta and crying, she'd tried to comfort her.

"I'm sorry for your loss," Zora said. "I know you two were close."

MK nodded. "I just can't believe she did that."

Zora scowled. Was she still talking about Marquitta?

"What did she do?" Zora asked.

"She—" but then MK snapped out of her grief and looked at Zora with disgust. "No, I'm not talkin' to you about this. Go bother someone else."

"MK, I just want to help."

She snorted. "You want to help? Go back to Memphis and leave me alone." She motioned toward the door then turned to face Zora. "And in case you haven't noticed, Jabari's mine now. So stay the fuck away from him!"

She stormed out of the room, slamming the front door as she did so. From then on, MK's vitriol came in the form of sharp glares, rolled eyes, and pointed sighs. She ignored everything Zora said and barely acknowledged her existence.

Orion was much the same. Instead of vitriol, he met Zora's attempts to talk to him with disdain. And when she tried to push through and talk to him, he used his powers on her, the power of persuasion. When he told her to go kick rocks, Zora had done just that.

If it hadn't been for Birdie pulling up and stopping her, she would've kicked the large boulder that sat at the base of the magnolia tree that grew on the sidewalk in front of their house.

Weeks had passed by since Zora first arrived in Savannah. As the nights grew longer and the air crisper, Marquitta's murder remained a vast puzzle with a thousand missing pieces. Zora tried to uncover the identity of YN by searching through Whitley's Instagram and TikTok, but she only came away with even more of an attraction to a woman who may have murdered someone. And it was the same with Jabari—she didn't know where to start when it came to confirming his alibi or to finding out whether the House Heads whose spell books he owned had actually gifted them to him or if he'd taken them.

Zora was about to update Birdie on her progress one night after the club closed when Birdie insisted on an impromptu training session. Zora's palms were sweaty when Birdie teleported them to Bonaventure Cemetery. They stood just inside the gate, and Zora's stomach flooded with acid while her heart beat triple-time in her chest.

"What're we doing here?" Zora asked.

"We're here so you can suppress the dead."

"But I'm still learnin'—"

"Think of it as on-the-job training," Birdie said. "It's been a few weeks. You've got your red brick dust and wormwood on you, and you've already used the spell for expelling a ghost. You can do this."

All the hairs on Zora's arms and neck stood at attention, and her throat felt like it was constricting. I can't do this, I can't do this, I can't—

Zora whimpered as Birdie recited the spell for illumination. "Iniji, Iniji, catch fire, catch fire."

A circle of light roughly twelve feet illuminated the path before them as they walked. Spanish moss swayed in the breeze. The moon was full, and stars dotted the sky. Apart from their boots clicking against the road that suddenly split in two, the cemetery was silent. Not many graves occupied the space where they stood, but Zora's body tingled with the kinetic energy in the air and she knew they weren't alone.

They walked further into the cemetery where the gravestones grew taller and grander. It wasn't until Zora stood before a grave with a large cross that the dead began to appear.

She stepped backward, trying her best to be quiet, but her

boots crunched on the gravel of this road, which was unpaved unlike the rest. This was a fool's errand because Zora knew that no matter how quiet she was, the dead would always find her.

"You can do this, Zora," Birdie said calmly. She turned toward Zora, and Zora's breath came out in jagged spurts as a group of ghosts staggered toward her, their movements herky-jerky.

"Zora, you know what you need to do. You have the red brick dust and wormwood to repel them, but you can suppress their presence so you don't have to deal with them altogether."

Zora nodded. She knew what she had to do but she didn't want to close her eyes. What if they touched her and she couldn't see them? She grabbed her pouch of dust and tried to slow her breathing. The ghost of a young woman about her age stood before her, and Zora tossed some of the dust at her. She disappeared, but another quickly replaced her. If she didn't do something fast, Zora knew she'd run out of the dust sooner than later.

With a final whimper, Zora surrendered and closed her eyes. She could feel their presence near her, could feel the air shift as they reached out to touch her.

She focused on a point in the center of her head just as Birdie taught her. Then she inhaled deeply and imagined pushing the ghosts away. Once she could visualize what it would be like to remove them from her space, she let her breath, her intention, and her energy go. She imagined it pouring out of her from every side, and when she opened her eyes, the ghosts were gone.

Tears sprang to Zora's eyes as she beheld the empty cemetery. It was quiet. Peaceful.

"They're gone. We're alone," she cried.

Birdie smiled and pulled Zora into a hug. "I knew you could do it."

Zora sniffled. "I never thought I'd be able to just walk around without them hovering over me."

"You see what a lil' magic can do? The more you practice, the easier it will be to maintain this barrier around yourself. Of course, you'll still need to use the red brick dust and wormwood while you're sleeping, and there's always the spell to send a ghost to the afterworld. But Zora," Birdie said as she pulled away from Zora and looked at her. "Always remember that you're in control. You have the tools you need."

"I'm in control," Zora repeated.

"Say it like you believe it, Zora."

Zora turned to face the empty cemetery.

"I'm in control!" she screamed. "I'm in control!"

She spun around in a circle, her head tilted up toward the night sky and the crescent moon. A giggle forced its way out of her and before she knew it, she was laughing and crying all at once. Finally Zora had the peace she longed for, even if it was only for a short time.

When she was done she looked at Birdie, at this woman who had changed her life.

"Thank you."

"It's my absolute pleasure, baby," Birdie replied. She held out her hand and Zora took it, and in a flash they were gone.

Amanda Ross

Chapter 13

"There a few things a witch can't accomplish—one is tax evasion, and the other is living forever."

Spell Book of Guillermo Prudencia, 2015

Zora caught her first break at three in the morning, almost a month after the Autumnal Equinox ritual. She was in the attic, pouring over spell books from House Heads past, when she found the spell book of Booker Transcendence. Amid the diary entries about hiding his magic from the neighbors, recruiting new witches, and his affection for Mobley, Booker had recorded a spell for a compulsion.

It was a simple spell that would allow the spellcaster to ask questions and be told only the truth by whoever they spoke with. However, the spell only lasted for a few hours. And witches who knew these types of spells existed could protect themselves from them by wearing amethyst or ingesting lavender and diluted jimson weed.

This could be it, she thought, as she copied the spell into her own spell book. This could be the thing that helps me solve Marquitta's murder.

She found an amethyst crystal in the attic, in an antique-looking curio cabinet near the door. She tucked the palm-sized stone in her pocket. That night, Zora nailed her routines: one classic burlesque and the other leaning more on her dance background. Though both sets were met with standing ovations, thoughts of Booker's spell drowned out the applause. After she left the stage for the final time, Zora got dressed then snuck out the back entrance.

Once outside in the crisp night air, Zora checked out her surroundings. Except for a stray cat that lingered near the dumpster and loose leaves that twirled in the wind, the coast appeared clear. She patted her pocket to ensure the amethyst was still there, and once she confirmed its presence, she exhaled into the night.

"Okay, let's do this," she said.

She grabbed her spell book from her bag and opened it. She cleared her throat and said the spell: "I call for Kikwat's kiss so that the words that leave my lips compel the truth from those with whom I speak. Grant me their honesty, and I will bear the cost of knowing." After she finished, Zora looked around, expecting there to be some sort of spark or drama. But there was nothing, and when the door opened and Safi and Livia stepped out to smoke, Zora nodded to them and slipped back inside.

She found Jabari first. He sat as he so often did, on an L-shaped couch surrounded by Divinities and Soliloquies. When the witch who'd been sitting next to him moved away, Zora took the opening and sat directly beside him, her thigh pressed against his. He lifted a brow and looked at her, surprised.

"To what do I owe this honor?" he asked. Zora smiled coyly and leaned into him.

"I just wanted to ask you something really quick," she whispered, forcing him to lean in closer to her to hear her over the music.

"And what's that?"

"Do you find me attractive?"

He licked his lips and answered, "Yes."

"Did you like my routines tonight?"

"Yes."

"Were you really at the gym when Marquitta was killed?"

He looked at her, his eyes low, then whispered in her ear: "Yes."

"And those spell books near your altar—were they really gifts or did you take them?"

"I was personally handed each spell book I have on my shelves."

She pulled away and looked him over once again, taking in the iridescent durag with the long train that hung over his shoulder, the black, silk track suit and shiny Doc Martens. Jabari Divinity looked at her with complete sincerity, giving Zora no reason to disbelieve him. Learning this truth about him felt good, but it also felt like a punch to the gut. Because if he hadn't done it, then there was more of a possibility that it had been Whitley.

Before Jabari could say anything else, Zora patted his leg and left. She searched for Whitley but couldn't find her until she stepped out on the patio. The smile Whitley gave Zora was so pure that Zora hesitated. Could she really use this spell on the woman she liked? Could she really manipulate Whitley into telling her the truth? But hadn't she just done the same thing to Jabari? Hadn't she also made a promise to Birdie to solve Marquitta's murder?

Zora squared her shoulders and seated herself at the table next to Whitley, her back facing the street. As always, Whitley looked gorgeous, dressed in black pants, a white t-shirt, and a black leather jacket.

"You know, for someone who doesn't like to be around the witches in the Triarchy, you sure are here a lot," Zora teased.

"I'm here because I want to see you," Whitley said. She

blinked rapidly, as though surprised by this admission. The revelation still made Zora's stomach fill with butterflies.

"I'm glad you're here. It's nice having someone I can talk to." Zora paused. "I wanted to ask you, you mentioned that there wa camera footage in the salon on the day Marquitta died?"

"Yes, I showed it to the cops already."

"Does it show you in it?"

"Yes, it does."

"Good. So you didn't have anything to do with Marquitta's death?"

"No, I didn't. I didn't kill Marquitta," Whitley said, knitting her brows. "Zora, what's—"

"I just need to know one more thing . . ."

Zora sighed and prepared herself for Whitley's answer.

"What did you do that made your family send you here?"

Whitley inhaled sharply before answering: "My ex-girlfriend Yvie cheated on me with Nina, my former boss at the salon I use to work at. So I cursed Yvie with Glass Foundation, which turne her bones brittle, made them easier to break. And I turned Nina invisible for a few days. My dad found out when Yvie landed in the hospital with broken bones after she fell while doing crow pose."

Zora tilted her head.

"The one where you balance on your arms and lift your feet up," Whitley stated. "Anyway, Yvie's sister was the head of the House of Libre, and she told my family and then I got in trouble. My aunt volunteered to take me in, but I only got to keep my powers and not be exiled from the community on the condition that I never go back to LA again." She finished off her drink. "I can't believe I just told you all of that."

Zora found herself at a loss for words. She'd hoped that

whatever Whitley had done, it hadn't been bad enough to prove she was capable of killing. But to curse someone like that, to hurt someone like that, it took a certain amount of rage that Zora wasn't sure she could rule Whitley out as a suspect even if she'd been compelled to tell the truth.

"It's okay," Zora said, squeezing Whitley's hand to comfort her. "I'm sorry that happened. Your ex sounds like a bitch, and so does your old boss. But even though all that happened, I'm glad you're here."

Whitley smiled wistfully. "You know, I'm starting to feel the same way, too."

The spell wore off shortly after, much to Zora's relief. She hated feeling like she was betraying Whitley's confidence, but she had to know, and she didn't have time to waste.

That night as Zora came home, she wandered through the hallway replaying her conversations with Jabari and Whitley in her mind. Then she passed by Birdie's open bedroom door and stopped. She noticed Birdie sitting on the window seat, staring out at Forsythe Park.

Zora knocked on the door frame. Birdie turned toward her and smiled, but the sadness in her expression made Zora's skin tingle.

"Everythin' okay?" she asked.

Birdie sniffled.

"Got a call from the detective working on Marquitta's case. She said they've got no leads, that the trail's gone cold. Zora, please tell me you've got something."

Zora flinched as her stomach started doing flips. She slid her hands into the pockets of her sweater.

"I . . . I don't have much yet."

Birdie shook her head. "I should've known better."

"What?" Zora asked, though she felt like she knew what Birdi was trying to say.

"I should've never relied on a necromancer so green. I should've pulled some strings, called in a necromancer from Atlanta or something. I don't know what I was thinking."

"Birdie, I can still help. It's just taking me longer to—"

"No, Zora that's okay. You tried, but . . . it's been weeks and you're not even close to solving this, are you?"

The desperation in Birdie's eyes made Zora's heart ache. She wanted nothing more than to tell Birdie that she knew exactly who had taken her fiancée away from her. But all Zora could do was tell the truth.

"I've got a few suspects, and I've been pouring over the spell books you gave me trying to find a way to break the curse on Marquitta, but I . . . I'm even farther away on that than I am on solving her murder."

Birdie whimpered as tears slid down her cheeks, leaving traces of her pain.

"Okay, thank you for being honest with me." She leaned her head against the window. "I'm tired now, please go."

"But—"

"Just go," she said sternly.

Zora's eyes were glassy as she walked into her room and shut the door. She tried her best to hold back the tears as she undressed, but they flowed uncontrollably as she showered. In all her years of using her powers, Zora may have felt afraid, but she'd never felt so ineffective, so useless. What she wouldn't give for the power to erase Birdie and Taemar and everyone else's pain, to answer the question of who killed their beloved.

With her eyes now dry, she lay in bed and sighed, her body relaxing beneath the blankets. She grabbed her phone and began scrolling through Twitter, but something made her pause. She thought back to what Jabari had said about the spell books.

"I was personally handed each spell book I have on my shelves."

It had been such a weird way to answer the question of whether the spell books were given to him or not. At the time, Zora hadn't thought much about it, but now she wondered. She opened Instagram and searched for Jabari, who she was already following. Though she'd done a deep dive on Whitley's social, she hadn't done one on Jabari's. But unlike Whitley, whose presence likely had been scrubbed with pictures of her ex and her boss totally removed, Jabari seemed to have never deleted much of anything.

She stopped at a photo of him and a short man with a bald head. The caption read, "With tha one and only @guillepru." Zora tapped on the person's screen name and recognized the name from one of the spell books: Guillermo Prudencia. Zora was happy to have found the page but when she saw the profile caption, she blanched.

It was an in memoriam, and it stated the House Head passed away at the end of 2018. Zora Googled him and found that he'd died of some unknown illness. Maybe it's just a coincidence, Zora thought, remembering how Jabari told her he had left Miami around that time. She went back to his Instagram page and found a photo of Sabrina Bounty. When she navigated to her page, Zora was shocked to find that the same thing had happened to her earlier that same year. She had also died of an unknown illness.

She then found a photo of a woman she recognized from a few photos around the house—Mozelle Transcendence, who had been House Head before Birdie. When Zora realized she had died of an unknown illness, too, Zora did the math. Sabrina died in April 2018, Guillermo in December 2018, and Mozelle in mid-2019. And Jabari had either just arrived or left not too long after the witches passed away.

Could he have been responsible for their deaths? If so, what was he trying to achieve? Birdie had told Zora that Heads were elected by houses or the former Head, but that witches still tried to overthrow them. Even if he had tried to overthrow them, and he was trying to overthrow the House Heads here so that he could take over, why would he have killed Marquitta and not Birdie or Whitley? Zora locked her phone and stared at the ceiling.

"None of this makes sense," she said as more questions flooded her brain.

Sleep eluded Zora, and after hours of tossing and turning, she sighed and resigned herself to another night of searching for answers she wasn't sure she'd find. She crept downstairs and made some tea before heading to the attic. She flipped through Booker's spell book but found nothing. Then she turned her attention to one from a witch named Dottie Transcendence, and though she found a useful spell for communing with spirits that she copied into her own spell book, she came up empty.

Traces of the sun peeped through the window as Zora looked through a dusty, fragile book from a witch named Shepard Transcendence. He seemed to have been the House Head after Booker, and a necromancer. Within the spell book she found a wealth of knowledge, including a spell for memory restoration. Was this spell the key to breaking the curse on Marquitta?

Zora closed her eyes and thought of her, and soon the ghost stood before her.

"Hello," Zora said, exhausted yet determined. "I'm going to try a spell to fix your memories."

Marquitta nodded at her and Zora turned her attention to the spell.

"Narya, goddess of the mind, one who holds the key to memory, I call upon you to unlock the door that blocks us from Marquitta's memories so that we may pass over the threshold of knowledge." She held out her hands and Marquitta placed hers atop Zora's. Zora braced herself, expecting to see the moments before the woman's death. But there was nothing. No memories, just inky, black darkness.

Zora looked at Marquitta, who just stared.

"What the fuck?" Zora whispered. She waded back into the ghost's mind again and saw the same darkness. Somehow, instead of restoring Marquitta's memories, Zora had erased them all.

She hustled to her room and dressed quickly then ran out the door to her car. She sped the few blocks between Transcendence house and Soliloquy house, and when she knocked on the door, she was relieved when Whitley was the one to answer it.

"What're you doing here? Don't you know how early it is?"

Zora looked at her phone. It was barely seven in the morning.

"I'm so sorry, but I . . . I need your help."

Whitley crossed her arms and stood rooted in place, keeping Zora outside on the porch. Zora knitted her brows, wondering why she wasn't letting her in.

"Oh, and why's that?"

"Well, I tried a spell and it backfired."

"And now you need me to help undo the mess you made while

trying to solve Marquitta's murder?"

Zora's heart skipped a beat. "I—"

"You should have just told me that's what you were doing thi
whole time. I would have helped you," Whitley said, her cheeks
reddening.

"I couldn't tell anyone. I had to treat everyone like they could
have done it," Zora replied.

"Bullshit. Then how come Niko and Taemar know?"

Zora winced. "They . . . figured it out. I didn't tell them."

"And were you treating them like suspects, too? Huh?"

Zora looked down at her boots.

"So, why I am a suspect? Look at me, Zora."

Zora's eyes were glassy when she looked up at her. Whitley
stood with her fists clenched and her eyes wide.

"You've got motive."

Whitley chuckled, but there was no mirth to it. "Oh, okay, so
because I didn't worship the ground Marquitta walked on like
everyone else in this fucking community I had motive?"

"Y'all didn't get along. You fought. You've got a judge and
a detective as regular customers. And you've . . . you've cursed
people. You're a powerful witch who was being bullied by
Marquitta. I couldn't not consider you."

Whitley's lower lip trembled. "You know, I thought you
wanted to spend time with me because you liked being around
me."

"I do! That hasn't changed." Zora stepped closer, but Whitley
held up her hand.

"No. I was just a suspect to you. You tricked me into telling
you why I was sent here even though I specifically told you I
didn't want to talk about it. You made me tell you the thing I am
the most ashamed of, the thing I feel so much guilt around I can

barely . . . you tricked me."

A tear slipped from the corner of Zora's eye. "I'm sorry, Whitley. I just had to know. I promised Birdie I'd solve Marquitta's murder."

"Well, let me make this easy for you then." Whitley stepped back and gripped the door. "I didn't kill Marquitta. I didn't like her, but I didn't kill her. As for the spell you fucked up, you can figure it out yourself."

And with that, Whitley slammed the door, further separating Zora from the truth, and possibly from love.

Chapter 14

"Out of everyone, necromancers have the most to lose when their minds are clouded with anger or stress or fear. It takes so much concentration to keep the ghosts at bay that one stressful situation or being pushed into fear can burst that concentration like a bubble, and all the ghosts come flooding back, for they ached to be away from you."

Spell Book of Marquitta Transcendence, 2020

Everyone was still asleep when Zora shuffled through the front door of Transcendence house. She made a fresh pot of coffee and sat on the patio, still smarting from Whitley's rejection. How had things gotten so fucked? First, she'd upended her life and moved to a new city, taking a chance with a group of people she didn't know at all. And now, not only was she still unsure who had killed Marquitta, but she'd also lost the trust of the woman she liked.

She was on her third cup of coffee when Taemar joined her, dressed in purple sweatpants and a matching hoodie.

"You good?" he asked as he set his coffee mug down and slid a chair back from the table.

"I fucked up, Tae," she whispered.

His brows shot up. "How?"

She told him about Marquitta's memories, how the very moment of her death was gone and how when she tried the memory restoration spell, it had backfired.

"Now I can't even try to piece things together from what she'
done before. Everything's just . . . gone."

"Have you asked Birdie for help?"

"She's the last person I can tell this to. She all but told me to
stop trying last night. This would kill her."

"Well, what about Whitley?"

Zora groaned. "She's pissed at me."

"Why?"

"Because I used the compulsion spell on her."

"Oh, girl," Taemar said. He scoffed and rubbed his forehead.
"Why would you do that?"

"She and Marquitta didn't get along! She knows people in
high places. And she for sure cursed not one but two people,"
Zora explained, flailing her arms as she spoke.

"Do you really think she could have done it?"

"I . . . I don't know. But I'd give anything to take what I did
back. I like her."

"I know," Taemar replied. He gave her a knowing look before
sipping his coffee. "Well, there's nothing you can do about this
now. Guess we'll have to do this the old fashion way."

"I already tried that."

"Yeah, but you did it by yourself. Now I'm involved. We'll
figure this out."

"Thanks, Tae," Zora quavered.

"Don't mention it. But first, let's get some food in our bellies.
Taemar finished his coffee and stood. "You down for some
biscuits and gravy?"

"Of course." Zora grinned, her confidence slowly returning.

After breakfast Taemar insisted they walk to Forsythe Park,
saying the walk would help get their minds right, and burn off

some of the carbs from breakfast. But after hours of walking and talking, they arrived at the same place: either Jabari was guilty or Whitley was. Yet, neither Taemar nor Zora could pinpoint a solid motive. The rest of the day passed by in a flurry of rehearsals and prepping for the night's routine.

As always, Nightingale's was packed. Most of the witches in the Savannah Triarchy were in attendance, except for the one witch who Zora wanted to see most. But Zora put on a show, both in the group routine set to "Lonely Little G-String" and in her own dance, which closed out the show. She smiled and waved as she exited the stage, trying to hide the other performance she was putting on.

Her smile now gone, Zora walked to the dressing room, where MK sat with Livia, Chansi, and Deja.

"Here she come," Deja announced, her eyes following Zora as she walked to her locker, while Livia and Chansi clapped and whistled. Zora ignored them. She had too much on her mind to worry about whatever they had to say about her.

Zora pulled a shimmery, lavender jumpsuit out of her locker and slipped it on. Then she sprayed herself with perfume. Once she fluffed her hair with her pick, she slid her purse on her arm and closed her locker.

As she turned, she ran directly into MK. The woman wore a murderous glare as she stood with her hands on the hips of her turquoise dress.

"Can I help you?" Zora asked, unfazed. She looked beyond MK to the other dancers, who tried to pretend they weren't eavesdropping.

"You could help me by keepin' your hands to yourself."

"Huh?"

"You heard me," MK spat. "I know you've been spendin' a lot

of time with Jabari lately, learnin' things you shoulda been knew
but I kept my mouth shut 'cause there's nothin' more pathetic
than a witch who don't know how to do shit."

"So, what's your point?" Zora replied, exasperated by the
woman's need to dance around the subject.

"Bitch, don't interrupt me. You believe this girl?" MK said,
looking toward the other dancers and pointing toward Zora.
"First you come on to my man, then you try to be cute when
you get called out. I told you to leave him alone, but apparently
desperate bitches like you don't listen."

Zora rolled her eyes. *Is that what this is about?* she thought.

"If anybody's a desperate bitch, it's you."

MK's jaw tightened. "What did you just say to me?"

"Look, I don't want Jabari. I never have. You two got
whatever it is you got goin' on. I'm not the one you should be
worried about."

"The fuck is that supposed to mean?"

"Are you kidding?" Zora asked. "Do you really not know that
Jabari spends most of the time he's here flirting with everyone?
Hell, he's sat and felt up half of Divinity house while you're up
doin' your set. If I were you, I'd be directing that anger toward
him, not me."

MK's hand connected with Zora's cheek, knocking her back
into the lockers.

"Oh shit!" Chansi yelled. She and the other dancers stood,
trying to get a better view.

Zora looked up just as MK swung again, but she ducked and
the woman's fist connected with her locker.

"Ah, fuck!" MK yelled. Zora pushed her, where she connected
with a long bench and fell backward, her feet tumbling over her
head. Zora rounded the bench as MK stood and split in two.

Fuck, Zora thought. She tried to land a punch, but one version of MK dodged her. The other's fist connected with Zora's arm, making it go numb instantly. Zora grit her teeth as she grabbed a hold of the witch's hair and brought her knee up into her nose.

The other version of MK rescued the one caught in Zora's grip and punched Zora again, sending her down to the ground.

"Still got somethin' to say, hoe?" MK snarled. Both versions of the witch stood over Zora.

"Yeah. Fuck you, bitch," Zora growled. She stood and cocked a fist back just as Birdie entered the locker room.

"What the fuck is happening in here?"

"She started it," MK said, as the two versions of herself merged.

Zora scoffed.

"Bitch, you came at me!" she yelled.

She and MK stepped toward each other, standing so close that their bodies touched. Birdie broke them apart and stood with her arms extended toward them.

"I don't give a shit who stared it; I'm finishing it. You're done. This ends now." She looked from Zora to MK, waiting for them to nod. When they did, she continued. "I don't know what the hell caused this, and frankly I don't care. You need to leave right now and I'm docking your pay for tonight. I don't want to see you around this club for the rest of the night and at home? You'd both better make yourself scarce. If I get even a whiff of y'all fighting, you're both done. Out of Transcendence house. Do I make myself clear?"

"Yeah," MK agreed, her voice full of vitriol. She glared at Zora for a moment longer before she opened her locker, grabbed her purse, and left the locker room.

Birdie looked at Zora not with anger, but with something

worse—disappointment. It was written in her frown, in her crossed arms, in the way her eyes passed over Zora as she stepped around her and exited the locker room.

Ignoring the stares and whispers from the other dancers, Zora picked up her bag off the floor then rushed out the room. She kept her eyes fixed on the front door, even as Taemar called out to her from the bar.

Sheets of rain poured down on the cobblestones underneath Zora's feet as she left Nightingale's. She slid into her car, soaked from the rain and from life. As soon as she pulled out of the parking lot, she slammed her hand against her steering wheel and screamed. *How could things be so incredibly fucked?* she thought. How had she gone from possibilities to problems so quickly?

She parked her car at Transcendence house but walked to Forsythe Park, knowing that home, where she could see MK, Orion, and Birdie's cars, was the last place she needed to be. As she walked, an umbrella shielding her from the rain, her phone buzzed. She pulled it out of her purse to see texts from Taemar asking what the fuck happened between her and MK, a text from Jabari wondering where she was, and a text from Keith chastising her for not telling him she'd up and moved to Savannah.

Zora couldn't deal with any of them and dismissed the notifications. She wandered around the park, her mind twisted and racing with thoughts of the fight. She couldn't believe MK had the nerve to blame her for Jabari's attention. After all, wasn't he the one she was dating? Why wasn't she in his face? And why, after seeing that MK had split herself in two, and after knowing how catty MK had been toward her, had Birdie suspended them both? Nothing made sense to her in that moment, not her family, nor the witches who were supposed to be her community, nor the man standing by the fountain dressed like a civil war reenactor.

Once the image registered in her brain, Zora stopped in her tracks. She could feel the man's gaze upon her as she walked past, and after a while she began to feel his presence. But when she glanced behind her, he wasn't alone. A woman walked beside him, and when Zora turned her attention back toward the front, another ghost began walking toward her.

Ghosts. They're all ghosts, she thought. Zora's heart jackhammered in her chest and she walked faster, hoping to lose them, but it was no use. They continued following her, and soon even more ghosts joined them.

She veered to the right on Abercorn Street and dug her hand into her purse, searching for the red brick dust and wormwood that would protect her. She grabbed the bag and sped up, but in her haste, the bag slipped out of her hands, spilling its contents. Zora gasped and looked back at the mob of ghosts on her tail. She looked at the ground, the rain already washing away the red brick dust and wormwood.

She called Taemar but there was no answer. She dialed Birdie but hung up just as fast, knowing there was no way she'd come to her rescue. She called Niko, who answered on the third ring.

"Zora, girl, what happened?"

"Niko? Niko, can you come get me?"

"What's wrong?"

"I'm near Forsythe Park. My mind's all messed up, and I can't concentrate enough to block out the ghosts. They're—"

Zora cried out as one of them made contact and she felt herself pulled into the memory of a bar fight. She saw broken bottles and smelled whiskey and gun powder, and then the person who'd touched her was on the floor with someone's fist in his face. She surfaced from this memory only to be bogged down by another. Somehow, she'd stopped walking and the ghosts who followed her crowded around her, their hands reaching, some making contact, their memories flashing before her eyes s⊘ rapidly that it made her dizzy.

Scenes of war and fighting and murder and sickness played out in her mind and she cried out for help, tears running down her cheeks in a deluge. She fell to her knees, her umbrella falling out of her hand, and curled up in a ball as the rain beat down on her and the mob of ghosts clung to her, her mind awash in their bloody, tragic ends.

Zora didn't know how long she lay on the ground before she felt another set of arms on her shoulders. She screamed and batted the hands away.

"Zora, it's me! It's me," Niko said, kneeling in front of her, hi⧸ eyes wide with worry. She shivered and sobbed as he wrapped h⧸ arms around her. "It's okay. It's gonna be okay."

He helped her stand and wrapped an arm around her as he guided her to his car. They drove the short distance to Soliloquy house, all the while Zora flinching at the sight of the ghosts that dotted the streets. When he parked in front of Soliloquy, Niko ran out of the car and opened Zora's door before helping her out. As he had when he led her out of the park, he held her in his arms, and she nestled between his neck and shoulder. Zora walked up the stairs with trembling legs and when they stepped into Soliloquy house, her legs buckled. Niko picked her up and guided her past the living room to the kitchen.

"Here, let's sit." Niko helped her into a chair then got to work making tea. Zora's shoulders and back ached, and she fought back the vomit that crept up her throat. Though she tried to calm her breathing, it escaped in ragged spurts. Just as the panic began settling in, the kettle whistled and Niko set a cup of chamomile tea before her. Then he slid onto the chair opposite her. "What happened?"

Zora shook her head. "Fight with MK, got suspended, tried to walk it off. Birdie taught me how to suppress the ghosts but I was so distracted that I just . . . couldn't . . . I . . . couldn't . . ." She tried to swallow the lump in her throat. "I dropped my red brick dust and then I just . . . I was so scared."

She buried her face in her hands and sobbed. She shed tears not only from her fear of the ghosts but also for everything that had gone wrong.

"It's okay; it's okay," Niko soothed. He slid into the chair beside her and rubbed her back. When she stopped crying, he stood and grabbed a box of tissues. Zora pulled three tissues from the box and blew her nose with one then carefully removed her lashes before wiping her face with another. She dabbed her eyes with the third tissue.

"God, I must look like a mess," she said, sniffling.

"You do, but you're still beautiful."

Zora looked up to see Whitley standing in the doorway, her hair back in a red bonnet, a silk robe clinging to her voluptuous frame. She walked over to the table and joined them, grabbing one of Zora's hands in hers.

"I'm gonna give y'all some time," Niko said before leaving the room.

Both Whitley and Zora nodded at Niko then locked eyes with each other.

"I'm so sorry," Zora said. "I shouldn't have used that spell on you."

"No, you shouldn't have."

Zora's breath hitched. She bit her lip, trying to stave off a wave of fresh tears that threatened to spill.

"But I forgive you. I know you want to do right by Birdie, so now that I know what you're doing, I can help you. That is, if I'm not a suspect."

Zora laughed. "We'll just have to see."

"I guess so," Whitley replied. She looked at Zora for a long while before speaking.

"You know, I meant what I said. You are beautiful."

Zora stared back at Whitley, her eyes filled with wonder. "So are you."

"And even though there's still a part of me that wishes I was in LA, I am happy that I've met you. Because if I wasn't here, I wouldn't get the chance to do this."

Whitley leaned in toward Zora, and their lips met. Instantly she felt as though her body were on fire. Butterflies rattled against Zora's rib cage as she reached a tentative hand out to cup Whitley's cheek. Her lips were so soft, her kisses so sweet, and Zora never wanted it to end.

When Whitley pulled away, Zora wanted more, but she just gazed at the woman and held her hand.

"I've been thinking about doing that for a while now," Whitley said.

"Me, too," Zora replied.

They laughed, their heads bowing together and their foreheads touching. The fear Zora once felt subsided and, in that moment, she allowed herself to just be.

Chapter 15

"No one knows a witch's spell better than themself. After all, they're the ones who tested their success, and it's an unfortunate truth that not every spell succeeds."

Spell Book of Titus Soliloquy, 1910

Sunlight poured through the window in Whitley's bedroom, illuminating the gold lamps that rested on her nightstands. Zora lay awake in Whitley's canopy bed, tucked under blush-colored sheets. Though Whitley had tried to comfort Zora by holding her all night, yet again sleep eluded her. No matter how hard she tried, the events of the day before kept playing on a loop in her mind. *How am I gonna fix this?* Zora thought. Is it even possible to fix? She rolled onto her back and wiped the sleep from her eyes before sitting up. As she turned, she noticed the empty space beside her. She also noticed the house was quiet.

Zora stood and stretched but no matter what she did, the tension that had settled in her limbs never faded away. She dreaded walking down the stairs and winced with every step, yet the black and white portraits that lined the walls somehow comforted her. Even though she didn't know the individuals' stories, their eyes exuded confidence and strength, which Zora held on to as she inched down the staircase.

She found Whitley in the kitchen, spatula in hand, making breakfast. The smell of bacon, eggs, maple syrup, and coffee made Zora's stomach lurch. Had she even eaten last night? Zora couldn't remember. Seated at the table were Taemar and Niko, a pot of coffee, creamer, and sugar on the table between them. Each one held a spell book open in front of them.

"Hey," Zora said, her voice hoarse from sobbing. They all looked up at her, and Taemar stood and wrapped her in a big hug. Zora allowed herself to relax in his grip.

"How you doin'?" he asked. He pulled away and looked down at her.

"Oh, you know, I'm in my flop era," she quipped. Taemar scoffed and walked her over to the table. Zora sat down beside him. "What y'all doin'?"

"We're trying to help you solve this thing," Whitley said. Zora looked over to her, in awe of how beautiful she looked in the early morning light. Even without makeup, she was stunning. The memory of the kiss they shared came to her, and Zora's heart leapt as Whitley smiled at her before turning back to the stove and flipping a pancake.

"How? I completely erased Marquitta's memories, and I tried the compulsion spell on Jabari and Whitley. Neither one of them did it."

"Well, I'm glad to finally be crossed off your suspect list," Whitley began. "But I wouldn't rule Jabari out just yet."

Zora tilted her head. "But—"

"The compulsion spell works unless the recipient is wearing amethyst or has ingested lavender and diluted jimson weed," Taemar explained.

"Yeah, I know that."

"Well, was Jabari wearing amethyst?" Taemar asked.

"I didn't see any."

"And for the record, I wasn't wearing any last night," Whitley added.

"He probably had some lavender and jimson weed, then," Niko said. "If I was trying to hide somethin' from a bunch of witches and I knew the compulsion spell existed, I'd be drinkin' that every day."

"Also just to clear things up, I didn't drink that shit either," Whitley interjected. Zora nodded. That left Jabari as the prime suspect.

"But how do we know that he had some?" Zora asked. "He said he was at the gym, so how can we confirm that?"

"With some good ol' fashion flirtation, baby," Taemar replied as he winked at her. "I went over to the gym earlier this mornin'. Now mind you, it's a men's only gym so you wouldn't have been able to get in, but I used my wiles to charm the front desk man into telling me what I wanted to know."

Niko rolled his eyes and sighed around his cup of coffee. "And what wiles are those?"

"Well, if you play your cards right, baby, maybe you'll get to see 'em later," Taemar teased. A smile played on Niko's lips as Taemar watched him with such intensity.

"Alright, you two, save the foreplay for later," Whitley joked. She set a steaming hot plate of bacon, eggs, and pancakes in front of Zora.

"Over easy, right? That's how you like your eggs? I asked Tae," Whitley said. Zora looked at her and nodded.

"Thank you."

Whitley squeezed Zora's shoulder before turning back to Niko and Taemar. Taemar looked from Whitley to Zora and smirked.

"Anyway, as I was saying. Jabari was at the gym that day, yes, but he left around two."

"And? That's right during the time Marquitta was killed," Zora said.

"But times of death are approximations," Taemar replied. "If he left at two, went home, showered, he could have gotten to Transcendence just after three."

Zora poured herself some coffee and considered this possibility. The timeline made sense, and he had motive, being the jilted lover. But it had been years since Jabari and Marquitta had been together and from what Zora saw, he didn't seem to be pressed about her at all. He had his pick of any witch he wanted, so why would he still be upset about Marquitta leaving him?

"Why would he kill her, though? I mean, I know they used to date and Marquitta left him for Birdie. Why would he wait all th time to get his revenge? He seemed to have moved on, right?" Zora asked. She took a bite of food and her stomach lurched. She was so hungry.

"What if he hadn't, though?" Whitley asked. Zora looked over at her as she sat down and held her cup of coffee in both hands.

"Are you suggestin' they was havin' an affair?" Taemar asked giving her a sidelong glance.

Whitley shrugged.

Taemar scoffed and rolled his eyes. "Girl, no. No, Marquitta would never. She loved Birdie too much for that."

"That doesn't mean she didn't still love Jabari," Whitley said. "Look, I know I haven't been a part of the Triarchy very long."

"No, you haven't," Taemar shot back. Niko put a hand on Taemar's forearm and looked at him as if to say "chill."

"But that's precisely why I'm saying what I'm saying. You all have been so close for so long that you might not be able to see the things that an outsider could. Yeah, Jabari is a lover, and he's loved a lot of the witches in this community. But there's something about the way he would look at her, talk about her, that just felt...like more. Like she mattered to him more than anyone else. And at the Vernal Equinox ritual, I saw them together."

"Together? Like... were they fuckin' or something?" Niko asked. Whitley rolled her eyes.

"No, not like that. But after we set our intentions of new beginnings, I saw them talking together in the kitchen and their body language, the way they looked at each other . . . I don't know. Something about that just felt like . . ."

"Like?" Taemar questioned.

"Like maybe they'd rekindled their romance," Whitley disclosed, looking him directly in the eyes. Taemar was quiet as he sipped his coffee, but Zora could tell he didn't believe Marquitta would cheat on Birdie.

"I'm sorry, Tae, but it makes sense. If they were havin' an affair, maybe Marquitta wanted to end it or if he was pressurin' her to leave Birdie and she wouldn't, maybe that made him snap."

"Or maybe he was pressurin' her to start an affair and she didn't want to? Why are we assuming she'd just willingly cheat on Birdie? Y'all didn't see them like I saw them," Taemar stated, his voice raising. Niko pressed his hand against Taemar's shoulder and looked at him.

"Look, let's all just chill," he said. "Whether Marquitta and Jabari were having an affair or not, the signs point to him. But we can't just accuse him . . . we've got to get proof. So instead of focusing on the potential affair, we should be thinking about how we'll find out the truth, either by getting Jabari to confess or by helping Zora fix Marquitta's memories."

Taemar and Whitley glanced at each other, each of them nodding briefly as though signaling they were going back to their respective corners. They ate breakfast in silence, and Zora wondered how they'd confirm that Jabari had killed Marquitta once and for all. Clearly, he was protecting himself against compulsion and probably other magical spells that would force him to tell the truth.

The other alternative involved finding a way to break the curse on Marquitta's memory. She hadn't been able to find a spell or potion that would break the curse, but what if that wasn't what she needed to do? What if she just needed to start by finding the curse itself?

She thought about all the spell books she'd read so far. Many belonged to Transcendence witches, and she'd looked at Whitley's aunt, Bonnie Soliloquy's book as well as that of the Houses' founding member, Titus. But many other spell books dwelled in this house from other Soliloquy witches long passed. If they searched only for that spell, then they could narrow it down.

"I have an idea," Zora said, breaking the silence. The group dropped their utensils and leaned in, eager to hear Zora's thoughts.

They made a list of all the House Heads they could think of whose spell books they'd have access to. Taemar went back to Transcendence house to collect the ones he could, while Niko and Whitley collected all the ones in the Soliloquy house and brought them to the table. As they stacked the spell books in piles, Taemar returned, this time with Birdie in tow.

A spike of anxiety hit Zora when she noticed the woman standing beside Taemar.

"Uh, we'll be . . . somewhere else," Whitley said, pushing Niko toward the door.

Taemar looked at Zora and mouthed "you've got this" as he followed Whitley and Niko out of the room.

"Hi," Birdie said.

"Hello," Zora replied, fidgeting with her hands. "Listen, I'm sorry about what happened at the club last night," Zora continued. "I shouldn't have let MK get a rise out of me like that."

"That's okay. It happens to the best of us."

"And I'm sorry I couldn't get you answers about Marquitta before. But I've got help now and a plan that might work."

"That's what Taemar said . . . that's why I'm here. I want to help." She set a box of spell books on the floor and began pulling them out and setting them on the table.

Zora nodded. When Birdie returned the gesture and smiled, warmth spread all over Zora's body. *I can do this,* Zora thought. *We can do this.*

"Okay, well, I think we're ready," Zora called.

Whitley, Niko, and Taemar came back in the room, joking about Niko trying to eavesdrop. The group shared a quick laugh then Zora revealed her plan: they were going to find the curse used against Marquitta. Once they located it, Zora would summon the ghost of the witch who wrote it and find out how to break it.

"I'll have to remove the warding against ghosts," Whitley mentioned, eyeing Zora. "Are you sure that's what you want?"

"What other choice do we have? I have to find out how to break this curse. I've come too far to let my fear stop me."

Whitley nodded, though Zora could tell she was worried. "What if the answers aren't in any of these spell books?"

"Then we'll have to figure out a way to get to the spell books in Divinity house," Zora replied. She looked from Whitley to the rest of the group, who all wore worried expressions on their faces. She thanked the gods none of them could read minds because her thoughts matched their faces.

For the next few hours, they searched every spell book in their possession for the curse that had stolen Marquitta's memories. But as they set aside book after book without finding what they were looking for, Zora slowly resigned herself to the fact that what they needed existed somewhere else. As Taemar made their third pot of coffee, it became clear that Divinity house held all the answers.

Birdie came up with the plan: Niko, Zora, and Taemar would drive to Divinity house. Using his shapeshifting powers, Taemar would sneak in and let Zora in, while Niko kept watch across the street. A coffee shop sat across the street from Obsidian Auto Body, the shop that Jabari owned and where many of the Divinity witches worked. Birdie and Whitley would keep an eye on them from there, and if everything went to plan, Zora and Taemar would find the answers they needed and be in and out without being seen.

As Taemar and Zora approached the door, he looked around before shapeshifting into a ladybug and flying beneath the door. Minutes later, after searching the home to ensure they were alone, he unlocked the door and let Zora in, locking the door behind her. They stood in the foyer, listening for the sound of footsteps or a door closing. When there was nothing, they tiptoed to the basement and carefully descended the old wooden steps. The room smelled like incense with an undercurrent of dust.

Taemar coughed in his arm before turning to the twin bookshelves on either side of the altar. They slowly began pulling volumes from the shelves, skimming the pages and searching for the curse. As they did, Zora startled at any sound, her temples and ears throbbing as she waited for the moment they'd be caught. She poured over five spell books, but none of them bore the curse she'd need to fix Marquitta. Crestfallen, she sat back on her haunches and put back the spell books she'd read.

"I think I found it," Taemar whispered loudly.

Zora stopped putting books on the shelves and scooted over toward him. She looked at the spell book Taemar held open for her, her eyes landing on a curse written in blocky letters, all caps, with red pen that smudged in some places. It required the blood and tears of the person being cursed, which would be mixed with crushed up holly berries and made into a paste that would be put on the eyelids, temples, and lips of the person being cursed, making it impossible for the recipient to see or to speak their own memories. Because memories were all ghosts had, the spell endured after death.

Zora snapped a picture of the spell with her phone and flipped to the front of the book to find the name of the witch to whom it belonged.

Sabrina Bounty. One of the witches who passed away shortly after Jabari arrived at her house. *We've got him,* Zora thought. She stifled a gasp as she heard the front door close.

"Shit, put this back," she whispered. She and Taemar tried to put the books back as quietly as they could. But when they heard footsteps growing closer, they stared at each other, the fear apparent in their eyes.

"Hide," Taemar whispered. Zora looked around and slid underneath the altar table using the cloth as a shield, while Taemar ran to open the door in the basement that led to the patio before shifting into a cat. He meowed as the basement door opened and the light clicked on.

"Oh, hell, what're you doin' in here?"

Teague walked into view and scooped Taemar up in his arms "Damn man, I be tellin' these guys to keep this door closed but they hard headed."

Just put him down outside and go back upstairs, Zora thought. But instead Teague cradled Taemar in his arms as he closed the door and walked back upstairs. He turned off the light and Zora sat in the darkness, afraid to move and unsure how to get Taemar back.

Chapter 16

"When a witch commits a crime against man, it's up to House Soliloquy to decide their fate. When they commit a crime against the gods, Divinity is judge and jury. But when the crime they commit breaks the laws of man and of the gods, all three houses have a responsibility to act. The witch must be stripped of power and exiled from the comfort of the Triarchy."

Savannah Triarchy Charter, Savannah, Ga, 1900

Zora remained pressed against the wall beneath the altar for nearly an hour. Each time she thought she could move, she heard footsteps, or a door closing, or music playing overhead. When finally the house was quiet for longer than ten minutes, she crawled out of her hiding place. Despite the fall temperatures outside, Zora had sweat through her shirt, and her bangs and the hair at the back of her neck stuck to her skin. She tiptoed to the side door and stood for a moment, waiting once again for confirmation that she was alone. When minutes passed and the house remained silent, she opened the door slowly and looked out onto the courtyard, which sat empty in the afternoon sun.

She sighed with relief and walked out of the house, closing the door behind her. She spotted a gate on the side fence that led to the street and ran for it, opening and closing the gate as quietly as she could before she sprinted down the street toward Niko's car. Zora pulled open the door, breathless, and startled as Niko jumped in his seat. He looked at her then behind her and seeing that she was alone, he unhooked his seatbelt.

"Holy fuck? What's wrong? Where's Tae?"

"Teague came home," she said as she slid into the passenger seat. She took several deep breaths and tried to calm her wild heart. "Niko, weren't you watching?"

"I was! I didn't see him and I didn't get anything from Birdie or Whitley about one of them leaving." He held his phone up, showing a blank screen. "Where's Taemar?"

"He had to shift into a cat to distract Teague and I don't know what happened to him," she replied in one breath.

Niko whimpered. Zora looked around them, but the streets appeared empty. Yet her mind raced. Could Taemar be in danger? Could he have accidently shifted back and was now fighting against Teague to leave?

She felt like her throat was constricting and she could tell Niko looked just as frantic as she did. She checked her phone and wondered if she should call him.

Then the door behind Zora opened and both she and Niko jumped. Taemar slid into the back seat, a pained expression on his face.

"Tae, are you okay? I was so worried."

"I'm okay, but I never want to be touched by that man again. He smells like Marlboros." Taemar gagged and Zora chuckled before heaving a relieved sigh.

They drove off and once they were far enough away, Niko asked: "So, did you get it?"

Zora nodded and smiled. "We got it. We fuckin' got it!"

The altar in Soliloquy house was set up in a drawing room on the ground floor. While it had initially been in the attic, Whitley mentioned Bonnie had struggled to climb both sets of stairs toward the end of her life and had it moved before she died. The room carried a similar vintage vibe as the rest of the house.

Paintings similar to the one over the altar at Divinity house hung above the altar, and Zora did her best to recognize the gods by their description: there was Yamala, goddess of fertility, rebirth, and breath, Iniji, goddess of fire, vengeance, and war, and Narya, goddess of mind, memory, and dreams. Zora recognized the same painting of Geddemin as Jabari had, and beside it appeared Baygre, the creator of life and the earth god.

A green cloth covered the altar, which was stacked with white candles, crystals, and jars of herbs and potions. The room smelled like mint and cannabis.

A round wooden table sat in the center of the room. Each of them grabbed a chair, with Whitley sitting facing the altar.

Zora held her spell book open in front of her on the spell for communing with the dead, which would allow a ghost to speak easily, instead of in short sentences or sounding like a skipping record. Now that the wards were down, the ghosts of Soliloquy house made themselves known. She recognized one of them as Titus Soliloquy, the founder of the House. He leaned against the door frame, hands in his pants and his hat drawn low. By the window stood the ghost of an older woman with a Jheri curl and an '80s style dress and large glasses. And behind Birdie stood Marquitta, looking beautiful and devastated all at once. Though their presence unnerved her, Zora breathed in through her nose and out through her mouth slowly.

I am not afraid, she told herself. I am not afraid.

She closed her eyes and thought about the photo she'd seen of Sabrina Bounty, thought about her long limbs, expertly arched eyebrows, high cheekbones, and ochre skin. She thought about her long, blue-black hair and soon she smelled Black Opium perfume and clove cigarettes wafting throughout the room.

Sabrina Bounty, Head of the House of Bounty, stood across from Zora, just over Whitley's shoulder. She looked at Zora expectantly, her dark eyes sunken and her pupils dilated so much that it made her eyes look completely black. Zora's heart beat so fast that the sound reverberated in her ears and her temples throbbed. Her face and chest felt hot and as she looked down at her spell book, the words blurred for a moment before settling.

It's okay, she told herself. It's okay.

"Is she here?" Taemar asked.

Zora nodded once and began the communing spell.

"Spirit come to me, lend me your ear and I will lend you mine. Commune with me as you do with Geddemin at the gates of the afterworld. Tell me truth, and I will tell you no lies."

The air in the room crackled and became chilly. Whitley's eye widened slightly, and she adjusted her glasses.

"Is she here?" Whitley whispered. Zora nodded.

"Hello, Sabrina," Zora said.

"Took you long enough," the ghost rasped.

"I need your help," Zora said, ignoring the ghost's comment. "I need to know how to undo a curse you created."

Sabrina was silent for a moment. "Was the curse placed on one of you?"

"No, on her," Zora pointed to Marquitta, who locked eyes with Sabrina. "It was cast before she died."

"Well, that is tricky, isn't it?" Sabrina lifted her hand to her chin. "Usually, it's broken by saying the curse in reverse, meaning instead of asking Narya to remove memories asking her to restore, while a paste of ginkgo, turmeric, peppermint oil, and squid ink is applied on the eyes, temples, and mouth of the cursed. But, I guess in this case . . ." Sabrina trailed, pacing around the room, before turning back to Zora, eyes wide. "You'll apply those things to yourself, since you're the one searching for the memories. And you'll need to change the wording slightly to reflect that the memories will pass to you."

Zora scoffed but she could tell from Sabrina's expression that she wasn't kidding. She asked Whitley for the ingredients and a mortar and pestle. Then she mixed the paste, trying not to gag at the awful, briny smell of it. She placed the paste on her eyelids, temples, and lips. The mixture tingled, and she looked down at the spell book and said:

"Narya, keeper of the memories of all," Zora paused, wincing and trying not to gag as the mixture got in her mouth. "Plant her memories like seeds so they may regrow within her. Let them flourish and be whole as they once were and allow me permission to receive them."

Zora held out her hands, palms facing up, for Marquitta to take. When she did, her memories flooded Zora's senses so much so that it made her head snap backward. She inhaled deeply, as though preparing to dive into a large body of water. Her vision shimmered before settling.

Suddenly, she was no longer in the altar room of Soliloquy house, and it was no longer mid-October. Now, Zora stood in Birdie's bedroom. A fan oscillated in the corner, its metal blades making a churning sound that filled the room. The open curtains billowed each time the fan passed by. Despite this, Zora could feel the mid-day heat, and sweat streamed down her back. The blankets and bed sheets were in disarray, laying halfway on and halfway off the ground. A pair of black boots with silver buckles sat at the edge of the bed, one shoe laying on its side. Clothes were strewn about the room and just as Zora wondered why the room was empty, the bathroom door opened and Jabari and Marquitta stepped into the room. Both were naked, and Zora momentarily marveled at both of their chiseled physiques. Marquitta knelt down to pick up her bra, dress, and panties and began dressing in silence.

Jabari planted kisses on her neck and hugged her hips, tryin to pull her into him, but she moved away.

"You good?" he asked. She didn't respond as she slipped her dress over her head and smoothed it down over her hips.

"Fine," she replied. Zora could tell the comment annoyed hir by the way he pursed his lips and knitted his brows.

"You don't seem fine. C'mon, we've got some more time. Wh don't we try again?" He flirted. Marquitta once again shrugged out of his grip and walked toward her vanity and began picking out her afro. Sensing her disinterest, Jabari began dressing, all the while staring at her. "You sure you okay? Seems like you got somethin' on your mind."

Marquitta sighed. She turned toward Jabari and clutched he pick in her hands, as if for comfort.

"I can't do this anymore."

"Of course, you can. We just did. Twice," he said with a smir But Marquitta winced, and the flirtatious expression on his face died, replaced by confusion.

"No, I mean, I don't want to do this anymore," she gestured between them. "I don't want to hurt Birdie."

"You don't want to hurt Birdie," he repeated. "But you're oka hurtin' me? You said you wanted to break off the engagement, be with me."

"I know, and I'm sorry. I just don't want that anymore." She began to walk past him and around the bed, but he caught her by the elbow and turned her around to face him.

"And what about our plan, huh? What about getting rid of Whitley and Birdie and combining the houses? The two of us, overseeing all of the witches in Savannah?"

Marquitta's eyes became glassy and she looked down at the ground. Zora's heart began to pound as she felt the energy in the room shift. Marquitta mumbled something and Jabari lifted her chin.

"Don't you believe in us?" he asked, his voice grief-stricken and his eyes wide, searching her face for a response.

"I don't want to do that anymore either," she replied. "I'm sorry. We have to be done with all of this."

She pulled out of his arms and stood before him for a moment. "I'll always love you."

He chuckled, the sound bitter as he bared his teeth. "But not like you love her."

Marquitta shook her head. Again, she turned to walk out of the room. A range of emotions flashed over Jabari's face until it settled on rage. He and Zora noticed the scarves and belts and purses hanging on hooks on the inside of the door. As Marquitta stepped over the threshold of the room, Jabari's arm snaked out toward the scarves and in one fluid motion, he grabbed a yellow one dotted with red roses and wrapped it around her neck, pulling her back into him.

Zora gasped at the action.

"Zora, what's wrong?" she heard Whitley say. But her voice sounded so distant, even though Zora knew she was just right there before her. She didn't respond, only blinked away her tears as she watched Marquitta claw at Jabari's hands. The woman choked and sputtered, her eyes bulging and her mouth wide. Jabari pulled the scarf tighter around her neck with such force that he fell backward, his body hitting the floor with a thud. Marquitta fell on top of him and writhed, but Zora could tell she was beginning to lose her strength.

Seconds later, her arms went limp. Her eyes stared at the door, unblinking.

Suddenly, Zora came out of the memory and it felt like coming up for air. She screamed as she did so, all the anguish she'd felt watching Marquitta's murder now fully expressing itself. She'd seen more murders in her life than she could count. She'd seen ones more gruesome, bloodier ones, ones that served as fuel for her nightmares. By the time she was nine, she knew what a body looked like when it was burned or drowned or stabbed to death.

She'd cried tears for the victims, for the families, but never had a murder affected her this deeply. She sobbed, the pit in her stomach growing bigger and bigger, and she wondered if she'd never be okay again. She wondered if this was truly what it felt like to lose someone you loved. Was this confusion, this sense of hopelessness, this feeling of time standing still, what each and every person she'd helped experienced?

She locked eyes with Marquitta and she could see the ghost's anguish at having to relive her last moments again. Zora wondered if she felt any guilt for her affair, if she had any regrets for deciding to let Jabari in her bed again.

"I'm sorry," Marquitta whispered. But Zora didn't respond, could only cry while the rest of the ghosts in the room looked on.

"Zora, what did you see?" Birdie asked, her voice already

pained.

"Yeah, it's okay; you can tell us," Taemar added.

All of them were talking to her, asking what she saw and who had killed their beloved Marquitta. Only Whitley remained silent. She stood from her chair and walked out of the room. When she returned minutes later, Taemar, Niko, and Birdie were still trying to coax Zora into telling them what happened.

Whitley placed a box of tissues and a glass of water on the table before her. Then she pulled her chair beside Zora, sat down, and began rubbing her back. Somehow, this silent comfort made Zora feel like she could breathe again. After a while she stopped crying, but her eyes were puffy and her eyelids felt heavy. Her head felt fuzzy and her nose was so stuffed up that it was hard to breathe. She blew her nose and took a sip of water. Then Zora took a deep breath and nodded.

Birdie sat across from her, tears spilling from her eyes, her mascara leaving dark trails down her cheeks. She looked at Zora like she was bracing for a punch.

"Tell me," she whispered.

Zora looked from Birdie to Niko, then Taemar, Sabrina, and finally, Whitley. Amid her anguish, a spike of relief shot through Zora at discovering the woman she wanted to be with had not been the one to murder Marquitta Transcendence. But somehow, the realization that it was Jabari still made her stomach churn and acid rise in her throat.

Though she'd considered him a suspect from the beginning, it was one thing to wonder, and another thing to know. Now she knew, and she hated all the times she'd delighted in his compliments, or thought about how handsome he was. She wasn't ready to tell everyone the truth, but she had no choice.

"It was Jabari," Zora confirmed.

Birdie gasped and brought a hand up to her face. "But why would he do that? Why would he kill her?" she questioned.

Zora grimaced. "They were having an affair. It sounded like maybe she told him she wanted to be only with him and—"

Birdie stood and stormed out of the room. Zora scowled and looked at Taemar before they both stood and followed Birdie out of the room. She stood by the threshold, tugging on her boots an slipping into her jacket.

"What you doin'?" Taemar asked. Birdie didn't reply.

"Where you goin'?" Zora asked. Whitley and Niko emerged from the altar room and stood back watching the scene. Marquitta hovered beside Zora.

"I'm sorry," the ghost repeated, the room icy from the intensity of her emotion.

"Birdie, please, talk to us!"

The witch stopped and turned toward Zora. Her mouth was set in a grim line and her eyes were bloodshot, but Zora had never seen her look more resolute.

"What's there to talk about? The love of my life was having ar affair with Jabari. And she got herself killed because of it."

Marquitta whimpered and Zora looked at her, wishing she could comfort her. Birdie picked up on Zora's behavior and eyed the space beside her. She strode over and reached into the empty space.

"Is she here? Is that who you're looking at?" Birdie demanded.

"Birdie, I know you're upset, but let's just—"

"Upset?" Birdie interrupted. She looked from the space besid Zora to Zora herself then to the rest of the group. "Upset? I'm more than upset. I'm fucking angry! I'm livid. How could she do this to me? How . . . Marquitta, how could you do this to me?"

"She says she's sorry," Zora translated. But somehow that only made things worse.

"Sorry? That's it?" Birdie exploded. "You're sorry? I loved you more than life itself and all you have to say is sorry?"

"It's not that easy for ghosts to talk. That's why I had to cast the communing spell on Sabrina. It gives them the energy they need to speak."

"Well, cast it on Marquitta. I need to talk to her."

"You won't be able to see her unless I do a spell to make her visible to you."

Birdie gripped Zora by the arms and shook her. "Then do it, please. I need to talk to her. I need to ask her why."

"I don't think that's a good idea," Zora replied.

"Zora, just do it! As your House Head I'm ordering you to—"

"Birdie, that's enough," Whitley shouted. Birdie released Zora and turned to Whitley, who stood at the foot of the stairs. The other Soliloquy witches, Kimayah, Chansi, and Devo, stood at the top of the stairs watching the scene below.

"This doesn't involve you, Whitley."

"Well, you're in my house, so technically it does. Look, I know you're angry and you have every right to be. But summoning the ghost of your dead fiancée to berate her for cheating on you isn't going to make you feel better."

"It's not about feelin' better," Birdie said, taking a step toward Whitley.

"Then what's it about?"

"Revenge. I want them to hurt just as much as I do right now. I want to look Marquitta in the face and tell her everything I have to say without having to use an intermediary. And then I want to go to Divinity and drag Jabari out of his house by his crispy, relaxed hair and beat his ass in front of everyone."

"And what then, huh?" Whitley asked, her arms folded. "Will that make you feel better?"

"Just stop talking! I'm tired of hearing you run your mouth."

"Birdie, she's right," Taemar added. He put a hand on her shoulder. "You have every right to feel how you feel and it's going to take a while for you to move past your anger. But gettin revenge is not the way to process your feelings and I think you know that. You have to make peace with the past."

"So, you're taking her side now?" Birdie shrugged Taemar's arm away.

"Girl, it's not like that and you know it."

"I do know that none of you are helping me. Jabari killed not just anyone—he killed a witch. He broke the laws of man and of the gods. And I'm not supposed to do anything about that?"

"No one said anything about letting that man skate by. But you're not just any witch. You're a House Head, and there are laws we must abide by no matter how we personally feel. Jabari will pay. He'll be stripped of his powers and exiled from the magical community," Whitley replied, her arms folded.

"Fuck the laws! That man took everything from me. He's got to pay and losing his magic isn't enough."

"Birdie, please. At least if you're plannin' to go to Divinity, le us come with you," Taemar said.

"Now you want to help me?" Birdie spat. From the look on Taemar's face, the words felt like a punch in the gut. "I'll take care of this myself. It's what I should've done this whole time anyway."

"Jabari isn't just some sound witch. He was powerful enough to cast Sabrina's curse on Marquitta. And none of us could figur it out for months. You goin' in with no plan, just hatred, could g you killed," Zora reasoned.

"Yes. Birdie, let us help you do this the right way, as outlined by the Savannah Triarchy," Taemar pleaded.

Birdie looked around the room, her gaze finally setting on Zora. "I'm sorry. But I don't got time to sit here and think on how to do things by the book. Jabari has to pay."

And then, in the blink of an eye, Birdie disappeared and Marquitta's ghost followed with her.

Amanda Ross

Chapter 17

"Witches are to be loyal to their House above all."

The Spell Book of Booker Transcendence, 1900

When Birdie left, the sun was on its slow decline in the west. Now, the crescent moon hung high in the sky and stars sparkled against the inky blackness of the night. Whitley talked them all down from following Birdie, but no one seemed able to keep still. Zora paced around the living room, twisting and untwisting the edge of her black and red flannel shirt around her fingers. Niko occupied the kitchen, yellow rubber gloves on and a sponge in hand, scrubbing the counters over and over. Whitley attended to the Soliloquy witches in the altar room, filling them in on what was happening.

Though they weren't speaking to each other, Zora could tell they were all thinking the same things: Had Birdie gone to Divinity house as she'd planned? Had something gone wrong and she'd been incapacitated, or worse, killed?

After the first hour, Taemar had argued with Whitley about doing recon. "I have to know she's okay. She's my House Head and my friend. My loyalty will always be to her, not you."

"Fine. But stay in your shape and just observe. Even if you see her getting her ass beat, don't act. It'll be better to have a plan."

Taemar left without responding. He hadn't been gone long but for every minute that passed by, the dread that had coiled in Zora's stomach unraveled. Even though Zora had reversed the communing spell, Sabrina Bounty still lingered along with Titus Soliloquy and the older woman. All three stood near the window and watched the scene before them in silent fascination.

"This is taking too long," Zora said. "Where's Taemar?"

Seconds later, the door opened and Taemar stepped in. Zora stopped pacing and Niko looked over at his boyfriend and heaved a relieved sigh, his blue curls falling in his face as he leaned forward.

"Whitley, he's back," Niko called. Whitley emerged from the altar room and stood in the door frame between the foyer and the living room.

"Well? Was she there?" she asked. Taemar shook his head.

"I looked through all of their windows and I didn't see her. I even changed shape from a bird to a snake and slithered into their altar room, but it was empty, so they aren't holding her, at least not at Divinity. I also went back to Transcendence, but Birdie wasn't there either."

"Where could she be?" Zora asked.

"I'm here." Birdie appeared in the foyer, her black silk suit looking wrinkled but no worse for the wear. Her eyes were puffy, and her voice was hoarse.

"Thank the gods you're alright," Taemar said as he wrapped Birdie in a strong embrace. She leaned against him for a moment before patting his back. He pulled away and led Birdie into the living room. As Birdie positioned herself on the couch, Zora sat down by her side.

"Where'd you go?" Zora asked.

"I went to Tybee Island," she said. "To the beach. Marquitta loved the ocean and it's where we had our first date and where I proposed to her. And I just shouted at the ocean and at her and the gods. I said everything that I wanted to say to her. You know,

I've had this picture of her in my head as this perfect woman, this sweet, sexy, smart goddess who loved me as much as I loved her."

"She did love you," Taemar reassured Birdie, placing a hand on her knee.

"I'm sure she did. But somehow it wasn't enough. If it had been, she wouldn't have cheated."

They sat in silence for a moment, everyone unsure of how to respond.

"But I owe you all apologies. I was messy earlier and I'm sorry." Birdie scanned the room, making eye contact with each of them. Her eyes stopped on her fellow House Head. "And Whitley, you're right. I can't do this alone. We need a plan."

"Then it's a good thing for you I've already been thinking of one," she replied. "C'mon. Let's get something to eat and talk this through. I'm starving."

"Me, too," Zora and Niko spoke simultaneously. They looked at each other and smiled.

"I don't think I have much of an appetite, y'all," Birdie said.

"Well, I've definitely worked up one with all this runnin' around I've been doing," Taemar began. "Besides, we're all going to need our strength for this one. So, what do you say?" he asked, extending a hand to Birdie.

She hesitated for a moment then placed her hand in Taemar's. "I guess I can eat a little something."

"I know the perfect place," Whitley mentioned as she grabbed her keys and purse.

Half an hour later, they sat on the balcony of a restaurant across from the Savannah River. The city lights glistened on the river as a gentle breeze pushed its waves forward. Glass of wine in hand, Whitley strategized how they could take down Jabari.

"Tomorrow is Halloween, and tomorrow night we'll be at

Divinity carrying out the ritual to honor the dead. All we have to do is act natural from now until then, and after the ritual we confront him. Then we strip his powers and exile him." She took a sip of wine and smiled, seemingly pleased with her idea.

"But what do we do if he tries to recruit the Divinity witches to help him?" Niko asked.

Whitley shrugged. "Then we'll be ready. We'll have us, plus the rest of Soliloquy house."

"But what about MK and Orion?" Zora asked. "Seems to me they're more loyal to him than Transcendence. At least, MK is."

"That's right. I don't trust them bitches as far as I can throw 'em," Taemar added. Zora sipped her rum and Coke and looked to Birdie, as they all were.

"You're right. Let's leave them out. We can't risk them tippin' Jabari off, and if they are loyal to their house, as they should be, then we'll have two more witches on our side."

"We need to be prepared for them not to be," Taemar warned. "Orion's persuasion could seriously fuck us if we aren't."

"Titus Soliloquy has a spell to combat persuasion in his spell book. If I remember correctly, it just requires spelling a piece of jewelry or an article of clothing and keeping it on while interacting with witches who use persuasion," Whitley said.

"So, we're really doin' this, huh? We're really going to take down Jabari Divinity?" Taemar marveled.

The gravity of what they were planning seemed to finally hit them all as Taemar's words echoed in their minds. When their food arrived, they ate and finished their drinks without much conversation. The chatter spilling over from other patrons' tables all but mocked the stillness at theirs. All the while Zora wondered how she could lend her powers to this fight. As though reading her mind, Birdie spoke.

"Zora, this will be an especially powerful day for you."

"Why?" Zora asked, nearly choking on her words. Halloween had never made her feel powerful. More ghosts lurked around, making trick or treating or going to Halloween parties impossible for her. Now, she knew it was because the veil between this world and what she now knew was the afterworld was at its thinnest. Despite her working so hard over the last month to learn not to be afraid of them, the thought of so many ghosts roaming around still frightened her, especially after what happened the other night. She shuddered as she remembered the barrage of ghosts clamoring to touch her.

"Because Halloween is the day when the veil between this world and the afterworld is the thinnest. They'll be ghosts aplenty, but you'll be able to use their energy to help you fight," Whitley added.

"And . . . how do I do that? We never covered how to use ghostly energy in my magical trainin'." Birdie gulped down the rest of her gin and tonic. "I'm sure if you commune with my fiancée, she can fill you in."

The energy among them shifted at the edge in Birdie's voice. While they all looked at each other and contemplated what to say, Zora looked at Marquitta, who hadn't left Birdie's side the entire evening, her face a picture of despair.

After dinner they all headed to Nightingale's and tried to follow Whitley's advice to act natural. Birdie put on a show, dressed in a black lace gown that reminded Zora of a Victorian widow. Whitley and Niko sat in the audience as Taemar tended bar.

Zora feigned excitement for their group number to "Tombstone Blues," but pasting on a smile and exuding sex as she stripped the black velvet gloves and corset to reveal a rhinestone bra and panties felt like a Herculean effort. But completing her own numbers proved to be worse because she didn't have anyone to hide behind, not to mention the whispers and stares from the dancers who wondered if there'd be a rematch between her and MK.

When Zora finished her dance, she ignored the dancers backstage and met Taemar at the bar.

"Shoot. I deserve a gods damn Oscar for this performance I'm puttin' on tonight, baby," he whispered.

Zora slid onto a barstool and nodded. "Tell me about it. I didn't realize how much work it took to smile before."

He slid a bottle of water toward her and she sipped it. Her stomach dropped as she heard the clicking of heels against the hardwood floor and noticed Jabari striding toward her. She looked at Taemar, eyes wide, before plastering on a smile.

"Another excellent performance tonight, Zora," he said as he embraced her. He smelled sweet and spicy, like rum and cloves and smoke.

"Thank you," she replied. He pulled away and looked down at her with such lust that it sent a shiver down her spine.

"Can I get you anythin'?" Taemar asked.

Jabari shook his head. "No, thanks. I'd just like to sit here and talk to this beauty for a while."

Zora sipped her water, trying to hide her distaste.

"I'm pretty tired from the set tonight. I was planning to head home early," Zora lied.

He waved a hand at her as though trying to dismiss that thought from her mind. "I still want to get to know you. The last time we spoke we spent more time talking about me and Marquitta."

Zora's stomach ached at the mention of Marquitta's name.

"I'd really like that Jabari, but the truth is . . ." Zora began. He looked at her expectantly. The truth is you're, you're a fuckin' murderer and I'm about to help you lose your powers, she thought. "The truth is . . ."

"The truth is, Zora's with me."

Zora and Jabari both looked over to see Whitley standing there, leaning against the bar, her curves poured into a gold lame dress. Jabari scowled and looked from Zora to Whitley.

"This true?"

Whitley walked over and wrapped an arm around Zora's shoulder, and the feeling of Whitley's body against hers made Zora's body quiver.

"Yeah. It's very new, but we've got a thing goin' on," Zora replied. Whitley nuzzled against Zora's neck and Zora smirked at the warmth of her face against her neck, as she took in the woman's perfume.

Jabari pursed his lips.

"I know you want to spend more time with Zora, but you'll have to do it another time. She's coming home with me," Whitley purred. She pulled Zora into the most passionate kiss she'd ever experienced. The kiss set her whole body aflame and it felt like the rest of the world faded away. Her nipples stiffened and her groin throbbed when Whitley's tongue lightly prodded Zora's lips, opening them and caressing her tongue. She brought a hand to Zora's cheek and caressed it. When she pulled away, Zora's mind and body pulsated. Whitley looked at Jabari as though daring him to respond.

He smiled but the gesture didn't reach his eyes.

"Well, far be it from me to stop . . . whatever this is," he said, gesturing between them. "Guess I'll see you both at Divinity house for Halloween."

"Yeah, we'll be there," Whitley smiled. Jabari turned on his heel to walk away. Once he was out of earshot, the smile faded from Whitley's face and she fanned herself. Zora caught her gaze and Whitley bit her lip as she looked Zora up and down.

"Uh, is someone gonna tell me what the fuck just happened?" Taemar asked, his brows lifted.

"What happened is between me and Zora," Whitley said. She leaned in to Zora and whispered in her ear: "Do you want to come home with me?"

She pulled away and Zora could see the lust in Whitley's eyes. Zora wasn't a virgin. She'd had sex before, but she'd never felt the kind of attraction she felt to Whitley. She wanted this woman with every fiber of her being, down to her very marrow.

Zora nodded and let Whitley help her off the stool and out of the club. Some of the witches traded glances at the sight of the two women together as Jabari's eyes burned with envy.

Whatever was to happen at the Halloween ritual would happen. Zora could think about that in the morning. But for now she only thought about feeling Whitley's naked body pressed against hers.

Chapter 18

"Halloween can be a necromancer's dream or their worst nightmare. With more ghosts around seeking their light, it can be easy for a necromancer to become overwhelmed. But if they can focus and harness the energy that ghosts give off, they become nearly unstoppable."

Spell Book of Marquitta Transcendence, 2021

Zora spent the night in Whitley's bed once more and though she barely slept once again, this time her exhaustion was worth it. This time, she woke up naked and blissful as she looked into the woman's dark eyes as sunlight trickled into the room. The ambience seemed nothing short of divine. Their arms wrapped around each other and Zora reveled in Whitley's warmth.

"Good morning," Zora said.

"Yes, it is," Whitley replied, her hand on Zora's lower back. She kissed Zora and rolled over on her back.

"Are you ready . . . for tonight?" Zora asked.

"You sure know how to pillow talk," Whitley quipped. Zora grimaced. "But no, I'm not. A part of me suspected that Jabari had been the killer, but I didn't want to believe it. I still don't."

"I suspected him, too. I guess I hoped that the worst thing he did was break too many hearts and sometimes have a bad temper. But once I realized only you, Birdie, or him could have done it . . . I stopped hoping. Because I couldn't bear the thought of you having killed Marquitta."

Whitley caressed Zora's cheek then pulled her in for a kiss. Her lips were soft and though her kisses weren't forceful, there was a hunger to them that took Zora's breath away. When they pulled apart, Zora sat up and leaned her head on her arm and looked down at her lover.

"How do you think tonight's going to go?" she asked.

"We'll fight, we'll win, and we'll take him down," Whitley said. Her voice wavered slightly and it made Zora's heart skip. Even she was nervous. And if an experienced and powerful witch was nervous to face Jabari and likely all of his house . . . what was Zora to feel?

Zora scoffed. "C'mon, you know it won't be that easy. We've seen this movie before. We go in, someone dies, maybe one of us since we just slept together before the big fight."

"Okay, well this isn't a movie and if it was, it certainly wouldn't be written by people looking to bury their gays. We're all going to come out on the other side."

Zora nodded and allowed Whitley to draw her into her embrace. As Whitley traced her fingers along Zora's body, Zora quivered and melted into Whitley's arms. They made love again, and this time more passion surfaced in their kisses and in their movements, more hunger.

After their morning session, they showered and dressed, bringing thoughts of Marquitta's final moments to Zora's mind. Reluctantly, Zora returned to Transcendence house to gather her costume and the things she'd need for the night. She knew Taemar had stayed at Soliloquy with Niko and that Birdie was likely at Nightingale's or on her way to Soliloquy. But it surprised her to find the house completely empty, and she wondered where MK and Orion were. When she returned to Soliloquy house,

Birdie, Niko, and Taemar sat at the table and Whitley prepared brunch.

All of them looked up at Zora as though trying to hide their smiles and Zora rolled her eyes, realizing that they either had heard or had been told about their night together.

"Bet you're glad you stayed in Savannah, huh, Zora?" Taemar asked. Whitley sucked her teeth and patted him on the arm.

Zora nodded. "I am."

Her cheeks warmed as the table whooped and whistled, which made Whitley smile sheepishly and turn toward the stove.

They ate tacos for lunch and discussed their plan of attack as they dined. Afterward, they prepared their potions and spells. The Halloween ritual began as soon as the sun set, so they had only a few hours to prepare their attack and themselves.

First, they warded themselves against Orion's powers. Each of them opted to spell a piece of jewelry, with Birdie choosing to use the bird charm she always wore and Zora choosing a black choker that complemented her costume. Then they prepared potions that temporarily bound the powers of whoever was hit with the potion.

Yet, Zora couldn't find anything in Marquitta's spell book on how to channel ghostly energy. She had tried to summon Marquitta to ask her but when Birdie had referred to her as her "fiancée" the night before, Marquitta had disappeared shortly after and didn't reappear despite Zora's attempts.

As they all spoke about the spells in their arsenal and what each of them did, Zora's mind wandered elsewhere. She wondered how she could use her powers to win this fight. She wondered if she ran out of the potions they were preparing, if she'd really be able to face Jabari, who could use sound waves to hurt or to heal, or MK, whose astral projection ability always made it an unfair fight.

Geddemin, please lend me your strength, she thought.

They drove to Divinity together as the sun dipped low in the west, casting everything in golden light. Spanish moss swayed in the breeze, and the street lights buzzed as they turned on. When they parked, they sat for a while in silence, as though trying to gather the strength for what they were about to do. Birdie was the one who spoke first.

"Remember, our primary goal is to take Jabari's powers and exile him. Don't start the fight, but be prepared to have to finish it."

They nodded and hopped out of the car, all of their heels clicking on the sidewalk. Zora admired Birdie's costume, a black, hooded catsuit with sequined lining, an homage to Grace Jones. Taemar and Niko dressed in brightly colored zoot suits, and Whitley paid homage to Dorothy Dandridge and dressed as Carmen Jones. Zora was in awe of her beauty as she walked through the side gate of Divinity house. She held on to that image of Whitley for a moment, knowing the atmosphere would soon change.

Unlike the last ritual, everyone was already outside, seated at a long, u-shaped table covered in a black tablecloth decorated with ornate candelabras, golden candles, magnolias, and fire lilies. The candle flames gave the yard an eerie feel as they danced across the faces of the seated witches.

When he saw them, Jabari looked up and smiled, but the gesture didn't seem kind to Zora. He stood and strode toward them, his black and green cobra costume accentuating his slim but muscular frame. He hugged Birdie and kissed the air beside her cheeks and complimented her outfit. If Zora hadn't known what was to come, she would've thought no animosity existed

between them. He did the same to Taemar and Niko, and finally
Whitley.

Then he turned his attention to Zora. "I've got to say, Zora,
I do think you've got the most interesting costume here. What
made you decide to go as a demon?"

Zora smiled tightly. She selected her costume weeks ago when
she was first told about the Halloween ritual. She glanced down
at the black corset dress she wore, with the high slit and tulle
skirt that trailed on the ground, showing off the hooved boots
that perfectly matched her medium brown skin. She wore an
ornate black and gold choker and a set of rams' horns that curled
over on themselves and ended by her ears. Her hair was down
and teased, and her makeup was immaculate.

"My mother told me when she found out about my powers
that I was consorting with demons. So I figured I may as well
dress up as one."

Jabari smiled ruefully and gestured to the table.

Zora took her seat beside Taemar and Niko. Like the equinox
ritual, the House Heads had to cover their faces before beginning.
Each of them slipped a black veil over their heads before walking
to the firepit and as they did so, the conversation around Zora
ground to a halt. Every witch turned their attention to the House
Heads as they began the ritual. Whitley conjured a matchbook
and handed it to Jabari, who lit the kindling in the firepit as he
spoke.

"Tonight is All Hallows' Eve," Jabari began. "It is the time
we honor our dead, beseech the gods for their peace, and thank
them, for our times have not yet come."

Whitley conjured a cluster of magnolia and fire lilies and
Birdie pulled a dagger from her sleeve. As Whitley held the
flowers in her hand, Birdie drew the blade across her palm and

squeezed some of her blood on them.

"I, Birdie Transcendence, beseech the gods to hold my beloved Marquitta in their arms and grant her the peace she deserves."

The edge in her voice made Taemar shift in his seat. Zora and he exchanged glances before turning their attention back to the ritual.

"I also thank the gods for my life and the lives of the witches in my house," Birdie finished.

Whitley tossed the flowers that Birdie had bled on into the fire. The flames sparked red and climbed higher before settling, and Zora began to feel that same feeling she had at the equinox ritual—like her entire body buzzed and her eyes watered and her heart felt full to bursting. She wondered how many of these witches still felt the same after seeing so many rituals take place.

For the next phase of the ritual, Whitley held out the cluster of flowers in her hand to Birdie, who took them and held them before her as a bride would a bouquet. Whitley ran the dagger across her palm and said, "I, Whitley Soliloquy, beseech the gods to hold my beloved Aunt Bonnie in their arms and grant her the peace she deserves. I also thank the gods for my life and the lives of the witches in my house." She trickled her blood onto the flowers and watched stoically as Birdie then tossed them into the flames. Again, they sparked red and surged up before settling.

Finally, Jabari took the dagger from Whitley's hand and held it aloft as he ran it across his palm and spoke. "I, Jabari Divinity, beseech the gods to hold the ones I love in their arms and grant them the peace they deserve. I also thank the gods for my life and the lives of the witches in my house." His blood oozed onto the flowers in Birdie's hand. She tossed them into the firepit swiftly, and for the third time, the fire glowed red before settling. The heavy scent of lilies and magnolias mixed with the coppery tang of blood permeated the air.

Then the three House Heads pressed their hands together before their chests as if in prayer. They tilted their heads back and spoke in sync: "We bleed for those who can no longer. We eat for those who can no longer. We drink for those who can no longer. We revel for those who can no longer. May our love reach them on this night when the veil between our world and the afterworld is thinnest. Gods, we beseech you."

The red glow returning, the flames climbed higher before settling and Zora knew that their part of ritual was complete. They all would eat and drink and revel until the fire died down. The House Heads ambled back to their seats, each of them sitting in the center of the table with Jabari in the middle.

Some melancholic tune began playing, and Zora thought about how it seemed to match the tone of the events to come. Bottles of champagne had been set out before them to pour into their glasses and pass along. Whitley handed Zora a bottle and they looked at each other as their fingers touched, and Zora wished they could be anywhere else holding onto each other and talking until the sun came up. She poured champagne into her glass and passed the bottle to her right, to Taemar, who followed suit. Once every glass was filled, they all lifted them toward the fire and repeated the words the House Heads had recited before taking their seats.

"We bleed for those who can no longer. We eat for those who can no longer. We drink for those who can no longer. We revel for those who can no longer. May our love reach them on this night when the veil between our world and the afterworld is thinnest. Gods, we beseech you."

They sipped their drinks then retreated into the house to

get food. When it was her turn, Zora entered with Whitley, but despite filling her plate with fruit, cooked vegetables, and salami and cheeses, Zora's stomach was sour. She picked at the items on her plate as the yard filled with laughter and raucous conversation. Even Taemar and Niko joked with the witches beside them. As Whitley and Birdie spoke with Jabari in lively tones, Zora marveled at their abilities to compartmentalize things. She'd never been able to separate things like this in her mind; when she was younger and knew she'd have to raise the dead or attend a funeral or speak to a ghost, she agonized for days before. She'd barely eat, toss and turn at night. By the time she reached her late teens, she'd gotten used to poor sleep and surviving on water and small meals. Eye creams and concealer became her best friends, and she thanked the gods for them now as she stared at her reflection on her phone. She didn't look as tired and worried as she felt, but when she felt Whitley squeeze her thigh, she sighed.

"Just relax," Whitley whispered against her neck. "It's going to be okay."

Zora nodded and closed her eyes as Whitley planted a kiss on her neck before turning back to her plate and the conversation with the other witches at the table.

As the night progressed, the fire began dying down. People had gone in for their second plates, had poured their second and third glasses of champagne, and Zora looked down at her mostly untouched plate with disgust. Jabari seemed to notice her mood and reached a hand around Whitley to touch Zora's shoulder.

"You good, beautiful?" he asked.

Zora nodded. "Yeah, just got a migraine. Crept up on me, so I'm not feelin' my best."

He stared at her for a long while, and Zora wasn't sure if he believed her. But then he nodded and turned back to his plate. Birdie cleared her throat and Zora's heart skipped as she watched the woman lean back in her chair, holding onto her glass of champagne in one hand and crossing the other over herself.

"Well, I'm happy to announce that I've recently found out who killed Marquitta," Birdie blurted out. Several witches paused what they were doing, and the conversations happening around them became whispers of interest and speculation.

"We're doing this right now?" Taemar whispered. He set his fork down and wiped his mouth with his napkin.

"Is that right?" Jabari asked, his voice even. Whitley sucked in a breath.

"Mm-hmm. I found out exactly what happened to her. It's an interesting story, would you like to hear it, Jabari?"

His teeth clenched. But he nodded.

"So, it turns out that the witch everyone thought was so perfect really wasn't. She was having an affair."

Gasps and murmurs filled the room as the witches looked around trying to figure out who could've been sleeping with Marquitta.

"When she tried to break the affair off, she was killed. Strangled to death with her own scarf."

Zora shuddered as she remembered the sound Marquitta had made when she was being killed.

"And would you all like to know who that was?" Birdie asked, her voice raising. "Would you like to know what witch had the nerve to steal my girl and then kill her?"

"Birdie, please, we're completing a ritual. This is disrespectful," Jabari said.

Birdie whipped around to face him. "Disrespectful? Like how you and Marquitta were fuckin' for months behind my back?"

"Oh shit!" cried one of the witches. They all began murmurin
and whispering to each other.

Jabari shook his head.

"I don't know what you talkin' about, Birdie," he said
nonchalantly. "I was at the gym when she was killed."

"No, you weren't. You were in my bedroom, stranglin' her."

"Why would I kill her? I loved her. She was my girl before sh
was yours, remember?"

Birdie glowered. "All the more reason why you had motive to
kill her. And you did, because she wanted to break it off. Isn't the
right?"

Anger slithered across Jabari's face, but soon his mask of
indifference slipped back on. "I didn't kill her."

"But you didn't deny that you were fuckin' her," Birdie
pointed out.

Jabari shrugged. "So?"

Zora's eyes widened as Birdie slapped Jabari across the face.
MK rose from her seat, but Orion grabbed her arm and shook hi
head. She looked at him and sat back down.

When Jabari recovered, he looked almost amused, as though
he pitied Birdie. Zora clenched her fists beneath the table. *How
dare he,* she thought.

"I suppose I deserve that," Jabari said. "I'm sorry for the pair
our affair is causing you but please, Birdie. I didn't kill her."

Birdie bared her teeth and opened her mouth to speak
but Zora spoke first. "Yes, you did. I saw it." Everyone turned
their attention from Birdie to Zora, and their whispering and
fascination at the situation continued.

Jabari scoffed. "This is where you got your information? A
witch who hasn't even had control of her powers for a month? I
thought you were better than that, Birdie."

His words felt like a slap, but Zora didn't back down. "I may be a novice, but I still found a way to break that lil' curse of yours that erased Marquitta's memories. You know, the one you got from Sabrina Bounty's spell book that's sittin' by your altar downstairs?"

"Shit, I just saw that spell the other day," said one witch.

"Could he really have killed her?" asked another.

Jabari looked over at his house members then back to Birdie and Zora. Again, his mask of indifference slipped as he tossed down the fork and knife in his hands against his plate, the clinking sound so loud amid the group that it silenced the whispers. Now, everyone's full attention rested on the three House Heads in the center of the table. Jabari plastered a smile back on his face and grabbed the bottle of champagne that sat on the table before him. He refilled his and Birdie's glasses before tossing the bottle into the flames of the firepit. The glass smashed and the flames climbed higher before subsiding.

"So, you think you somethin' because you figured the curse out, huh?" he asked, craning his head to look at Zora. "Well, you got me. So, what're you gonna do about it?"

"This," Birdie said. This time she punched Jabari, hitting the bridge of his nose and making him fall backward out of his seat. He dropped his champagne glass on the table, the glass shattering and spilling champagne on his and Whitley's lap. Whitley scooted to the side but remained quiet. Jabari stood, his hands clutching his face, blood spilling between his fingers. The rest of the witches around them began shouting. Many of them voiced support for Jabari and yelled obscenities at Zora for getting him in trouble, as though she'd been the one who'd deliberately killed someone.

Birdie stood up and looked at Jabari, her nose almost level

with his. "Jabari Divinity, you've broken the laws of man and of the gods. In accordance with the Savannah Triarchy charter, your powers will be stripped and you'll be exiled from the witch community. What happens to you after that is up to the gods. Whitley?"

Birdie turned to look at Whitley. Just as the witch stood, Jabari punched Birdie in the stomach, causing her to double over. She teleported to the other side of the table, her back to the fire, just as Jabari made to punch her again. She reached over the table and tried to grab him, but he met her attempt with a spell.

"Father Baygre, hear my cry, protect me from the one who wishes me harm. Lock her in your icy embrace until I am soothe by Iniji's protection."

Zora screamed as Birdie's body was quickly encased in ice, her face a picture of fear. She reached out a hand to try to break the ice, but Taemar pulled her back.

"Uh-uh," he warned. "If you break it, you might end up killin her."

"At least someone has some sense tonight," Jabari mocked.

"Fuck you," Taemar said through gritted teeth. "If you hadn't done what you done, this shit wouldn't be happenin.'"

Jabari grimaced before turning his attention to the rest of the witches, including MK and Orion, who looked seconds away from leaping over the table to grab Zora.

"This one here is right," he said, gesturing to Zora. "I killed Marquitta."

Gasps, murmurs, and sharp looks of disbelief traveled around the table.

"And MK and Orion helped me cover it up."

Taemar and Whitley's heads snapped over toward MK and Orion, who cowered under the gaze of the other witches. *Not so tough now,* Zora thought.

"I've lived with the guilt of my decision since the moment it happened. But I knew that I couldn't turn myself in, neither to the Triarchy nor to the cops. Because my life isn't just about me. It stopped being about me when I became House Head."

"Oh please," Whitley scoffed as she shot out of her chair. "You're not above the laws of men and of gods just because you're a House Head."

Jabari sighed. "You really don't get the importance of our jobs here, do you, Whitley? And why should you? You were sent here after cursing your ex-girlfriend and her lover. By rights, your family should have stripped your powers and exiled you, but instead they shipped you off to your aunt, and you were allowed to become House Head, weren't you?"

"I—" Whitley began, lifting her hands in supplication. "That's . . . I didn't kill anyone. What I did was so different than you—"

"Was it, though?" Jabari stood and began pacing around the table, his arms behind his back. "I mean, we both did something terrible to the ones we love, and now we have to live with that regret forever."

Some of the Divinity witches began nodding their heads and murmuring their support for Jabari.

"Jabari, just stop. You murdered someone and not only covered it up but also looped in two members of her own house to help you, making them accomplices. I came clean about what I did, I didn't lie, and I didn't use a cheap spell like Father Baygre's embrace on the person who confronted me."

"No, you didn't. But isn't it weird that the second you arrived in Savannah, your dear aunt Bonnie started gettin' sick?"

"That's true, I remember when Bonnie got sick," said Deja. "Miss thing arrived not twelve hours before."

The Divinity witches nodded in support, and though they remained silent, Zora could tell the Soliloquy witches had been thinking the same thing.

"Shit. I bet Whitley was makin' plans to be House Head befo Bonnie was even cold in the ground," said Raheem.

"That's not true," Whitley said. But the damage was done. Many of the witches around the table whispered and murmured to each other about Bonnie Soliloquy and her illness, and her final days. They cast harsh glares toward Whitley, who stood as tall as she could, but Zora could tell she was diminishing under the scrutiny. She had to do something.

"That's rich comin' from you," Zora interjected. Jabari stopped pacing. "Three of the House Heads of houses you used t belong to died either shortly after or just before you left. Sabrina says go fuck yourself, by the way."

Jabari balked at Zora's comment. "Yes, well. Unfortunate consequences of power, I'm afraid. It's always someone tryin' to come for you when you become House Head. Now's no different Divinities," he spoke as he turned toward his house. Every member stood at attention. "I've confessed my sins. I'm askin' fo your forgiveness, for your absolution. I'm a murderer, but haven I also cared for you? Haven't I also gotten you jobs and kept a roof over your heads? Food in your bellies? Haven't I nurtured your magic and your relationships with the gods? Even you've benefited from that, Zora."

She grimaced then looked at Birdie. Taemar and Niko stood beside her, discussing spells that would break her out of her confinement.

"So I ask you. Will you have my back and help me fight against those who wish to take me away from you? Who wish to leave you without a House Head or replace me with someone who won't treat you half as good as I do? Or will you abide by the laws of man and of the gods and turn me over to her?"

The Divinity witches looked at each other before turning toward Zora and Whitley.

"We fight," yelled Teague. Zora watched in horror as a Cheshire cat-like smile spread across Jabari's face. And suddenly, the Divinity witches were upon them. Zora barely had time to turn before Teague grabbed her by the hair and pulled her down to the ground. She punched him in the jaw and scrambled to grab the power binding potion from her cleavage. Her hands were clammy as she gripped the small glass vial then crushed it into his chest.

"Fuck!" the witch yelled and slapped Zora across the face. Her ears rang but she knew she couldn't sit and wait until she felt normal again. She had to get away. She rolled under the table then crawled out the other side near the firepit. He followed her and she grabbed a bottle of champagne and broke it over his head, hitting him twice before he fell on his face, unconscious.

She looked to the side and observed Taemar fighting with Safi and Livia, while Niko appeared nearly knocked out by a taller, more muscular Divinity witch. Niko pressed a hand against the witch's belly and used his hydromancy to suck the water from the witch's veins. After a few seconds, the witch fell to the ground and his skin shriveled, but he seemed to be still breathing.

Zora dodged an ice shard hurled at her from a witch at the far end of the table. When the witch rushed toward her, Zora tossed her chair at her, making the woman fall over and nearly knock the firepit down. She sprinted around the table, dodging hands reaching out for her and bottles and glasses being thrown her way as she started toward Jabari and Whitley.

They were fighting in the copse of trees at the far end of the yard. Zora watched as Whitley conjured a knife and threw it at him, the blade finding purchase in his shoulder. He grunted before pulling the blade out and tossing it on the grass. Blood oozed from the wound, staining his costume crimson. He lifted his hand toward her and she screamed, his magic making her double over.

Zora inched closer to them but suddenly all the air was knocked out of her as Deja tackled her to the ground. She rolled Zora onto her back and straddled her. Zora grunted and twitched as the witch placed her hands on either side of Zora's head, sending bolts of electricity through her body. Her whole body buzzed and her limbs moved even after the witch lifted her fingers.

"I've never killed anyone with this power before. I've always wanted to know what happens," Deja said, her voice sickeningly excited.

"Iniji, come to my aid. Consume my enemies with fire and purge them of their misdeeds!" Zora rasped, hoping the spell she'd read in one of Mobley Divinity's spell books seconds before she left Soliloquy house was correct. She pressed a hand against Deja's face as she repeated the spell. The witch released Zora's head and rolled over onto her back. Soon she was enveloped in a fire that wouldn't kill her but would leave her writhing in agony until the spell was reversed. Deja screamed and pressed her hands against the flames, which only intensified the pain.

Zora's body shook for another moment longer before settling. She sat up and tried to stand, but MK's boot connected with her head, knocking her down on her side. MK rolled Zora back onto her back and straddled her.

"I'm so glad I get to finish what I started the other night," she spat. She punched Zora in the eye, and Zora returned the gesture, making MK's body jerk to the side before she recovered. The music that had been playing had stopped, and the sound of deafening screams and breaking glass and harshly-shouted spells replaced it. She heard Niko scream and as she tried to look in his direction, MK's hands encircled Zora's neck, cutting off her air.

"This is kinda poetic, for you to be a necromancer and also die the same way Marquitta did," MK sneered. Zora's hand reached out and felt along the grass for something, anything, to help her. Her hand grasped a shard of glass and she winced as it gouged her own hand as she gripped it tight. She raised it and dug the shard into MK's hand, blood spurting across Zora's dress and neck. The woman shrieked and fell off of Zora before astral projecting.

"Oh fuck," Zora groaned. Her own blood trickled onto her dress and onto the ground as she once again tried to stand. She was barely on her feet when MK looped an arm around her waist. The second version of her stood before Zora and held the broken shard she'd removed from her hand up toward her throat. "Perhaps a slit throat is more appropriate, since you be talkin' all that shit," MK growled.

Zora's breath escaped in spurts. Her jaw ached and she could feel blood seeping from her nose onto her lips. *How am I going to get out of this?* she wondered. She looked out at the scene before her, at Taemar in wolf form, biting a chunk out of the leg of the witch who'd been punching Niko. Jabari and Whitley still fought. Whitley conjured a bat and swung it, but Jabari used the sound the bat made as it sliced through the air against her, seemingly sending a wave of pain down through her arms. She screeched and dropped the weapon, her arms going limp. She conjured weapon after weapon but nothing seemed to work against Jabari.

Zora heard her shout a spell meant to halt someone in their tracks but all it did was give Jabari more sound to turn back around on her. Her stretched out his hands toward her and Whitley lifted off the ground before being flung against a tree. Zora watched as blood poured from Whitley's nose, mouth, ears, and eyes. She couldn't hold on for much longer, Zora knew.

I have to end this, she thought. *But how?*

Hovering near the tree line stood the ghost of the gangster Zora had seen when she first stepped into Divinity house. The bullet hole in his face looked even more ghastly in this light and she extended her bloody hand toward him, as though luring him toward her. Right away, he appeared beside her, gazing down at her eagerly.

"Help me," Zora rasped. He nodded toward her hand and she lifted it to his face. He stuck out his ghostly tongue and lapped at the blood, and for a moment, he was corporeal. MK, seeing this ghost materialize out of nowhere, shouted "What the fuck?" seconds before he punched the version that stood before her in the jaw.

Zora grabbed the power stripping potion and broke the vial against MK's arm. The woman shrieked and pulled her hand back, drawing the second version of herself in. She moved to strike Zora, but she punched MK across the face, causing her to spin on her heel and fall backward, landing on her face.

The ghost faded back to his former form and nodded at Zora. She stood and looked down at her palm and remembered an entry from one of the spell books she read about ghosts craving a necromancer's life. She'd read it and thought it strictly meant they wanted to kill her, but what if it only meant they wanted a taste of life again? To touch the people and things around them, to feel the air on their skin and the sun on their face? And what if she didn't need to craft a spell to force their hand to help her? What if all she needed was to give them what they craved? Life?

She tried to ignore the way her entire body ached as she realized what she had to do. She had to save Whitley. She had to save them all. She closed her eyes and dropped her defenses, letting all the ghosts near her come to her. When she opened them, Sabrina Bounty, the gangster ghost, Mobley Divinity, and Marquitta stood before her.

"Hear me. I will give you a taste of what it feels like to live again if you help me save my friends."

Every ghost nodded. "Do not kill the ones who hurt them, just neutralize them. There's only one person here whose life may not last the night." She cast a glance toward Jabari, who stood over Whitley.

Zora bent down and picked up the shard of glass and cut her other hand. Then she held her palms up and allowed the ghosts to drink. One by one, they became whole again. "Go."

Sabrina, Mobley, and the gangster walked amongst the other witches and helped Niko and Taemar. Several witches ran at the sight of them. As they did, Zora turned to Marquitta.

"Are you ready to face him?" she asked, and a wicked smile split her face in two. Zora turned and ran, stopping short of the fight.

"Jabari!" Zora bellowed. He stopped just as he was about to deliver the crushing blow to Whitley. He turned toward her and gaped when he saw Marquitta standing beside Zora.

"So, you've learned the cost of necromancy," he said, gesturing toward the twin wounds on Zora's hands. "No matter. I'll take you down just like I did this one."

Just as he was about to turn to finish Whitley, Marquitta moved in front of him and punched him, sending him onto his back.

"Get her out of here," Zora said to Marquitta, pointing towar Whitley.

Marquitta hesitated. "Are you sure?"

"Yeah, I need you to keep her safe while you're whole. I'll dea with him."

Zora turned her attention back to Jabari as Marquitta helpec Whitley up and slung an arm around her shoulder and walked back toward the house. Then, Zora stood over Jabari, rage surging through her body.

"So, is this the moment where you take my powers?" he mocked.

"This is the moment where I get revenge," she replied. She kicked him in the stomach, making him draw his legs into himself. She kicked again, but this time he grabbed her leg and pulled her down. She grunted as she hit her head on the ground. The movement stunned her, knocking the breath out of her and making the edges of her vision go white for a second. Jabari crawled on his stomach until he reached the knife Whitley had stabbed him with. His hand gripped the handle and he turned back to Zora, pulling her left arm down and pressing his knee into her hand. She yelped as his knee connected with her wound

"You may be feelin' yourself for figuring out how to get ghost to do your bidding, but you've only figured out half the equation He drew the knife up her arm, splitting the flesh. A deluge of blood erupted from the wound and Zora screamed at the searing pain. Each of the ghosts Zora summoned before suddenly knelt before her and fell to their knees, greedily lapping up the blood. Zora tried to move her arm but they gripped it so tightly that it started going numb. "You see, once you give these ghosts a taste they always want more. And like vampires, they'll come back an come back and come back, wanting to feast on your blood. If you don't learn how to control them when they're in this state, they could kill you."

Marquitta was the last to appear, and Zora looked at her pleadingly.

"Nice to see you again, baby," Jabari flirted. "I miss you. Well, parts of you."

But the ghost wasn't listening. It wanted Zora's blood.

"No, please, stop, please. Sabrina! Mobley! Marquitta! Help me!"

Jabari chuckled and walked away, leaving Zora with the specters who were upon her now, their ghostly tongues lapping her blood. Already she was feeling lightheaded, the world above her spinning. Her mind swam and she tried to remember the spells she'd learn to stop a heart, but her thoughts came and went, unfinished. Tears streaked down her cheeks and she begged Geddemin, Iniji, and any god listening to help.

It was Marquitta who came to her aid, the answer to her prayers. She pushed the ghosts off Zora and charged them.

"Bind your wounds," she rasped as she fought off the ghosts to buy Zora some time. With her free hand, Zora ripped the tulle from her skirt and wrapped it around her arm and tied it off. Then she did the same with her hands. She tried to stand but her legs wobbled and her vision twisted like a kaleidoscope. She leaned against the tree and tried to steady her breath and refocus as she heard the ghosts behind her crying out for her blood. She had to put up her defenses. If she didn't, they'd come for her again.

Zora closed her eyes and forced herself to focus on forming a protective bubble around her. She tried and failed and tried and just as she felt the ghost of Sabrina looming over her shoulder, her hand outstretched, the bubble formed around her. The ghost bumped against it with a shriek. The gangster, Mobley Divinity, and Marquitta all joined Sabrina as she tried to push and strain against Zora's defenses. In her weakened state she could feel them knocking against the walls she built, but Zora knew she had to stay strong. She had more work to do, and she needed their energy.

Zora turned her attention to the last House Head standing.

She took a deep breath before she pushed off the tree and followed behind Jabari, who was unleashing his powers on Taemar and Niko as they stood trying to reverse Father Baygre's embrace. She stopped short of the scene, taking advantage of his distraction. She closed her eyes visualized a beating heart in her minds' eye, saw it pumping, saw blood flowing in and out.

She held up her palm toward Jabari's back and began the spell. "Baygre, Yamala, Narya the creators of life, breath, and mind."

Jabari turned on his heel as he heard her speak.

"What're you doing?" he demanded.

"I am the daughter of Geddemin, the originator of death."

His eyes widened. He extended a hand and turned his power on her, and Zora doubled over as she felt the full weight of it crushing her insides. But she did not stop. She had to finish. "Here is one that they must know."

Jabari leaned in toward her, bringing both hands to face her. Zora screamed. Sweat beaded on her brow, her hair sticking to her cheeks and neck, but she didn't back down. She threw her full weight into her power, closing her eyes again and envisioning the ghosts that surrounded her. She thought about all of their memories, their most painful moments unfurling in her mind's eye. And she let the pain that came with those visions in. She let their pain and horror and grief mix with hers until she felt it all rushing through her veins.

When she opened her eyes, the effects of Jabari's power barely felt like pin pricks. Zora Transcendence grit her teeth as she finished the spell. "Grant me the power to still his mind, to halt his breath, to reach through skin and bone and marrow and stop his beating heart so that I may deliver him to my parent's doorstep."

"No!" Jabari screamed. He ran toward her but stopped short as Zora closed her hands into fists.

Jabari Divinity's eyes rolled back in his head. He gasped and clutched his chest before falling dead at her feet.

Zora knew her task wasn't done, however. She knew Jabari's ghost would return soon enough. And with his anger, he'd be able to hurt her, probably even kill her.

Taemar and Niko looked on anxiously as Zora planted her feet and watched for his spirit. When it appeared seconds later, his brow furrowed and his hands out and ready to grip her neck, she shouted the banishment spell: "I call upon Zephyrym, the god of wind and change. I call upon Yamala, goddess of rebirth and first breath, and I call upon Geddemin, the god of death themself. With the strength of the gods within me, I cast the specter before me away from this place, away from this world, away from life itself. I cast you to the gates of the afterworld where you will meet Geddemin firsthand. May they judge you harshly, you murderous mothafucka!"

Jabari's face contorted into an expression of pure rage before his ghost vanished in a cloud of red smoke, and Zora hit the ground as the smoke cleared.

Chapter 19

*"No witch can survive in this world without community.
When Birdie first said it to me, I didn't think it was true.
But now I know that was the most important lesson I've
learned so far."*

Spell Book of Zora Transcendence, 2022

irdie's pale pink dress billowed in the wind. They all stood on the beach and stared at the waves, Birdie holding the urn of Marquitta's ashes in her hand. It'd been a week since Halloween. During that time, they'd healed their physical wounds but not their mental ones. Zora had taken a life and the way Jabari had looked when he died, eyes flat, mouth open in terror, haunted her. She woke up in the middle of the night sweating, and though Whitley was there to calm her, she suspected it would take a while before she felt okay again.

But she was grateful for the people in her corner. For Whitley, who'd been patient and kind and kept Zora company in the early morning hours when she couldn't go back to sleep. For Niko, who made her laugh and brought her coffee. For Taemar, who talked her through her panic attacks and held her as she cried. And for Birdie, who made sure she ate and showered and honored the gods. And she encouraged Zora to meet up with Keith, who was home on a long weekend after midterms.

They'd sat at Lulu's, in the same place Zora had been sitting when she met Birdie. He'd been hurt and angry, having found out she was in Savannah from their mother. He sat across from Zora with his back pressed against his chair, his thumb tapping against his coffee mug.

"I thought we were closer than that," he said.

"I didn't know where I was going after I saw her. I didn't war to worry you."

"Well, worry me, Zo. I'm your brother. We're supposed to worry about each other."

Zora chuckled as tears sprang in her eyes. "I know. I worry about you. I spent so much time consumed with how my powers affected me, how Mom and Dad affected me, that I didn't think about how all of it affected you."

Keith nodded and ran a hand across his face. "It sucked. For real, it fuckin' sucked. I don't think Mom forgave me for the role played in keeping your secret."

"It should never have been like that," Zora murmured.

"No, it shouldn't have. But it was. We can't change it, just move forward. I'm in college now. I've got my own friends, a girlfriend," he said sheepishly. Zora leaned forward.

"For real? Keith that's so great!"

"And you?"

"Well first, I need to see a picture of this girlfriend. And second, I'm the happiest I've ever been."

She told him about dancing at Nightingale's, about living wit Birdie and befriending Taemar and Niko, about how she liked Whitley and how she just knew they were something special.

When they finished having coffee, they promised to keep in touch, and Zora invited him over for dinner. They shared a laugl as Zora told him not to get too comfortable because he might want to stay forever.

That night, they buried Jabari Divinity in Bonaventure

Cemetery under the first full moon of November. There was no fanfare or eulogy extolling his virtues. Just the witches who fought against him on one side and the ones who fought for him on the other. Despite this division, there wasn't a dry eye in the space as they watched his coffin lower into the ground. Birdie cast a spell to cover the coffin with fresh dirt. Atop of his grave they planted white snapdragons to purify the space.

A few days after the funeral, Birdie and Whitley held another ritual—one to strip the powers of MK, Orion, Teague, Deja, and all the other witches who fought on Jabari's side. Zora watched in solemn wonder as the witches whose powers she'd envied and even feared a little were taken. When the ritual was complete, the witches had twenty-four hours to pack up and move out of their respective houses. When MK and Orion left, they glared at Zora the whole time, with MK intimating their beef wasn't over.

Nightingale's was temporarily closed, given that half the dancers and the DJ had their powers stripped and were exiled from the magical community. Birdie had started actively recruiting dancers, teleporting around the country in search of more dancers with magical abilities. The witches who hadn't fought, or who'd fought against the Divinities, were still able to work. Kimayah Soliloquy, who'd been at Obsidian Auto Body since it was opened, became the manager. Whenever a customer came in asking after Jabari, the staff would shrug and say he blew town like he'd done so many times before. Though deciding on Kimayah was an easy solution, one space was harder to fill.

Whitley and Birdie spent endless conversations debating on who to make House Head. Given that Safi was the only Divinity who hadn't fought against Soliloquy and Transcendence, there was hardly a way for them to select their new House Head. They communed with the gods, but Taemar and Zora both thought it should be Niko. After all, he'd been close to becoming the Head before Whitley, and he was much beloved by everyone still remaining in the Triarchy

But Zora shoved thoughts of her brother and Jabari and the new House Head out of her mind as she stood on the beach beside Birdie. Taemar, Niko, and Whitley rounded out the group and they all held hands as they waited patiently for Birdie to release Marquitta's ashes into the ocean.

"You know, I used to think she was perfect. I'd wonder how someone so like the goddess Yamala could want me. But now I know she wasn't. She was petty and selfish and mean," Birdie said, looking at Zora, who smiled tightly. She looked beyond her House Head to the ghost of Marquitta, who wept into her hands. "And she was unfaithful. She shared her body, mind, and heart with someone else, and I don't know that I can ever forgive her."

"I love you, Birdie, I always will," Marquitta said. Zora sighed, her heart aching for the women who she'd come to care for. Birdie looked at Zora as though she could tell that Zora was in contact with Marquitta.

"She said she loves you," Zora offered. Birdie's eyes watered. She clung to the urn as though depending on its weight to keep her upright.

"Where is she?" she asked Zora. "I need to say see her."

Zora nodded. She knew Birdie would want to speak to her lover despite what she'd said to the contrary over breakfast. She pulled a small pocket knife from the pocket of her oversized flannel and pressed it against the barely healed cut on her right palm.

"What're you—" Whitley began. Zora held a hand up.

"It's ok, I need to do this. We all need to say our goodbyes."

Whitley looked to Birdie, then Niko and finally Taemar. Each of them nodded, Taemar's lips set in a grim line. He winced as Zora ran the knife across her palm. Blood trickled out of the wound and Marquitta lapped at it, and within seconds she was corporeal.

Birdie gasped as she saw her lover standing before her. She set her urn down then reached a hand out and touched Marquitta's shoulder. When she realized she could make contact, she drew her into a tight embrace. When she pulled away, her mascara-tinged tears left streaks down her face.

"I'm sorry, baby," Marquitta said. "I didn't want to hurt you but I know I can't take back what I did and I—"

Birdie hugged her again, this time more fiercely. The women held each other and wept briefly before Marquitta broke away.

"I don't have much time like this," she said. Birdie's expression was pained but she nodded and cleared her throat.

"I meant what I said about how angry I am with you. How you've hurt me and how I don't know if I can forgive you. But I don't know how to be without you. You were always the calm that quieted my chaos, and it feels like one of my own limbs has been chopped off. And the truth is, in some fucked up way, it was easier not knowing what happened because then I had somethin' to focus on. Solvin' your murder gave me purpose, and now. I don't know what to do with myself."

Marquitta caressed Birdie's cheek. "You'll live. That's what you'll do. You'll live for yourself and for me and you'll travel and try new things and fall—" her voice broke. "You'll fall in love again."

Birdie shook her head. "I don't know if I can. You were the love of my life and though I'm still heartbroken from what you did I will live for you and when my time comes I will accept it gladly because it means I will get to look upon you and hold you and kiss you again." The women pressed their foreheads together before sharing one last kiss. When Marquitta pulled away, Birdie picked up Marquitta's urn and clutched it before turning away.

Marquitta turned toward the group, first locking eyes with Whitley.

"Marquitta, when we first met, I hated you," she said. Taemar sucked his teeth and started to speak, but Niko held a hand out.

"Let her finish."

"But despite everything, despite our disagreements, our vitriol, I always respected you. I always admired your power, your strength, the way you loved Birdie. The way you loved this community. When you died I cried and I missed you when you were gone. I think... I think I'm going to miss you forever."

Marquitta chuckled and squeezed Whitley's hands.

"Marquitta, I miss gossiping with you in the salon," Niko began. "Seeing you dance was like watching a sculptor painting. Such beauty, such vulnerability. I'll miss the way you made me feel talented, the way you taught me how to properly use my spell book, how you taught me to make sweet potato pie. May you find the peace you so deserve in the afterworld."

The ghost drew Niko in for a brief but tender embrace. When she turned her attention to Taemar, Niko leaned in to Whitley and cried, his blue curls falling over his face.

Taemar wiped at his eyes and sniffled. "I'm gonna keep this brief because y'all know I could give a whole dissertation."

Marquitta laughed. Taemar grabbed her hands and held them.

"Marquitta, you touched all of us in so many ways. You're the reason I went back to school."

"You gon' be an amazing therapist," she said. Taemar nodded

"When I wake up every day, I'll look at the sunrise with

gratitude because I got to live in a world with you in it, even for a short time."

Marquitta's form was fading. Zora knew she wouldn't last much longer as she was and so when she caught the woman's eye she immediately drew her in to an embrace.

"Thank you," she whispered into her ear.

"No, Zora, thank you. You've helped me more than you know."

She looked at Zora, her eyes watery but full of peace. She let Zora go and stepped back toward the water.

"Be well, my love," Birdie said. "May you find peace in the afterworld."

Marquitta Transcendence smiled at the group one last time before closing her eyes. Then, she shimmered away, her ghost gone and floating on the wind. They stood in silence, listening to the waves crashing on the beach. Zora couldn't feel Marquitta's ghost anymore. As though reading her mind, Birdie spoke:

"She must in the afterworld now."

Zora exhaled laboriously as tears spilled from her eyes and her throat felt tight and sore. As a soft breeze swept through, Birdie opened the urn of Marquitta's ashes. She stepped toward the ocean and tossed them in, some of them carried away by the wind. Birdie dropped the urn and held on to Taemar and Zora's hands as she watched the waves lap up what remained of Marquitta Transcendence. Whitley wrapped an arm around Zora and Niko stood by Taemar's side, holding his other hand.

They stood like that for a while, holding on to each other and staring at the waves. Zora marveled at them, her community, her family, and in that moment, she realized she was home. And she wasn't anxious nor was she scared or trying to put on a poker face. She was wholly and completely herself, comfortable in her own skin. Zora looked back at the waves knowing that whatever happened next she would face it—they would face it—together.

Acknowledgements

Many people think writing is a solitary practice but if there's one thing I've learned in my two years as a published author, it's that community is everything. There are many people who helped this book come to fruition: my family, including my husband, my mother, brothers, and sisters. Each of them listene as I gushed or lamented about this book. Each of them cheered me on, listened to various passages, and helped me think of way to promote my work and put myself out there. I am eternally grateful for their support and love.

I am also grateful for my author community, many of whom have become my dearest friends. Without their help, this book would be just a draft in the drawer. I would be remiss if I didn't especially mention my critique partner and my good friend C.M. Lockhart. Her constant support, feedback, encouragement, and willingness to do writing sprints at two in the morning with me helped make In the House of Transcendence as amazing as it is.

I also want to shoutout my editor, Erica James, of MasterPieces Writing and Editing LLC. She's been a constant part of my publishing team from the beginning and I am so thankful for her keen eye and the flair she helps me add to my work. Also, sending thanks to my cover designer, Tajae Keith, fo bringing Zora to brilliant life on the cover.

And finally, thank you to my readers. I'm still so surprised that there are people out there who actively seek out my work and aren't just reading it because I asked them to. You're the reason I write and why I look forward to every new idea that pop into my dome. Thank you for rocking with me and helping make my author dreams come true.

About the Author

About the Author Amanda Ross is an indie author who writes NA fantasy set in modern times. Her Witchkind series—*To Astera, With Love* and its sequel, *To Ilaris, In Desperation*—is filled with magic, humor, and social commentary. She also co-published the YA fantasy anthologies *Girls of Might and Magic* and *Kindred Kingdoms*. In addition to her authoring, Amanda is also an AuthorTuber, one-half of the horror podcast the *Horror Heaux Support Group*, and the Marketing Director of the Melanin Library. When she's not writing, Amanda can be found at the beach, reading or listening to her favorite podcasts.